Praise for *Portra...*

"...a page-turner unlike any historical novel, weaving passion, adventure, artistic rebirth, and consequences of ambition...a masterful writer at the peak of her craft."
        —C. W. Gortner, author of *The Confessions of Catherine de' Medici*

"In *Portrait of a Conspiracy*, Russo Morin's prose is as sharp as a Medici dagger...Thwarting danger, finding love, and creating masterpieces, [these women] remind us just how powerful the bonds of womanhood can be."
        —Marci Jefferson, author of *The Enchantress of Paris*

"This riveting book is filled with art, assassinations, retribution, and a sisterhood of fascinating women who inspire as well as entertain."
        —Stephanie Dray, *New York Times* bestselling
author of *America's First Daughter*

"In *Portrait of a Conspiracy*, Russo Morin's rich detailing transports the reader to the heart of Renaissance Italy from the first page."
        —Heather Webb, author of *Becoming Josephine*

"Illicit plots, mysterious paintings, and a young Leonardo da Vinci all have their part to play in this delicious, heart-pounding tale."
        —Kate Quinn, author of The Empress of Rome Saga

"A 15th-century Florence of exquisite art, sensual passion and sudden, remorseless violence comes vividly to life in Donna Russo Morin's new novel."
        —Nancy Bilyeau, author of *The Crown*

"Russo Morin's elegant command of language and composition left me breathless, but the story itself, with its flawless depiction of power, corruption, defiance, intrigue and retribution makes *Portrait of a Conspiracy* an absolute must read."

—Flashlight Commentary

"This riveting historical fiction novel [is] filled with art, passion, and violence. A portrait of the dangerous beauty of Renaissance Florence."

—*The Florentine*

"The action is fierce and the stillness is resplendent with intensity of being. The suspense is thrilling and intelligent. The writing is masterful."

—Open Book Society

"Elegant and Intriguing!"

—Red Carpet Crash

THE
Competition

Da Vinci's Disciples
BOOK TWO

DONNA RUSSO MORIN

DIVERSIONBOOKS

FIC
MORIN WOT

Diversion Books
A Division of Diversion Publishing Corp.
443 Park Avenue South, Suite 1008
New York, New York 10016
www.DiversionBooks.com

For more information, email info@diversionbooks.com

First Diversion Books edition April 2017
Print ISBN: 978-1-68230-806-6
eBook ISBN: 978-1-68230-805-9

To Carl,
For his unwavering belief,
For his calming presence,
For his love.

RENAISSANCE FLORENCE

A Home of Viviana del Marrone
B Home of Fiammetta and
   Patrizia Maffei
C Home of Lapaccia Cavalcanti
D Home of Natasia Soderini
   Capponi
E Home of Mattea Zamperini
F Home of Isabetta Fioravanti
G Home of Carina Tafani

H Santo Spirito
I Palazzo de' Medici
J Cathedral of Santa Maria del
   Fiore (Duomo)
K Baptistry
L Palazzo della Signoria
M Home of Soderini (Natasia's
   parents)
N Church of San Lorenzo

O Bargello
P Ponte alla Carraia
Q Ponte Santa Trinta
R Ponte Vecchio
S Ponte alla Grazie
T Porta San Piero Gattolinio
U Porta alla Croce/Gallows
V Porta a San Gallo

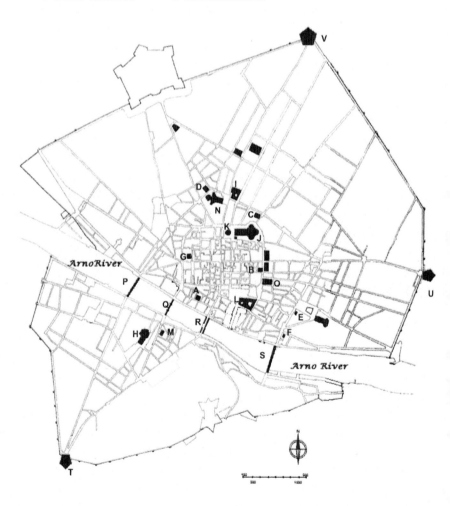

Personaggi

*denotes historical character

Viviana del Marrone – a founding member of Da Vinci's Disciples; the daughter of a long line of wealthy vintners; born 1444

Contessa Fiammetta Ruspoli Maffei – a member of Da Vinci's Disciples; daughter to one of the great noble houses of Florence; born 1442

Isabetta Fioravanti – a member Da Vinci's Disciples; a mainland Venetian brought to Florence by her husband, a once-successful butcher; born 1454

Lapaccia Cavalcanti – a member of Da Vinci's Disciples; widow of Messer Andrea Cavalcanti; born 1438

Natasia Soderini – a member of Da Vinci's Disciples; a member of one of the most powerful and noble houses of Florence; born 1462

Mattea Zamperini – a member of Da Vinci's Disciples; daughter of a deceased merchant; born 1461

Conte Patrizio Maffei – Fiammetta's husband; a high-ranking nobleman; born 1437

Patrizia Ruspoli Maffei – daughter to the Conte and Contessa Maffei; born 1464

Sansone Caivano – professional soldier from northern Venice; born 1450

Marcello del Marrone – son of Viviana; soldier; spice merchant; born 1461

Rudolfo del Marrone – son of Viviana; soldier; spice merchant; born 1463

*Lorenzo de' Medici – entitled *Il Magnifico* by the people of Florence; renowned Italian statesmen and unofficial ruler of the Florentine government; merchant banker; a great patron of the arts; Platonist; poet; born 1449

*Clarice Orsini de' Medici – wife of Lorenzo; daughter of Jacopo Giacomo Orsini, Lord of Monterotondo and Bracciano, and his wife and cousin Maddalena Orsini; born 1453

Andreano Cavalcanti – son of Lapaccia; once a member of the *Consiglio di Cento*, Council of One Hundred; born 1456

Carina di Tafani – daughter of a minor Florentine nobleman; born 1468

Father Raffaello, Tomaso Soderini – Natasia Soderini's brother; parish priest of Santo Spirito; born 1457

Antonio di Salvestro de' Serristori – a clerk for the *Dodoici Procuratori*, oversight committee of the Florentine finances; born 1457

Fabia di Testaverdi di Salvestro de' Serristori – wife of Antonio; born 1462

*Alessandro di Mariano di Vanni Filipepi, better known as Sandro Botticelli – Italian Renaissance painter of the Florentine School; belonged to court of Lorenzo de' Medici; born 1445

*Andrea di Michele di Francesco de' Cioni (Andrea del Verrocchio) – Florentine painter, sculptor, goldsmith; *maestro* of an esteemed and influential workshop; born 1435

*Lucrezia Donati Ardinghelli – daughter of fallen nobleman Manno di Manno Donati and his wife Caterina di Benedeto de' Bardi; wife of Niccolò Ardinghelli; born 1447

*Leonardo da Vinci – polymath; born 1452

If our fates must be decided, and not simply allowed,
we should be their masters.

Chapter One

"Inspiration, when it comes, comes on its own terms."

Specks of sand in a windstorm, eddying about, seemingly chaotic yet cohesive, unified within the calm, unseen core.

They stood apart in the vast crowd and yet together, a feat they had managed to accomplish ever since those fateful days. None could see them and know them as a group; society would frown upon it. Few of their number—in truth, but one—cared little for the caprices of society. Their truth had already rendered it specious. But if their truth were known—the deepest, darkest depths of it—they would all be dead, a brutal death at the end of the hangman's noose.

The boisterous throng swirled around them, ignorant to the revolutionaries they stood beside. With the crowd whirled the music, the voices, the change in the wind. Some of the women wore jewels and ermine trim, others simple muslin. Only in their smocks were their ranks and wealth negated. They stood united by what they had done, by all they created, and all they hoped yet to create. Such brazenness, such daring, such criminal activity bound them in a way little else could. They were—now and forever—united as Da Vinci's Disciples.

"Isn't it breathtaking, dearest?" Natasia twittered to her husband, Pagolo, squeezing his arm with a plump hand in her zeal.

Tall and stick-like to Natasia's round fleshiness, Pagolo Capponi shielded his slim, dark eyes from the midday sun as they watched the grand procession pass before them. "Yes dearest, splendid."

Viviana tucked her chin down, hiding her motherly grin; so much had changed, and yet some things never would. Natasia may be married now, as she had so craved to be, but her girlish giggles had not abandoned her.

Viviana stood beside the couple and they beside Fiammetta and Patrizio, the Conte and Contessa Maffei, she with her face a blasé mask, he with bright spots of happiness on his round cheeks. Beside them stood Lapaccia Cavalcanti, simply attired as always, an ash walking stick in her hand. The widowed noblewoman held the arm of another elderly woman, a noble as well, down to her luxurious trappings.

On Viviana's other side stood Isabetta and Mattea, both in their finest—if simplest—muslin, both with the kiss of the sun emerging on their pale cheeks.

Viviana was the middle ground between the *ottimati* and *popolo* of their group, the elite and the common citizens. She was a widow herself, that of a disgraced lesser elite, disgraced by his own hands, deceased by hers and those of the women near to her. She was as in limbo in life as she was between these women, not exactly knowing her place, not exactly knowing where life would next take her.

"About time things returned to normal," Fiammetta grumbled. Viviana wholeheartedly agreed with her, which did not happen often.

"Thanks to *Il Magnifico.*" Viviana felt gladness for him, and all of Florence.

Lorenzo de' Medici was not the man he had once been. The change came the day they murdered his brother in the great cathedral. It came when Lorenzo learned the murder was a conspiracy, with gnarled fingers that reached all the way to the Vatican. All goodness and light within him had been extinguished when he had avenged Giuliano's murder in a massacre of near to one hundred men. He ruled darkly in the wars that followed, and in the years that followed those wars. What with the pope's decree of excommunication upon *Il Magnifico* and all of Florence, the wars, and the plague, Florence and its citizens had suffered dearly in the intervening years. Lorenzo's grief and anger had hovered over the city like an ominous black cloud. Today, at long last, he had allowed a celebration to take place. And what a spectacle it was.

This *Festa di San Giovanni,* a celebration of John the Baptist, was unlike any the city had seen before. Under *Il Magnifico's* rule, as every facet of life had become, it blazed with both pageantry and eminence.

"Florence dons her golden gown once more," Isabetta said. "Would you look at that?"

One had no choice. Fifteen wagons drawn by fifty pairs of oxen filled the street, their clomping the air, the cheering of the crowd the ears.

The women leaned away from the heat of the many *girandole,* the wheels of fire in the shapes of ships and houses, their fires crackling, popping, and spattering the crowd with sparks.

Zigzagging their way through the wagons and platforms, the *spiritegli* hovered over all, their legs strapped to poles so tall they seemed to walk on air.

A banner upon the lead wagon identified the *edifizi* it carried: *Lucius Aemilius Paulus.*

"It is his vanity," Fiammetta said once more.

"It is his need to reassert himself," Viviana argued with a whisper, not for her sake, but for Fiammetta's; she had no wish for any to hear of her friend's continued anti-Medicean attitude. There were those who shared Fiammetta's feelings for the city's ruler. Most hid behind a façade of Medici support, in dark corners and shadows, for their own purposes and pernicious agendas.

Lucius Aemilus Paulus was the Roman conqueror of Macedonia, from before the birth of Jesus Christ. His return to Rome, with overflowing bounty, had made him immortal.

"No doubt *Il Magnifico* wishes to make an identification," Viviana raised her voice in concert with the rising roar of the crowd. "Lorenzo put much at risk to save our city, going to Naples, being held virtually hostage there for more than a year. His safe return, his success in saving Florence from further ravages of war—surely it is a bounty worth celebrating."

"Humph," was Fiammetta's response.

"Indeed, Florence is reborn," Mattea agreed with Isabetta. "Already women are wearing their finest again, and palazzos are being built. Yes, Florence is reborn. But can it be as if nothing ever happened? Can it be as it was before?"

Before. The word had a strange effect. Did they really wish for it to be so?

Viviana studied each face, watched as her friends' minds traveled back in time with her own. Lapaccia had never regained her health since the days and weeks she'd hidden in the convent. She had become what she had never been, no matter her age...an old, frail lady. Her son, Mattea's lover, wandered, hiding, the small price he paid for the small part he played in the conspiracy to kill Guiliano de' Medici and the attempt to kill Lorenzo. Mattea's longing, her fear was ever there upon her face, in her eyes that did not sparkle as they once had, upon lips slow to curve.

Isabetta in her widow's weeds, her husband whom she had loved and nursed for years now gone, though not so very long ago. A badge of guilt hung heavy on that woman's neck. But not nearly as heavy as one did on Viviana's, for Isabetta had not been the instrument of her husband's death; that part belonged to Viviana and Viviana alone. Was it truly wrong? No, she had never thought so, not for a moment. What she feared more was that she had killed something within herself when she killed him.

Fiammetta had slipped down the social ladder—an atrocity, in her mind, for staying on her perch was so very important to her. Her association with the Pazzi family—they who had led the assassination—had chipped away at her lofty standing. Watching her struggle to climb back up was like watching a child attempt to scale a mountain, a pitiable sight.

Only Natasia—sweet, young Natasia—had come away unscathed.

They had even lost their mentor, if only temporarily. They'd lost Leonardo da Vinci to the Duke of Milan, or rather his uncle Ludovico, who acted as regent for his eight-year-old nephew. The wars Florence had endured had left no one to sponsor him, which da Vinci needed in order to become the *maestro* of the studio that he deserved to be.

But something had happened, something glorious in the *before*. They had saved Lapaccia's life, even Andreano's, and they had created a masterpiece. It hung in the Palazzo della Signoria still, the towering building at their backs. It hung where the original masterpiece had hung and still no one knew the difference. The city and its keepers thought it a warning to all those who dare defy its leaders, most especially the Medicis, and so it remained upon its wall, an accusatory finger to be avoided. In truth, it was a living, breathing testament to the women's growing prowess as artists. It didn't matter that no one knew such beauty had come from their hands; at least that was what they told themselves.

Viviana looked to the sky, to the small prison at the top of the tower where she herself had spent a night. No one knew she and these women, Da Vinci's Disciples, had rendered the painting that hung in that tower.

No, it didn't matter. Or did it? The question had plagued Viviana more and more of late, as she searched for the same fiery purpose she had felt when helping to paint it. She now seemed to crave it, as the souse craved his wine.

Like her city, Viviana carried the scars of those days, yet like Florence, she too was healing. She closed her eyes, raised her face to the sun, and let it warm her. She let gratitude consume her, let the crowd and the cheering and the song and the laughter fade away.

"I purchased that chapel in Santo Spirito three years ago." The words spoken by the resonant, lofty voice of a man, somewhere close behind her, broke through her reverence and shattered it. "Now I shall finally be allowed to have it frescoed."

Viviana's eyes snapped open like a shutter in a gale. Through the haze, she saw the man who had spoken, knew his face.

But more importantly, she saw *it*, the answer to what came next.

Chapter Two

"Often with death comes freedom."

She lay in bed waiting for the sound of the rooster's crow. She did not need it to wake her up. Viviana had never finished yesterday.

Viviana's mind had refused to still, refused to stop imagining or dream. The few times she dozed, the journey of the unconscious took her through a house, each bright room overflowed with the herald of conquest. Not a one dispelled it.

She rose, dressed quickly, hurrying Jemma, her ever-stalwart maid.

"No, *cara*, the blue one," Viviana instructed as the young woman reached for a set of slashed sleeves to tie over Viviana's puffed-sleeved *gamurra*.

Viviana had abandoned her widow's weeds long ago, barely able to stand their gloominess for the requisite time. Especially as the gloom was not hers to wear in truth. Her wardrobe reflected who she truly was, elegant and unique, wealthy but in the comfortable sense. A widow, yes, but not one knocking on death's door. This blue gown was the perfect outer statement of her inner truths, with its deep V neckline allowing the delicate, pale blue embroidery of her *gamurra* to show through, its tight sleeves, tight to the elbow, ending in a profusion of hanging tippets that furled out as she walked.

She stared at herself in the smoky looking glass.

What have you to tell me? Viviana asked her reflection. *Have I changed much in the last five years, since I became free of him?*

Him.

She never said his name; she hated the taste of it on her tongue.

Her looks did not threaten to betray her. Not as her dead husband had.

She caught her own gaze again. Did she feel guilty? Yes, for her faith demanded she feel remorse and guilt. Though her guilt was for the truth. She was not remorseful, not for her actions that condemned him. Her cruel husband had been horrifically executed, she had seen to it, but for different crimes than those he actually committed. She ignored it, or tried.

"Where are you off to, madonna?" Jemma laced up the back of the gown. "You are not for church, not in this."

"I go to set a meeting," Viviana said, the words floating on a breath of excitement.

Jemma stiffened, stilled.

"A meeting?" Jemma walked slowly round to face her mistress, her still-cherubic features, hinting at the beauty of full womanhood just around the corner, scrunched with caution. "It is not just to paint then?"

Jemma's wisdom had grown as she had.

"Well, *cara*, it is and it isn't." Viviana pinched Jemma's cheek. "It is that and so very much more."

"*O Dio mio*. Something starts again, doesn't it?"

Fully dressed, Viviana spun to face Jemma, holding the maid by her shoulders, bestowing a smile upon her that held a glimmer of everything that was in her mind, every expectation, every possibility. "I hope so, dear Jemma, I do hope so."

Vague pronouncement made, Viviana grabbed her small silk purse, tying it to the slim belt just below her breasts, and headed for the door.

"Do you not want me to accompany—"

Jemma's words eddied to mumbles as Viviana closed the door behind her.

• • •

The raggedly dressed men who cleaned the streets filled them. The remnants of yesterday's *festa* bedecked the cobblestones with the residue of celebration; empty bottles of wine rolled down the uneven cobbles with arrhythmic chimes, abandoned ribbons and streamers now dotted the landscape with bursts of color.

Viviana walked past the men and the few other *fiorentinos* out and about at such an early hour. There weren't many; most were still recovering, she thought with an amused grin, heads too heavy with wine to lift them from their pillows. Others, perhaps those who had not embraced the celebration as devoutly, were no doubt in church.

Viviana strolled south toward the Ponte Vecchio, not at leisure, but in thought. The meeting would, by necessity, need to be properly timed. Setting a signal would signal that it was much more than just another day.

Her group of colleagues—women who had named themselves Da Vinci's Disciples—who dared to learn true art, rarely went a day or more without time in their hidden *studiolo* behind the church of Santo Spirito. Rarely could one of them go too long without the feel of the brush in her grip, the acidic scent of pigments in her nose, or the sight of the chisel and stone that cried out for her attention.

Viviana needed them all there at the same time, needed it to be a full coming together of the entire group when she shared her news. She needed Leonardo there as well. She would have to set the meeting time for at least a fortnight from now; it would take that long for the message to get to the artist and for the artist to make his way to Florence. The young man, a model Leonardo entrusted to carry such messages, was reliable, but he could only go as fast as the horse that carried him.

She approached the corner niche shrine of Saint Caterina— not their Caterina, not her cousin, who had been a prolific gifted artist, whose journals had first brought this group together, but a Caterina nonetheless. They had made this shrine theirs, had used it, the stones, flowers, and candles that they lay at her feet, to schedule their meetings.

Viviana looked up into the unseeing eyes of the saint. She

wished the saint could see. Viviana wished Caterina could see into the future, could tell Viviana if what she did—what she hoped they would do—was the right thing. Would it bring them that which they wanted most of all, to be revered for their talent? Or would it only bring more devastation into their lives? This very question had haunted her for most of the night, a specter refusing exorcism. Her answer now was still the one that had kept coming to her through the darkest hours.

Without another moment's hesitation, she began to set the signal: two candles, two weeks; three flowers, three days; eight stones on the east side, eight o'clock in the morning.

Viviana stepped back and studied her work.

The possibility became ever more real. Her blood pumped at the very notion.

She closed her eyes and pictured them, guessing at what their responses would be. Not all would be the same as hers. In her mind, she saw Leonardo again. Oh, how terribly she missed him.

The scarcity of da Vinci in her life—in their lives—had been far too great these past few years. He had been sent to Milan, so he told them, as an artistic emissary by Lorenzo de' Medici himself, taking with him a young musician, Atalante Migliorotti, and the musician's unique instrument created by da Vinci...a lute in the shape of a horse's skull. Artist, musician, and lute traveled to cement the alliance with Milan. Leonardo himself decided to stay.

She understood why, looking at it through his eyes. To watch others—Botticelli, Ghirlandaio, and even his own teacher, Verrocchio—receive the most prestigious commissions, was to watch too much passing by. Though his talent far outshone theirs, in Viviana's mind as well as many others', Leonardo floundered in the heated competition that was an intrinsic element of being an artist in Florence. His focus seemed forever expanding, buzzing from project to project like a bee in a profusion of blossoms. Life was his subject, and the world his canvas. It did not sit well with those whose commissions he did not finish. It did not compete well with those he competed against. What Leonardo needed most was the freedom—the financial and artistic freedom—to follow his mind, wherever that took him. It was a hard thing to come by in Florence in those dreary days after Giuliano's murder.

When the Duke of Milan made the offer through his uncle, though Leonardo had not shared the finer details with the women, only a few hints at a regular salary from the *stipendiati* of the duke's court, and a place to call his own, he would have been a fool not to go. He visited them at least once a month, sometimes more. It was not enough for Viviana. She missed his calm wisdom as much as she missed his expert tutelage.

Yet there was one she missed far more than Leonardo. Viviana stumbled against the pang of it, a jutting cobblestone upon her smooth path. She had lost him quickly as well, to those first skirmishes of war against the Vatican and Naples, to the battles to recapture Florentine-ruled lands in Colle Valdelsa, Poggibonsi, and Chianti. Sansone Caivano was a soldier, a highly sought after, highly paid soldier. She accepted his truth. Her sons were soldiers as well—or had been—yet they had returned. Though those lands still required military protection, she thought—hoped—Sansone would have returned, to the city he loved, to her and the promise of what they could be.

Perhaps her truth—what she had done—prevented him. Perhaps his unimpeachable honor kept him at bay. Perhaps he could not, would not return to her.

Viviana skidded to a stop midstride. Her fingers fisted in her voluminous skirt. She turned, looking, as if the truth lay somewhere nearby, awaiting discovery. She found something, but was it an answer?

In the ground-floor paned windows of the Palazzo Minerbetti, Viviana found herself.

There she stood, the sun bright on her face, her reflection unvarnished.

Was she deluding herself? Had the years been unkind, or had she aged so much in his absence that he would no longer want her? With a twinge of embarrassment, she admitted she saw little change—her eyes still bright, her skin still smooth, her body still firm. But there were younger, firmer, smoother women out there, women who craved a celebrated soldier like Sansone. Had he found temptation in another?

"Stop it," she chided herself aloud as she slapped a lone tear from her cheek.

If she would never see him again, it would wound her deeply, forming yet another scar on her tattered heart. She had survived the others; she would survive this one as well.

Wouldn't she?

Chapter Three

"Regrets are often found, not in what we have done, but in what we haven't."

Viviana pulled at the chain around her neck, inserted the key in the lock—a key that all members of her society wore about their necks—and turned it. With the click came her sigh.

She stepped into the studio, closed her eyes, and breathed deeply.

Viviana knew her smile and from whence it came. The pungency of linseed oil, saffron, and poppy seeds—just some of the ingredients used to make the paint—satisfied her more than that of a rose or a lily. She sniffed the dust of chiseled stone, relished the tickle it brought.

She opened her eyes; again, she sighed.

How different the studio was from before, before Leonardo and his tutelage. One couldn't say it was any less messy, but a more organized mess. The six worktables now gathered in the center of the room, rather than along its walls as they used to be, allowing for more shelves and storage bins, more mixing tables, and more room for Isabetta when she chose to sculpt.

A riot and mess of color was everywhere, as if it had leaked and slithered off their canvasses and onto the floors and the walls. Viviana cherished it all.

Her table, the canvas on its easel beside it, beckoned. She answered, rushing toward it, stumbling to a stop as the door she'd left unlocked swung open.

He was there.

"You came!" she cried, launching herself into his arms.

For seconds uncounted, thick with gratitude, they held each other.

Viviana laid her head upon his chest. He kissed the top of her head.

"I have missed you as well, madonna," Leonardo said.

Viviana giggled like a small girl, pulling away from him just enough to see his face, to see the long, straight nose, the full, curved, almost womanly lips, to see the amber eyes that held all his wisdom, his truth, his demons. It had only been a few months since his last visit; it felt like years.

She could have cried. Instead, she teased, "Well, I can see they are at least feeding you well."

The tall man threw back his head with a bark of laughter, his *berretto* nearly falling from its perch atop his long, wavy, golden hair.

"I eat very well, *cara*," he said, rubbing his belly. "You look well, my friend."

"I am, dear man, I am."

He squinted his penetrating eyes. "You are up to something." It wasn't a question.

Viviana raised her brows high, batted her wide eyes. "Me? Up to something? What could I—"

The click and whoosh were her salvation. Viviana had no wish to speak her thoughts, to share her dream, until they were all present. The opening door, the women flouncing in, crying out at the sight of da Vinci, saved her.

Viviana stood back and watched them huddle around him, each one hugging him, even Fiammetta. She looked upon them as she did when her children were little and played merrily together.

"Well then," Fiammetta hooted, fists on her wide, plump hips, where she seemed to prefer them to be, "who called this meeting and why?"

The moment was upon her; Viviana's heart quickened. She almost changed her mind. Almost.

"I did." She stepped into the center of the group. "I have a proposition." She shook her head; that wasn't right. "No, I have an opportunity for us, for the group." She quaked beneath the penetrating stares all trained on her.

"Go on," Fiammetta nudged.

Viviana sucked in a breath, straightened her shoulders, and began. "At *la Festa di San Giovanni* I overheard a conversation. It was between Antonio di Salvestro de ser Ristoro of the Serristori family and another man I did not recognize. Antonio has purchased a *cappella*—well actually he purchased it a few years ago." Viviana rambled; she knew it. She bounced on her toes as she babbled. "But now, now that *Il Magnifico* has released the city from its mourning, allowing building and business, and allowing the arts to flourish once more, Antonio wishes to change the fresco, to have it completely redone."

"Yes, I know Antonio and his family. What has that to do with us?" Fiammetta pushed, oblivious.

Not so Isabetta. "Hah!" she barked. "*Dio mio*, you are well and truly mad, Viviana, do you know that?"

Viviana cocked her head, brows waggling. Perhaps she *was* mad—a madness that demanded they do more, go further.

"I believe we, Da Vinci's Disciples, should bid on the commission."

"You *are* mad!"

"What are you thinking?"

"Us? You want *us* to do it?"

The words pummeled her; the women closed in on her, all save Isabetta. Leonardo too said nothing. Their instant objection brought out the fighter in Viviana.

"We have the talent; you know we do," she said, an accusatory finger pointing. "Do you not think so, *maestro*?"

Leonardo stood motionless, arms crossed thoughtfully.

"*Sì*, the question of your talent is an irrelevant one. The real question is one of consequences."

Leonardo said nothing Viviana had not already thought.

"It would mean the world will know of us," Mattea muttered. Viviana could not tell if her softly spoken words were in favor of or against the notion.

"Patrizio," Fiammetta moaned her husband's name.

"He is a good, kind man, Fiammetta." Viviana pacified her with truth. "I think he may be more understanding than you imagine."

The woman's deep-set brown eyes glared at Viviana. "Perhaps. But not until he roars."

"He won't—"

"Oh, he will." Fiammetta stomped away from her, trundled to her worktable. "He will, for the only way to tell him what you want us to do is to tell him what we have done."

"Surely that's not necessary," Isabetta snapped quickly.

Fiammetta spun. "But it is. In my marriage, it is."

"Pagolo." It was Natasia's turn to speak her husband's name; her blue eyes enlarged to the size of platters. "His position. I could not do anything more to jeopardize it."

"More? What do you mean—"

"He has just been promoted," Natasia carried on. "He has become one of *Il Magnifico*'s chancellors. A lower one, but still."

"How wonderful, Natasia." Viviana preened with happiness for them.

Under Lorenzo de' Medici's new regime, one very different from before his brother's death and the wars that followed, such young men as Pagolo, those of the lesser elite—secretaries, notaries—had gained a greater foothold in *Il Magnifico*'s organization. To become a personal chancellor to the ruler meant a place in his inner circle. They accompanied ambassadors on diplomatic visits, wrote their letters, and at times, so Viviana had heard, became involved in other negotiations, those Lorenzo meant to keep more private. Others went on to serve on powerful committees, such as the *Otto di Pratica*, which supervised not only Florence's diplomatic relations but the security of the territory itself. They were a powerful force in a city filled with powerful men.

"He will be against it." Natasia ignored Viviana. "It would be too much of a risk. It could be too much of a detriment to him."

"I don't agree," Isabetta said, softly yet firmly. "*Il Magnifico* is a different man these days. He is doing a great many things unheard of before. Why may we not do the same?"

"That's easy for you to say," Fiammetta sniffed.

"Perhaps. But there has been little easy in my life. And I have survived. I have thrived."

Isabetta's husband's illness had done more damage than merely take his life; it had almost robbed them of their small butcher shop, one Isabetta still owned; it had brought them to the brink of homeless poverty.

"My mother will be livid," Mattea said, but not without the hint of a sly grin on her thin, rosy lips. "She already believes me unmarriageable, at my advanced age. Twenty-three and still not married," she mimicked with a high-pitched whine. "She will say it will be the ruin of me." The still young, still beautiful woman rolled her azure eyes, bringing her gaze to land on Lapaccia. Lapaccia missed her son as much as Mattea did; to her, she was married, for her heart belonged to Andreano now and forever.

Viviana knew she must appease these women, remind them of what they promised never to forget.

"What is it we have always wanted?" She pulled each one close to her, forming their eternal circle. "We have always wanted more, wanted our talent to be more than a secretive diversion, is it not true?"

Three heads nodded. Viviana pushed ever onward.

"We forged a painting, one that still hangs in the Palazzo della Signoria, one that is still admired and talked about." Once more, a pointed finger swirled around their circle. "*We* did that. We put our lives in danger to save one of our own—"

"I did not want—" Lapaccia sputtered.

Isabetta stroked the woman's shoulder. "Of course you didn't," she said. "But you would have done the same were it one of us, wouldn't you?"

The eldest of the group did not hesitant for an instant. "Of course," Lapaccia replied.

"Women who do such things are not ordinary," Viviana continued.

"*We* are not ordinary," Isabetta chimed in.

Viviana bestowed a smile upon her. "We want our work, our talent, to be recognized, above all else."

The silence was one of agreement—very quiet agreement.

"And we do not do it for ourselves alone." Viviana turned to Fiammetta. "What of your daughter? She is a great talent, isn't she?"

Viviana fought unfairly; Fiammetta worshipped her daughter as much as she did her God. Using the girl was a ruthless tactic. "Do you not hope for better for her? Do you not wish, deep down inside you, that she should not have to hide her talent as you have hidden yours?" Viviana's blood rushed through her. Her words were no longer words of persuasion but of her truest passion; they enflamed her. "And what of our children's children, the daughters, shouldn't they have the opportunity to be a part of the artistic growth over-taking Florence?"

Isabetta nodded. "Should they continue to be denied it simply because of their sex?"

"It will have consequences, some grave, but some amazing, for us all." Viviana's blue eyes glowed with her mania. "But what is the point of all this if it dies when we die?"

There it was; the true crux of the matter, the true purpose of the creation of Da Vinci's Disciples. There was little any could say in opposition.

"May I make a proposition?" Leonardo's voice came from the corner near the paper-covered windows, where he had stood, all but forgotten.

Viviana opened the circle to him. "Of course, *maestro*. Your thoughts, your guidance, are greatly desired."

Leonardo came to stand with them. "I propose you all return to your homes and do perhaps the hardest thing you have yet to do." Considering all they had done, it was difficult to imagine. "You must tell your families, tell them all. Beyond a doubt truth bears the same relation to falsehood as light to darkness."

Fiammetta groaned; Natasia whimpered.

"Tell them all, and what Viviana proposes. If they are adamantly opposed you will have your answer."

"A perfect suggestion," Viviana said, believing that, while it may be difficult, each woman would ultimately find not only acceptance but encouragement.

"Agreed," Fiammetta was the first to acquiesce, surprising them all. The rest followed suit.

"And what if we can't…if I can't? What then?" Natasia asked.

"Then we will not do it," Fiammetta answered, though not for all.

Isabetta cocked her head. "Then *you* will not do it."

Fiammetta's head whirled round, frizzy red strands of hair coming loose from her bejeweled caul.

"You would do it without us?"

This silence bristled.

Viviana knew the truth of it, and she could not pretend otherwise.

"We must each do what our heart tells us to do."

Chapter Four

"Returning to your beginnings begins them again."

Each time he walked the streets of Florence, paths oft tread in another life, he wondered if the change he saw and felt was in him or the city.

It was never easy for Leonardo to return to Florence, but to return for them, for the women who looked to him, he ignored the unease. Falling out of Lorenzo de' Medici's favor had cast a pall on Florence, through his eyes, no matter the depth of his love of the city. But one could not—should not—blame others when the blame rested so precisely on one's own shoulders.

Lorenzo was correct; Leonardo admitted it, at least to himself. He had left far too many commissions unfinished, he had been unproductive, and he wrestled for control of his moods, losing far too often.

But why?

He asked himself the question often.

"Signore da Vinci," the man Leonardo passed bowed his head.

"*Salve,*" he replied, a word of cheer not so very cheerfully spoken.

A group of men seated at a café called out to him, "Good to see you in town, *maestro.*"

Leonardo dipped his head to them. Their respect a needed tonic.

They called him a master. But of what? Was it so very wrong of him to long to master more than merely painting?

Do we ask the sun merely to shine? Do we not expect it to warm us, to grow our food?

More calls of greeting came his way; in his ears they were but echoes, muted in the shadow of his own thoughts.

Although nature commences with reason and ends in experience, it is necessary for us to do the opposite, that is to commence with experience and from this to proceed to investigate the reason. I must experience all I can. Should I be persecuted for it?

"No," he said aloud, to himself, to all who would hear and all who could not. For it was the answer, it was the *why* of him. There was so much on this earth to know, to study, to recreate. He could not help it if his mind jumped from one thing to another and then another.

Leonardo wandered as his mind did, finding himself at the Canto de' Tornaquinci, where the streets of the Vigna Nuova and the Spada ended in the Via Tornabuoni. A bustling intersection full of life and shops that fed that life. The sight of a large apothecary arrested his perusal, not only for its size and the varied goods on display in the windows but for the name on the placard in the shape of a mortar and pestle with a snake winding upward upon a chalice: *Landucci.*

"Could it be Luca?" he mused aloud, but did not wait for the answer to come to him; he went in search of it.

Winding his way through the dark wooden cabinets, Leonardo scrutinized the quality of the medicinal herbs and the pigments, some of the finest he had ever seen. Aromas wound around him, acidic and earthy, floral and spicy. Forgetting his quest to learn the proprietor's name, he began to pick up vials, small and large, and basket them in the cradle of his arms. Once full, he made for the back of the long narrow shop.

"Signore da Vinci! It is you! You are here!"

The call found Leonardo before he found the man.

Leonardo found his smile. "'Tis I, Luca, and how good it is to see you."

The tall man came round from behind his counter to embrace Leonardo.

"You have come home Leonardo, *sì?*" Luca Landucci relieved Leonardo of his bounty and stepped back behind his counter.

"For a visit only, my friend. But what a surprise to find you here, and with your own shop. What became of the other and your partner? I noticed no other name upon your placard."

Landucci's face, still nearly free of creases though he was nearing fifty, puckered, and he batted the air with a long and agitated hand. "Ack, what a mistake that was. All that money to expand the old shop in the *mercato?* It was all mine. That Spinelli had not a cent to his name. I quit him and that shop." The slim man puffed up. "Took me far too long to recover, but recover I did, and splendidly I think."

"It is wonderful, Luca. I am very pleased for you. So life is good?"

Luca bellowed a laugh that shook the tiny bottles upon their perch. "It is a happy life, my friend. My business is good, my children grown well, and the wife," Luca shrugged his shoulders, crooking his peppery brows. "Eh, what can I say, *cosi cosi*. It is the way of wives, good days and bad days."

Leonardo laughed with his friend, thinking it was more the way of husbands. If they kept their wives happy, then they in turn would be so as well.

"Marriage is like putting your hand into a bag of snakes in the hope of pulling out an eel, eh?" Leonardo appeased but did not agree. "But God has been good to you. I am glad to hear it."

Da Vinci's own religion was that of reason, but this man's faith was all around him. Others might be unable to see it, but Leonardo could.

"Indeed he has," Luca replied as he began to weigh Leonardo's purchases, writing each down in the ledger before him. "In fact for some years I have been travelling to Ferrara, to hear Fra Girolamo preach. Have you heard of him, Leonardo? Girolamo Savonarola?"

Leonardo had heard of the fiery Dominican. He simply nodded.

Luca perceived none of Leonardo's indifference. "I hear he is coming to us, to Florence." The apothecary stopped his ministrations, and pegged Leonardo with a serious stare. "You should make it a point to hear him preach." The man took on an ethereal expression. "He has a special message. It speaks to me."

Leonardo began to wonder if he should hear this Savonarola for himself; any man that made such an impression was either a prophet or a menace.

"I will consider it, Luca," he assured the man.

Their business complete, the two old friends embraced once more.

"Florence misses you," Luca told him.

"And I Florence," Leonardo lied, if only a bit.

"Be well, my friend. Come see me whenever you return," Luca bid him.

With a one-handed wave, the other holding his box of purchases, Leonardo assured him, "I will, Luca. Indeed I will."

Once more upon the streets, once more Leonardo's amber eyes wandered the city. As the joy of seeing an old friend faded, he saw the opulence infesting Florence and knew it for what it was: the true motivating force of its inhabitants. They had no care for experiences, only for what they could attain. They were as unequipped to understand him as he was to conform. He was, and ever would be, more of nature.

Leonardo sniffed a laugh; the memory of the bird returned. He had been told it was no memory, but a dream, a fantasy. Whatever name it was called, it had made an everlasting impression.

It seems that I was always destined to be deeply concerned with vultures; for I recall as one of my earliest memories, that while I was in my cradle a vulture came down to me, and opened my mouth with its tail, and with it struck me many times with its tail against my lips.

The truth of the event, Leonardo did not question. Perhaps it was, however, an omen.

There would be many vultures who would come and slap their tails against him. It was for him to find one that would not slap so hard.

Chapter Five

"The stars of our own making shine the brightest."

"Mama!"

The cry reached out to her as soon as she cracked opened the front door of her modest palazzo. Viviana burst with joy at the sound.

"Rudolfo! You have returned!"

They came together, arms entwining, kisses abounding, while all around them men at work continued without pause, save for one: Viviana's eldest son, Marcello.

"Yes, he finally decided to return from his travels." Marcello came to them, kissing his mother on both her cheeks. "Apparently the women in the Far East have grown sick of him."

Still with one arm around his mother, the shorter of her sons poked the taller in the ribs.

The small, healed family laughed together, as they did so often ever since the poison infecting them had been extricated from their lives.

"Actually, Mama, I have found riches." Rudolfo released her from his arms only to pull her further into the ground floor of her home, their childhood home, where their business had started, where it now thrived. She had heard them talk of moving, of setting up an independent location; it was a wave of change flowing through the city. Less and less were the ground floors of Florence's great palazzos also the master's place of business. More and more were building or occupying dedicated structures of their own. Time marched on, no matter that the feet that marched had changed.

Viviana followed readily. "Your hair, Rudolfo," she cried, truly seeing him as the wave of utter joy at seeing him passed. "It is so long."

Rudolfo shook his head, and the long strands of dark wavy hair fanned about his face, falling onto his shoulders and a bit beyond. He fussed at the long tresses, pulling them back from his face.

"It is. The style is quite popular in the Far East." The last words he said sheepishly. Viviana looked to Marcello, who rolled his eyes yet again. They both knew what those words meant in Rudolfo's mouth: women.

"Look, Mama." He brought her to a wooden crate, the top already levered open, an earthy but still sweet scent wafting out, nipping the back of Viviana's throat. Rudolfo plunged his hand in, brought it out filled with small brown pieces, each made of a short stem and a larger top.

"They look like nails," she mused, picking one up, bringing it to her nose only to dash it away as her nose scrunched in response. "What are they?"

"These Mama, Marcello, these little ones are the key to our fortune."

They looked at him skeptically. Rudolfo had always dreamed of this business, this spice business, and of sharing it with his brother. Once the wars ended, since both had served their time, they both received permission to withdraw with honor. Both returned wounded, but not seriously. Marcello's right leg pained him now and again, especially in damp weather. Rudolfo wore a small scar on his left cheek, and wore it dashingly, embellishing its origin, especially to young and beautiful noblewomen. Free to be whatever they wanted to be, Marcello had at last given in to his brother's pestering, claiming that even on the battlefield, his brother had pestered him, and the dream of the business became a reality.

"They are cloves," Rudolfo told Viviana. When he told her their worth, both she and Marcello gasped.

"Are you sure, brother?" Marcello reached in, to touch one, smell one himself.

"Very sure, *mio fratello*," Rudolfo said, pointing to more crates further back in the cavernous room. "And there, in those, is nutmeg." He lowered his voice, leaned toward them. "They are as valuable as gold. It was quite the feat to get the grower to sell to me."

"You acted honorably, Rudolfo, did you not?" Viviana cared little for riches; to her honor held far more value than gold, no matter how much of it there was.

"Of course, Mama," Rudolfo assured her. "Finding it was the tricky part. But find it I did. Take a bite, Marcello. It cleans one's breath," he said to his brother, who still studied the peculiar plant in his palm.

"Truly?"

"Truly. Try it for yourself."

They both did, mother and son. Viviana's mouth felt as if something had burst in it, something fresh and vibrant but sharp.

"May I have a few?" she asked brightly, full of pride.

"Of course." Rudolfo scooped out a handful for her with a dashing grin. "They are especially useful to chew just before kissing." He laughed. "Though I'm sure that's not why you want them."

One side of Viviana's mouth rose mischievously, her eyes slanting upward.

A dark brow rose on her youngest son's face; she laughed with delight at his comical confusion.

"We must look to Milan and Rome, Marcello." He glanced skeptically at his grinning mother. "Few have found their way to these spices. Even fewer have returned with them, yet they are desired by nobles everywhere."

Marcello nodded thoughtfully. "I have just recently been making some headway with the spice sellers in Milan. I see no reason why we can't reach out to Rome as well, especially with these."

Viviana watched them, pride growing, though she knew it was a sin to feel it so strongly. It was the way of them. Rudolfo did the travelling, going places Viviana had never even heard of, finding more and new spices to sell. Marcello stayed in Florence, made the deals with those who sold spices in the marketplace. Both were perfectly suited to their tasks; Rudolfo loved adventure, and Marcello loved his city and his music. When business was slow, Viviana could hear him from her floor above, humming along to the music he composed.

They were happy, they were successful, and they were free—free of fear, free to be their true selves. It was all she had ever hoped for them. If only she could have the same.

"Well done," she nodded, pleased, "both of you. Let nothing hold you back, not even yourselves."

"*Sì*, Mama," they answered in chorus. They were accustomed to her words of wisdom, had grown up with them, and still they did not take them lightly.

"I am for my *cena*. Would you care to join me?"

Flippant words hid her hope. There had been far too many dinners alone at the table, and she saw too many of them ahead. Granted, it was better company than that which she used to keep, but still, loneliness was a poor companion.

"Not tonight, Mama," Marcello said, kissing the top of her head. "We are off to celebrate Rudolfo's return with some of our fellows."

Viviana put on a smile that stayed only on her lips and headed for the stairs to the private rooms of living above.

"But we will both be here for dinner Sunday," Rudolfo called out to her.

"That will be wonderful," she proclaimed, joyous once more. "You have been gone far too long."

"Oh, Mama," Marcello called, stopping her. She turned back. "Would it be…would you mind if I brought a guest with me, to Sunday dinner, that is?"

Viviana felt her mouth open, but her tongue seemed unable to form words. Her gaze flitted to Rudolfo, seeing her shock writ upon his face. Such a request could only mean one thing. A glimmer of the glories of the future burst into her mind, shattered the thoughts of the lonely meal she was about to take.

"Of course, Marcello. We will make a merry event of it." She turned then, climbing the last of the stairs with more vigor than before, her mind whirling, trembling with promises and possibilities.

As Beatrice served her meal, the dear cook and housekeeper still with her though she moved much slower these days, Viviana's mind strayed to the possibilities, wandered through the city, to the homes of her friends, to the promise of what they hoped to achieve that night.

• • •

In three homes—two palazzos and one modest house—in three different parts of the city, the same conversation took place, the same confession. In each home, the reactions varied; one quacked with outrage, one grew somber with concern, one became filled with fears and tears.

For all, it was a long night.

Not until the light of dawn did answers come.

Chapter Six

"The acceptance of a challenge is the first and hardest step of all."

Viviana had no idea who had set the signal. She had walked to the shrine every day for the past four. Seeing it there yesterday, seeing its message to meet today, set her fingers tingling. She passed another sleepless night, watching the rise of the sun and the waking of the world from a perch by her window, soft linen sleeping gown wrapped cocoonlike about her legs, forehead against the leaded glass, feeling it warm as the sun rose.

Now she paced the quiet studio, once more the first to arrive. Viviana could have worked on her painting, a portrait of her mama, the woman who had taught her strength, but she knew her hands were shaking far too much to ply a brush skillfully. Viviana stood in front of it, the outlines of her mother set against the completed background of the wine vineyard that had been her childhood home.

"What would you say if you knew, Mama?" she asked of the rendering, of her mother's spirit that forever lingered by her side. "Would you think me mad?"

"Perhaps a little."

Viviana spun; a real answer had come, from the man in the door. Leonardo stood with an impish grin on his long face.

With a laugh, Viviana greeted him. "*Buongiorno, maestro*. So you think me a little mad, do you?"

His small smile dissolved. He studied her with serious intent. "Why do you do this, madonna? Why do you want it so much?"

Viviana breathed deeply, letting the air out slowly as her gaze looked beyond this room, this moment. "Do you know what it is like to be known only as someone's daughter or someone's wife?" she asked instead of answering him, gaze locking on his face. "Do you know what it is like to have no sense of self or purpose?"

Leonardo took a moment of similar introspection. "I have borne many burdens, *cara madonna*, it is true. But that is not one of them."

Viviana did not flinch. "Then perhaps you cannot understand, but, in truth, I think you can."

Da Vinci nodded slowly. "But have you not suffered enough already? Have you not faced enough challenges to appease?"

"What is the point of life if we do not continue to challenge ourselves? What we did was madness, but the way it made me feel…"

Leonardo's lips curled benevolently. "When once you have tasted flight, you will forever walk the earth with your eyes skyward, for there you have been, and there you long to return."

"Exactly! Is it wrong of me to crave it once more?"

"Wanting more, wanting better, is never wrong, madonna."

Viviana dipped her head at his dispensation, accepting it. "But it is more. I am not that wholly selfish. It is for my granddaughters."

One pale brow jumped up Leonardo's forehead as if commanded. "Is someone in the family way?"

She snickered. "No, but soon I hope, I think," Viviana replied. Her whimsical mood faded, replaced by a furrowed frown. "But even if not, what of all the other women, the young girls standing before easels, dreaming. We have to make things better for them, no matter the cost. God gave us these gifts, these abilities, why wouldn't God want us to use them? Why should there be shame and secrecy in our using such gifts?"

Leonardo took a step closer to her. "You are called to a higher purpose than painting, Viviana." How rarely he called them by name. How deeply he could see into their souls. "Come," he said, breaking his spell upon her, "come show me your mama."

They stood before the rendering, *maestro* and apprentice;

Viviana memorized every comment, every suggestion he made. For those few moments, she forgot everything but the thrill of creation. Such private tutelage did not last long.

The women soon began to arrive. Viviana studied them with the same intensity as she and Leonardo had been studying her work. She could read little on any of them save Isabetta; Isabetta she understood without effort.

They gathered together. She held her breath.

"Patrizio has slept in a separate bed for the last four nights." Fiammetta broke the pregnant silence, sliced it with a sharp-edged knife.

Viviana felt her heart fall to the pit of her stomach.

"He is furious with me, with all of us, especially you, Viviana."

Viviana rolled her eyes; she was quite certain she had been made to be the villain in Fiammetta's story far more than she truly was. Her head dropped, chin to chest.

"But he is astounded by us, by what we have done. What we are going to do."

"Going to do?" Viviana dared to ask.

Fiammetta nodded, pudgy cheeks waggling. "So it would seem, Viviana. I not only have his permission, I have his pride."

Viviana threw her arms around the robust woman, squeezing her tight. If Patrizio agreed, surely they all must have.

Fiammetta chuckled, put Viviana an arm's length away. "There are conditions, however."

"Such as?"

The woman ruminated on it. "I am not exactly sure, to speak plainly. I think much will depend on public opinion, on what it will do to his position, his standing."

"It is the same for me," Natasia chirped, as was her way, graceful fingers fiddling with her bodice ribbons. "Pagolo was shocked beyond words. For hours he said nothing after I told him of what happened after Guiliano was murdered, what we did." She turned to Fiammetta. "He slept beside me still, though I didn't sleep at all. And not for the good reason."

The women giggled; Leonardo snorted.

"He worries most about what it will do to his family name, to our standing in society," she continued. "But the day after I told him, when I revealed that the unsigned painting in our bedchamber, his favorite in the whole house, was of my creation…" Her plump cheeks grew florid. "Well, he rewarded me then, and quite nicely too."

As if the room filled with chirping birds, so too did it fill with more twitters.

"I too have my husband's cautious permission," Natasia said.

"My mother has pronounced me hopeless, a lost cause," Mattea said, a dour declaration, yet spoken with a spark of merriment. "And it is true, I am hopelessly in love. I don't think that can ever—will ever—change."

Lapaccia offered a fey smile to the woman who could be— would be—her daughter-in-law, if Andreano could only find some way to return to the city.

"Her great concern is that I shall never find a suitor. As I am not looking for one, it makes little difference." She gave a shrug, tossing off her mother's concerns as she would a stray leaf that landed on her, weightless.

"I have only myself to answer to," Lapaccia spoke last. Her chin rose, but not without a quiver. "I will do what I can, as much as I can."

Viviana knew it was a matter of her health, as did they all, she was sure. Her asthma had plagued her more often since her months in the cold, damp convent. Lapaccia said nothing to disabuse them of the notion.

A somber shroud of reality fell upon them. It was a flashing, blinding moment and, like the lightning it mirrored, not one without apprehension.

"We need to make a plan," Viviana said, knowing the best way to dispel worry was to work through it.

"I have already thought of one," Fiammetta declared. "What?" she blustered, discovering every skeptical gaze had fallen upon her.

"Yes, I may have been initially opposed, but now, if we are going to dare this, then let us dare."

Viviana longed to embrace the woman again; so often the contessa's haughty attitude annoyed her, it was true. Not in that moment.

For the first time that day, Leonardo spoke to the group; he did not waste words. "It has long since come to my attention that people of accomplishment rarely sat back and let things happen to them. They went out and happened to things."

"Exactly!" Fiammetta exclaimed. "I will pay a call on the Serristori family, this Antonio. The man is such an upstart, I am sure his delight at my appearance will catch him off guard."

Viviana stifled a cynical bark. And there it was again: Fiammetta's pretension. In this case, however, it would indeed work to their benefit. Viviana had no doubt that, under the glare of the contessa, the man would be willing to spill all, slice a vein if impressing her meant a step up the social and political ladder he strained to climb.

"I will find out as much as I can of what he plans, when he will put the commission out to bid, and when he hopes for the work to begin."

"See if you can ferret out his ideas as well, what the fresco itself will entail," Lapaccia added, to which Fiammetta nodded.

"Yes, I will wring him of every tidbit, I assure you."

Not a one of them doubted it.

"What of your brother, Natasia, what trouble will he incur?" The young Mattea revealed her aged wisdom. They had yet to consider what it would mean to Father Raffaello, not only Natasia's brother but also the parish priest of Santo Spirito. Without his help and support, their studio behind his church would not exist; without his willingness to smudge the truth, they would have been caught long ago.

"Do we ask too much of him?" Viviana feared for the priest, for whatever the Vatican may to do him if they won the commission, if women painted openly in his church. She chided herself silently for her selfishness.

"Let us ask him, shall we?" Natasia announced with little worry, dashing away, only to return with the ever more rotund priest.

"*Buongiorno,* fair ladies, Signore da Vinci," Father Raffaello greeted them cordially.

With economy of words, Viviana told him what they planned to do, what they hoped they would be allowed to do.

When she finished, Father Raffaello met her words with a small chuckle and an even smaller shake of his head. "You astound me. All of you. I am surprised to even be surprised."

Relieved sighs sluiced the air like a caressing summer breeze.

"Will you suffer for it, if we somehow make it through the labyrinth ahead of us, if we are, indeed, allowed to do this thing?" Viviana interrogated him; she had to be sure. "Will you be criticized—chastised—by the Vatican?"

The priest did not answer her. He stepped away, walked a small circle, and then stopped. "The man has paid for the chapel, paid a great deal, much of which went into the Vatican's hands. It is his to do with as he wishes." It was the truth as well as the priest's excuse. "I am overcome by his insistence on having you ladies create the fresco."

Natasia rose up on tiptoes and kissed her brother's cheek. "Thank you, Tomaso. We need not keep you any longer. I shall stop in to see you before I leave."

"Of course," the priest replied. "I am, as ever, at your service madonnas, signore."

With a nod of his large, tonsured head, he bid them goodbye and left.

Viviana trembled with excitement; she gathered herself as best she could, though she could not stop moving, walking from table to table, touching the tools of their craft.

"I know not what will come of this, whether we will even be allowed to make a bid, let alone if we will win the commission. But in the very trying, we will accomplish so much, I feel it, I know it."

Her enthusiasm was infectious. They began to talk, all and at once, of what it would mean to women artists everywhere.

Only Leonardo remained quiet. When he spoke, Viviana wished he had remained so.

"And what of Lorenzo de' Medici?" His deep, flat voice threw a thick blanket over their joyous conversation.

"What of him?" Fiammetta bleated crossly. There went her fists upon her hips yet again.

"Antonio di Salvestro will have to obtain *Il Magnifico*'s permission for such an uncommon undertaking." Leonardo stated the case flatly, far too succinctly. "You will have to receive permission simply to make the bid."

Viviana's head fell back on her neck, and she reproached herself for not thinking of it, this truth. Like a stooping bird, her spirits plummeted.

"You know him best," Lapaccia quietly said. "What do you think his response will be?"

Leonardo's head shook almost imperceptibly. "Times have changed much for the man. Those who were once his most loyal supporters have turned against him and the actions he has taken toward Naples and the Vatican. The evidence of it has been made quite public. Remember the Frescobaldis?"

Some of the women nodded sadly, others grunted with disgust.

Just a short time ago, members of three families—the Frescobaldi, the Baldovinetti, and Balducci clans—actually confessed to a plan to murder Lorenzo de' Medici, thinking they were already found out, hoping their confession would find them mercy. It hadn't. They all hanged.

"Now he has looked elsewhere for support, to the lesser elites."

"Yes," Fiammetta huffed, "even from the *popolo*. His grandfather rolls in his grave."

"True," Viviana agreed, "but isn't Antonio di Salvestro just such a man? Surely that will serve our cause."

Viviana did not think *Il Magnifico*'s political movements were quite that egregious, though it was odd to see such men like Bartolomeo Scala, the son of a miller, as the Standard Bearer of

Justice. Many like him were filling highly ranked positions, more and more as the months and years of Lorenzo's reign passed.

"*Il Magnifico* grows ever more paranoid," Natasia ruminated. "I heard Pagolo and my father speaking of it just the other evening. My uncle is ever more excluded because he is deemed too powerful. He whines about it incessantly. Rather rude of him considering our family has never reached the same lofty heights as my uncle. The fabrications that…" She blinked, eyes shifting quickly among them, words shifting just as quickly. "Lorenzo is turning to those he believes he need not fear."

"He also looks to the very common for support," Mattea chimed in. "I heard just the other day of the butcher's son being made part of the Seventy. What better way to make regular citizens love him than to go against what the elite would want?"

"It is unseemly," Fiammetta snorted.

"Perhaps." Leonardo addressed Fiammetta's disparaging vehemence diplomatically. "But in this instance, it may work to your favor. These new men have new ideas. They know what it is like to rise up, to work to gain respectability. If we make Lorenzo see that you are only trying to do the same, that you may be looked upon with approval by such men, things may go well."

"I shall go to speak to him." Viviana said the words, the thought still flitting in her mind.

"You?" Lapaccia balked. "But your…"

"History?" Viviana supplied. "Yes, *Il Magnifico* and I have a history, a connection. It may not be the best, but any connection is better than none. Yes, I will go."

"And I," Isabetta declared righteously, stepping beside Viviana.

"And I will be with you," Leonardo said, as if he spoke of taking a stroll.

"You will?"

"He will see us sooner if I am with you," the artist explained. "He will listen more closely."

As much as Viviana loathed acknowledging that their femininity would delay things, that only a male presence could erase, she was grateful for it.

"Thank you, *maestro*." She dipped her head.

They all thanked him; their devotion to him grew with their gratitude.

"Might we practice a bit?" Mattea asked quietly as she sidled up to him. "We have not had a lesson in so long."

The painter looked down at her as a father might, with amusement and pride in his small grin and his glowing eyes.

"Of course, *picolina*. Why do we not begin at the beginning? Let us make some *arriccio*, shall we?"

The women were no longer women, but artists dedicated to their craft, to learning more of it, to perfecting it. They gathered round da Vinci as he measured out the one part limestone and the two parts sand that made for the best *arriccio*, the undercoat of plaster first applied to any wall to be frescoed.

His tutelage consumed Viviana, enthralled her, as always, but not so much that she did not notice Natasia's quick and quiet retreat from the studio. She gave it little thought, knowing the girl intended to visit her brother. Viviana turned away from the closing door, and turned back to where her soul belonged, to her art.

Chapter Seven

"One cannot truly learn, if one does not share such knowledge."

It was a day not any one of them wished to end. It was a day replete with invigorating triumphs and startling discoveries.

They had all remained in the studio long past their usual time; not a one knew where their path would lead them, but each knew that the tutelage they received that day—if they received nothing else—was worth taking the first step.

Viviana jostled along in her carriage without noticing which streets they took, who they passed, or how long it took to arrive home. She knew only that she must keep the knowledge fresh in her mind until she could render it immortal on the page.

At her home, she flew from the carriage before the driver could open the door for her. She flew inside her palazzo, up her steps, and into her salon.

"Mona Viviana? Is that you?" The call from Jemma came from the kitchen above.

"It is, Jemma. I am home."

"Do you wish your supper? You are very late. You must be quite hungry."

"Thank you, no. I have no appetite."

Not for food, was her thought.

Upon her knees now, Viviana ruffled through her *forziere*, the leatherbound trunk like that found in every household, in every room. Her fingertips brushed against them, grabbed at them, the journals of Caterina dei Vigri, her deceased cousin.

Viviana sat back, rubbing an open palm gently upon them, caressing the words they held, the freedom they had given her. These journals had started it all, the words, the tutelage found in them. She would pay them, and Caterina, homage. She would continue her cousin's work. Now it was her turn to add to the tutelage Caterina had begun. In that moment, it became her duty to continue to chronicle all she had learned, all she was learning.

Jumping up, she took herself to her desk, took up quill and ink, and turned to the first blank page in the last of Caterina's journals.

Leonardo da Vinci taught his disciples the art of creating a sinopia this day.

The words came, gushed from her like wine from an overturned pitcher, vigorous and sweet. Long into the night Viviana wrote; she wrote as Jemma came and lit the candles, kept writing when Jemma brought her food, she wrote as she ate.

Her hand cramped; her fingers became splotched with ink. But she did not put her head to her pillow until the words were upon the pages. Only then did she feel her work for the day had truly been finished.

As Viviana finally lay her head to rest, she knew this was not the last night she would spend at such a task, merely the first.

Chapter Eight

"Beginnings do not always begin at the beginning."

"Jemma, the gold candlesticks, if you please," Viviana called out as she circled the large table in the *Sala dei Pappagalli*. It had been a long time since she had set the table in the family dining room with such thought and care. The best crystal goblets for the wine, polished pewter trenches, pewter knives, and two-tined forks with red jasper handles brought out the brilliance of the red parrots on the wall. The fresco that named the room, once faded from neglect, had been reborn under her brush.

Never had one of her boys brought a guest to Sunday dinner. Oh, there had been many times since Orfeo's death that they had dropped in on her, a rakish group of hungry friends with them. Bringing a guest to a Sunday meal was something different entirely, something exhilarating and worrying and buoyant, all at once.

"Really, Mama, must it be this fancy?" Rudolfo stood in the doorway, leaning against it in that boyish, manly way of his.

Viviana went to him, kissed his cheek, then spun him round. "*Sì*, it is. And it will be the same for you."

She stepped back, critical eyes scouring him from head to toe. "Could you not have put on something less roguish?"

Rudolfo's head flew back in laughter. His mother was not so amused. Rudolfo's black leather *farsetto* was of the much shortened, newer style; his tightly fitted breeches displayed his thighs and more—*Too much more*, Viviana thought—and black leather ankle boots were more for the tavern than for the Sunday table, no matter the fineness of the silk *camicia* beneath.

She pushed him. "Go. Go to your room, and see if you cannot find something better."

"*Dio*, Mama," he pouted like a little boy, "there will be nothing to fit me."

"Just try." Viviana shooed him away with her hand, shaking her head with a laugh as he stomped off to his room. Some things never changed, and how glad of it she was.

Tempting aromas filled the house: roasting veal, sautéed peppers in stewed tomatoes, baking tortes, and dough in the shape of pinecones—one of Marcello's favorites—frying in olive oil. Only the best would do for today. Viviana hoped for only the best.

"Is this better?" Rudolfo returned.

Viviana barked a laugh, palms slapping her cheeks as she shook her head.

He stood before her, changed, yes, but not necessarily for the better. He wore brocade breeches now, but instead of ending just below the knee, they ended just above it. He'd replaced his leather *farsetto* with a deep gold silk one, unbuttoned, for the ends would not meet, wrists exposed as the cuffs ended far too soon. With one fist on one hip, the other behind his head, his pose was as comical as his clothing.

"No, no," Viviana laughed more, harder, unable to speak anything else.

"Well, you're looking fine, brother."

Mother and son spun. There they stood. In the door, opened without notice amid Viviana's laughter. There she stood.

In the time it took Viviana to walk the few steps to them, first impressions of the girl were painted into life.

Tall and willowy, dressed finely but modestly, her lustrous raven hair fell in soft waves to her waist. Large black eyes shaped like almonds slanted up just a bit at the corners. Her Roman nose ended just slightly above full lips, lips curved in a smile.

A beauty. The thought skipped across Viviana's mind. She

reached out to the lovely young woman, kissing both of her smooth, soft cheeks.

"Welcome to our home," she said.

She would always call it "their" home. In truth, in the eyes of the law, the entire building belonged to her sons, as dictates decreed at the passing of their father. Not once had either son uttered a single word of her vacating it, of her returning to the vineyards where she grew up, where she would be but an unwanted guest in the home now run by her uncle and his wife and their five children. To her boys this would be, forever and always, where she lived, her home. Viviana had intoned more than one prayer of gratitude for it, for them.

Marcello leaned down to kiss his mother's cheeks; she caught just the wisp of sweat on his upper lip. It told her all she needed to know.

"Mama, this is Carina di Tafani. Carina, please make the acquaintance of my mother, Viviana."

The young woman dipped a slight curtsy. "*Buongiorno,* Signora del Mar—"

"Please, dear one, call me Viviana." She still could not bear the name she carried, far heavier than any burden a donkey had ever lugged on its back. "If I may call you Carina?"

"Oh, *sì,* of course. It is my honor," the girl gushed, voice as bright as the twinkle in her eyes.

"Let us to table, shall we?" Viviana suggested, with a gesture of welcome into the dining room.

Her son and his guest stood with stiff twitchiness; such nerves needed a good dousing of wine.

It didn't take very long for them to fill themselves with food and wine, to fill the house with laughter as Viviana told Carina all the silly, oftentimes stupid things her sons had done over the years. She boasted too of their bravery and their accomplishments; both sorts of tales embarrassed her sons equally. She asked Carina only a few questions about her life, her family; Viviana did not want to appear a prying old widow, a parent overly concerned with petty details.

There would be plenty of time to learn all her truths, if Viviana was meant to learn them. It was a merry table, a joyful time.

Rudolfo and Marcello chimed in, trying to best each other with increasingly embarassing stories about the other.

Viviana picked up her goblet, made as if to sip slowly. Instead, over its rim, she watched them, her sons and this new, wondrous creature coming into her life. She felt the branches of her tree stretch and blossom with glorious blooms.

Time slipped away unnoticed beneath the warmth of enjoyment, until the sky began to darken.

Marcello stood and embraced his mother. "I do so hate to end this merriment, but I must return Carina to her family."

"Of course, of course," Viviana rose in his arms, walking the couple to the door, noticing Marcello's proprietary hand on Carina's lower back. She had raised a gentleman, indeed.

"It was the greatest pleasure to meet you, Carina," she said without a trace or twinge of artifice, for she felt the need for none. "It was lovely to have you here."

As they kissed each other's cheeks, Carina assured her, "It was quite the loveliest day. Thank you, Sig…Viviana. Thank you so very much."

"You'll come back? We did not scare you away, I hope," Viviana laughed, though her question was not wholly jocular; she knew herself to be gregarious, overly so at times, especially when her nerves tingled.

"I will count the days till I may return," Carina replied with genuine grace.

"*Buona notte,* Mama." Marcello leaned down once more to kiss his mother. "Thank you, so very much, for everything." These words he whispered, words of gratitude for her alone.

Viviana felt them pull on her heart as she put palm to his cheek. He made for the door.

"Oh, I almost forgot." Marcello turned back, his lopsided, childhood grin spreading from ear to ear. "Did I tell you, Mama? Carina, she is a painter."

Marcello's laughter carried him down and out the door as his mother stood utterly still at the top of the stairs.

● ● ●

He left them with a wink, a cuff to his brother's shoulder, and a jaunty step.

"Tomorrow, brother," Rudolfo bid them farewell as he ran off to wherever he cared. "Carina, *bellisima*!" He whirled around, kissed the tips of gathered fingers, and tossed them in her direction.

Carina giggled, sneaking a look at the sweetly handsome man beside her. His eyes deep brown in the growing dusk, twinkling as he tossed a smile at his brother.

"*Sì,* tomorrow, my silly brother," Marcello chuckled, as he watched his brother's form fade into the night. "He *is* silly," he jested.

"He is young and loves life," Carina murmured. "You all do."

Marcello turned to her, a wondering look on his face. "Did you enjoy yourself today?"

"Oh, yes, very much. Your mother is delightful." She grinned and kicked a stone with her toe; it jangled away from them over the cobbles. "It is lovely to see sons so close to their mother."

"When people survive great challenges together, there is a bond formed unlike most others."

They strolled in a peaceful cocoon of amiable silence. The city simmered in its summer glory; the chirp of crickets kept time to a man singing somewhere close by; laughter wafted out of opened windows upon the stream of aromas of cooking food; feet pattered here and there. Few stayed indoors on such a night.

Carina relived the day, the meal, meeting his family. There was so much more to them than she knew, she was sure of it. What she did know, with absolute certainty, was that she wanted to know all of it, all of them.

"We know who we are by how we survive," Carina replied thoughtfully, eyes unblinking as they held his firmly.

Marcello took a step closer to her; she tingled at his nearness, warmed at his grin.

"My mother has often said the very same," Marcello whispered.

Carina closed her eyes as he leaned down, as his lips softly met hers.

• • •

Dumbfounded, her heart still thudded in her chest. Viviana felt the same twitch of her fingers as she did before plying brush to canvas. What did it mean? What did Marcello mean by tossing such words at her? Perhaps more than one family would grow.

"Your boys are good men."

Viviana whirled round. Her knees almost buckled, but not in fear.

He stood upon the balcony, tall and lean, sinuously sensual; he stood in the opened door that welcomed the warm summer breeze.

"You've come." It was all she could think to say.

He said nothing. Nothing of where he had been, why he had been gone so long.

Sansone crossed to her, closing the gap between them in a few long strides. Grabbing her by the back of her hair, he pulled her gently to him. Her mouth opened in welcome. He kissed her, kissed her as she had dreamed he would, as she imagined he would for all those years. His tongue was a food on which she had longed to sup, on which at last she had been fed.

He kissed her face, her ears, her neck, the pleasure of it a wave of tingles that ran through every pathway of her body. Her knees quaked, no defense against the pleasure of his onslaught.

At last in his arms, and I am to faint. The passing thought made her laugh, an unfeminine guffaw. A second thought stifled her. Would he think she laughed at him?

But she felt the rumble in his chest, the firmness pressed against her.

His hands reached round to the back of her, and with the

whoosh of fine ribbon he pulled on her laces, slowly and ever more slowly as he reached lower and lower.

O Dio mio, she thought, *I wear my oldest chemise.* It was the very worst sort of thought for the moment, and once more, she laughed; she sounded like a donkey.

He pulled back from her. His eyes searched every inch of her face; she felt them wash over her. What he saw there, she could not tell, but whatever it was forced his lips upon hers, harder this time, not to be denied.

The door left ajar allowed egress for a breeze, sweeping the tangle of clothing and ties and laces and lace in a scatter of petals, whooshing softly as they fluttered down onto the stone.

Viviana stood before Sansone, now in nothing more than the cursed chemise, but its state had long been forgotten. He swept his hands down the sides of her, the tender skin between arm and breast, inward along the sides of her waist, outward over the full roundness of her hips. Then up again to cup her face, green eyes ablaze.

"Your room, Viviana. Your bed," he whispered.

She stood rooted, confused. With a shake she gathered herself, for she had almost laughed again, her nerves the cruelest foe, playful though they may have been. Instead of laughing, she led him to her study and the settee. She would not yet lie with him, not in that bed, no matter the ownership she had taken of it.

Viviana sat and patted the cushion beside her, tilting her head at the puzzlement writ so clearly on his sharp-boned face.

Sansone stood over her. With a gaze that never left hers, he slowly shed doublet, boots, breeches, and his linen undershirt, revealing slim firmness, hard curves, and glorious edges. In his naked splendor, he brought his hands to his hips, lovely creatures topped by the loveliest of dips between muscle and bone. Her eyes moved lower, bulged.

Her thoughts must have been etched upon her face, for he blushed, but not without a sensual half smile.

Viviana giggled, bit her tongue, bit off the frustrating urge to laugh that would not stop pestering her.

"Really, Viviana, this is not the reaction a man hopes for in such a situation."

She giggled again, helpless. She drew in her bottom lip and bit it hard. The pain dashed the cackles away. Once more, Viviana rubbed the space beside her.

He shook his head. He did not sit. He knelt, knelt before her, face-to-face. With a single kiss, he began to move. Pulling her chemise down, pushing it up, he revealed her body as the fabric puddled at her waist.

Oh thank the lord, she thought, so very pleased that the fleshiest part of her was covered, and again laughed. Viviana's eyes rolled up in her head. Why, oh why, did she keep laughing?

His lips, his tongue, traced the curves of her, the pointed tips of her breasts, the curve of her hollowed stomach, the edges of her hips, and then lower still.

She gasped. She planted her feet and pushed. She scurried up the small couch.

"What…what do you do there?"

Sansone dropped his chin, but not before she saw the twitching of his lips. Playful nerves became playful no more.

"Worry not, *cara*. It is the best place I could be." With smile unhidden, he pulled her back toward him by her ankles, opened her legs, and lowered his moist mouth to her once more.

She gasped yet again, but neither from shock nor nerves. She gasped until she cried out.

Above her trembling body, he rose in one long, lithe movement, until he held his head inches from hers. She dropped her eyes.

"Look at me, Viviana." Sansone nuzzled her neck with his nose.

Viviana shook her head, tangled hair swooshing softly upon silk.

"I have sinned."

"Open your eyes, *tesoro mio*."

She heard the chuckle in his voice as he called her his treasure. Her cheeks burned as she raised her head, as blue eyes found green.

Beneath his gaze, she could hold her tongue no more.

"I did not know."

He shook his head, the playful smile shrinking. "That, my dear lady, is truly a sin." Sansone lowered his lips to hers. "Taste yourself," he whispered into them.

She groaned. She could not squelch it, though she did try. Her hands threaded through his hair; her desire wound her fingers tightly through the dark gold floss.

Lowering his hips to meet hers, to match a rythm she did not know she beat, with slowness he allowed himself to dance in her forest. Viviana shivered with each pass of the smooth hardness. He tended her need; it was a creature she had not met, not for all her years.

She laughed. And this time so did he.

"You really shouldn't make me laugh while we do this," were the last words she heard him say. The rest, if there were any, were lost, as she was lost.

• • •

They talked deep into the night, as it turned and began its inevitable trudge toward dawn.

Sansone told her of the battlefield, of his wounds, showing her the deep scar that ran down the length of his right thigh. Viviana kissed it with a sigh, thanking all she believed in that it was only this wound he had needed to recover from, that he had not succumbed to infection as so many soldiers did.

They talked, wrapped in each other's arms, holding tightly as if afraid to let go, afraid they would not come back to this place, afraid they would fall off the small settee but not caring to move from it.

Sansone asked many things of her; of the years of her widowhood he had missed, of how much his absence had pained her.

"It seemed so unfair," Viviana whispered. She felt his head nod above hers, which rested on his chest. To have longed for him for years, to have the freedom to fulfill such longing, only to be separated by something as stupid as war.

"But you have been working, yes? You have been painting?"

Viviana raised herself up to gaze upon his face. Would she not share all, could she not, after what they had just shared?

She rose, pulling her chemise up with irrational modesty. Without a word, she left him, only to return with two goblets and a bottle of trebbiano. She filled both their cups with the white, light, fruity wine, and as they drank, Viviana told him all, sitting in her favorite chair across from him.

Her tale told, Sansone sat motionless. He had sat up halfway through her story; he had continued to drink.

When he finally spoke, she wished he hadn't.

"You put yourself in danger again," he said, almost flatly except for the jumping of his jaw.

Viviana swatted the air. "There is no danger in it. Yes, we may be ridiculed. We may lose whatever standing each of us has in the community. But that is not danger. Such things hold no true weight in a true life."

"You have not thought of all the consequences and repercussions." Sansone shifted forward on the settee. "If you succeed, if you win this commission, you will be taking work from other artists, men."

Viviana shrugged dismissively.

He grabbed her by the hand. She felt the jolt of both attraction and tension in the single touch.

"Do you know what I think? Do you know why Florence bursts with such artistic magnificence?" His green eyes pierced her. "Because they are hungry. Because there are so many artists here and only so many *concorrenzi* to be bid on. Their hunger drives them to be greater. A good thing. But men who lose work, lose money, and to women?" Sansone shook his head, looking away from her, to what she could only imagine. "Such men can be dangerous, far more dangerous than you think."

Carina's face burst into Viviana's mind. *She is a painter*, Marcello had said. One who, no doubt, painted as a pastime, as Viviana had done, longing for it to be more than that. She knew it was true by Marcello's laughter.

She answered Sansone with the same words she had said to the women, words of legacy, words of freedom. Viviana watched the effect they had on his beautiful face, watched his shoulders fall.

"You are not a normal woman, *tesoro mio*," he said at last.

She heard neither happiness nor sadness in his conclusion.

"Is it so very bad that I am not?"

Sansone studied her face for a long time. "If we love," he finally spoke, "we cannot love only parts of someone but the very whole of them, or it is not love at all."

Viviana breathed, as she had not when he studied her, a breath trapped by fearful premonitions. One word she heard loudest, as if he had screamed it louder than all the others. The word had never passed between them before. In her mind, what they had just done together had answered the question for her. Had it for him? She hated to ask, hated to feel the need to ask, hated the hidden weakness that lived within her that needed to be assured. But ask she did.

"And is it? Is it love?"

Sansone rose, comfortable with his nakedness, far more comfortable than Viviana was with it, for it captured her, brought a rush of desire she thought had surely been stoked. Looking at him, she realized it might never be. How did one satisfy seven years of longing? How could such longing ever slacken? Could such longing *ever* be satisfied?

He came to her, pulled her up to him, and pressed her to him tightly. Such an embrace she had never felt before.

Sansone's sharply carved face hovered inches from hers. "It is all that and more, *tesoro mio.*"

His mouth found hers; their bodies sealed the pact.

Chapter Nine

"At times, it is easier to face the dragon than to slay it."

They looked up before the palazzo that Cosimo I had built, the Medici palazzo. It punctuated the intersection of the Via de' Gori and the Via Larga where it bent slightly to the right, at the corner with the Via de' Gori. As one approached, the palazzo's form elongated diagonally, as if reaching out to the baptistery and cathedral of Santa Maria del Fiore. Palazzos in the Santa Maria Novella quarter of Florence were not merely palazzos but communes, connected blocks of palazzos inhabited by those who could afford to build them.

Here it had stood, this new incarnation of it, for not quite fifty years. Brunelleschi had submitted a design, only to have Cosimo instantly reject it for its ostentation; he had no desire to arouse envy among the citizens. Instead it had been Michelozzo di Bartolomeo who had blended the Tuscan Roman elements—the *pietra forte* and rustication—with the modern—the biforate windows and the massive cornice that capped it. The transition from the rustication of the ground floor to the delicate ashlar of the third only made it loom taller as one looked up, a physical representation of the intangible force that was the Medici, a force that impended ever higher, ever more powerful.

Viviana's knees quivered. She looked to Isabetta; the woman's face was far paler than usual.

"Come along, ladies," Leonardo urged them both gently. "It is, after all and in truth, just a home."

"Just a home." Isabetta sneered at him in derision. "Sometimes, *maestro*, you can be quite maddening."

"Thank you, my dear," Leonardo replied, not perturbed in the slightest. He rapped his knuckles quickly, twice, upon the carved wood door. Just as quickly, it opened for them, a man in the red and gold liveries of the house stepping aside as soon as he saw Leonardo upon the threshold.

"*Grazie*, Paolo. His study?" Leonardo asked of the man.

"*Sì*, signore." The man dipped his head, pointed the way forward, though it was only a formality; Leonardo knew his way around this palazzo, had lived in it for a few years when the troubles were upon him.

"This way, my dears," Leonardo said softly.

The eyes of those who had built the Medici dynasty locked upon Viviana from out of their frames. Each portrait hung on the polished mahogany of the entry hall. Piero the Gouty, Cosimo *Pater Patriae*, Giovanni di Bicci de' Medici, the last considered the founder of the family, of its power. Viviana walked stiffly past them, following their stares from the corner of her eye.

"How lovely." Isabetta's worshipful whisper brought Viviana's gaze forward, into the glorious courtyard awaiting them, situated just to the left of the palazzo's center. It was lovely indeed, a vista with the power to overcome all anxiety.

Four great stone columns anchored the quadrangle-shaped courtyard at each corner. Between each pair stood two more columns connected by graceful arches topped by a broad, horizontal band of sculptures. Pagan-themed medallions alternated with the centuries-old Medici crest, the six *palle* the family attested symbolized the dents upon Averado's shield, a knight of Charlemagne, he whom myth held had defeated the giant Mugello, and a knight to whom the Medicis claimed relation. Looking upward, one saw the inner exterior of all three floors, the blue sky, and the sun shining down through a wisp of cloud.

"How glorious it would be to paint here," Viviana murmured.

"You cannot imagine," Leonardo affirmed. He led them to the left, through the columns, and into the roofed portion of the courtyard. "Wait here just a moment."

Viviana's foreboding awaited her in the shadows. "Do not leave us…" But he was gone, through a door that closed quickly behind him.

The two women inched closer to each other, shoulders rubbing, gaining strength from the touch.

"We must be as emotionless as possible," Viviana whispered, as much to herself as to Isabetta.

"We are artists, we are about naught but conducting the business of art, the same as any man, any artist," Isabetta championed, chin jutting, shoulders rising. Viviana's jaw tightened, no longer with dread, but resolve.

"Come along," the call came, from Leonardo's voice, from *the* door.

United, the two women walked through it.

The opulent room, walled with the same glistening mahogany as the foyer and bedecked with exquisite tapestries, overflowed with an array of objects d'art and artifacts that filled almost every nook and cranny. Viviana recognized two ancient marble busts of Augustus and Agrippa. Not far from them, she spied what could only be authentic Chinese vases. Jeweled daggers, coins, medallions, and antique cameos lay everywhere, as if tossed casually aside. The most dominant objects, though, were books. Like strewn petals, they were scattered everywhere with no rhyme or reason, some open, some closed, piled one atop the other. Among them lay books of another sort, journals, some with their ink barely dry.

All were inconsequential in the face of their owner and the city's ruler, Lorenzo de' Medici. Viviana had only been this close to him once before, when he condemned her husband to death. She looked at him far more closely now than she had on that fateful day.

How could it be that he was, in truth, so plain in appearance? He had swarthy skin beneath a cap of straight black hair that fell to his chin, dark eyes set deep and close, a long nose seemingly squashed upon his face. Only average in height, yet he seemed to fill the room with his broad shoulders. Those same dark eyes pierced as sharply as his daggers.

"*Magnifico*, I present to you Madonna Viviana del Marrone and Isabetta Fioravanti," Leonardo graciously introduced them, with little attempt at curtailing his possessive pride.

As if rehearsed, they dipped into curtsies of the same depth at the same time.

"Fair ladies." The harsh voice brought them back up. Lorenzo stood and came round from behind his gilded desk to stand before them. His air of domination and preeminence expanded. At thirty-five his masculinity—the virility of him—was ageless.

He studied them as he might one of his artifacts; Viviana felt as if he were undressing them, so intense was his scrutiny. She suddenly realized she had no notion what Leonardo had said of them or why they were there. Lorenzo quickly freed her of her ignorance.

"My friend here tells me you have come with a request?"

They answered him with silence. Viviana could have kicked herself; they were utterly unprepared. "We have, *Magnifico*." She cleared the croak from her voice, fingers twining and twisting with each other. "I will tell you straight away, it is a request that you may find unique."

Lorenzo chuckled, with a quick glance at Leonardo. "Why does that fail to surprise me? Well, then, you have prepared me. Continue."

"We would—" Viviana began.

"Before we tell you of our request," Isabetta cut her off brusquely, taking a step closer to the powerful ruler, "we must tell you who we are, what we are."

Lorenzo's dark brows shot up his short forehead. Just the hint of a grin, a smirk, appeared on his thin lips. "Are you not two citizens of Florence, both widows?" He jutted his protruding chin toward Isabetta in her widow's weeds, yet made no mention of Viviana's husband; there was no need.

"We are that. But we are much more." Isabetta unfurled her shoulders, fingers clinching doggedly.

Lorenzo's eyes slanted as they roved over her, down then up; his grin widened. "I am tantalized. Tell me then, who and what are you?"

Isabetta looked sideways to Viviana, to Leonardo, finding strength in their steadfast gazes.

"We are artists, *Magnifico*," she began, softly respectful. "We are painters and sculptors who have studied our craft for many years, some for the majority of our lives. We have our own studio where we create masterpieces." Her voice rose and ended with commanding conviction.

Lorenzo blinked, glance darting between the two women before him. This man had experienced great power and blinding fear, war and death, pinnacled heights and hellish lows. Upon his face, Viviana swore she glimpsed surprise.

"I have been tutoring them for over six years." Leonardo saw it too, the man's surprise, his incredulity.

Lorenzo's sharp stare targeted the artist. Leonardo shrugged his shoulders in response. Lorenzo rolled his eyes heavenward, then back to the women before him.

"As you have no men to keep you appropriately occupied, I suppose there is nothing untoward in your activities," Lorenzo ruminated dismissively.

"We are not all widows," Viviana said quickly, perhaps too quickly.

"'We?' There are more of you?"

"Six in all, *Magnifico*," Isabetta avowed. "Three widows, two married, and one as yet to marry."

Lorenzo de' Medici, ruler of Florence and all its territories in fact if not in rank, took two steps back and leaned against his desk. "And the husbands of those married and the families of all, they approve of their womens' activity?"

Viviana tilted her head with a squint of her eyes, a thinning of her lips.

"Possibly 'approved' is not the most accurate word." She pictured Patrizio, Fiammetta's husband. "Perchance 'accepted' is more precise."

Lorenzo chuckled darkly at that. "And what is it you want of me, *artiste donne?*"

He called them women artists; it was a start.

"I…we have learned," Viviana began. This, their request, was hers to make. "That Antonio di Salvestro de ser Ristoro of the Serristori has purchased a chapel in Santo Spirito. He wishes to have the fresco repainted, with an entirely new design."

"It is typically done," Lorenzo replied.

"And we would like to bid on the commission."

Her words, their message, stopped *Il Magnifico* as abruptly as any army ever had.

"Surely you jest."

"We do not, *Magnifico*, we are serious, deadly serious," Isabetta said harshly with a look upon her face that begged defiance. Viviana nudged her with her elbow. Isabetta continued, this time more amiably. "We have the talent. We have the resources and the time. And the married women have their husbands' permission."

"*Dio mio.*" The blaspheme slithered through Lorenzo's straight rows of teeth. He rose up, walked to them, stopping only inches away. "I know women have little notion of politics, but…"

"In that, I must disagree." Viviana couldn't catch the words as they flew from her mouth. "We are all very aware of the state of our Republic, of your efforts to bring it back to its former glory." There was more she could say, more of their knowledge of Lorenzo's tribulations, but she captured those thoughts before they became words. Most men seemed to trivialize women further the more intelligent they deemed the women to be, as if such intelligence threatened their own.

Lorenzo's dark eyes narrowed. "Then you know there could be reprisals for such permission, were I to give it. Reactions that may not further my cause."

He spoke to them plainly, as he would to men. It gave Viviana hope.

"Or it could garner you greater power, such as that which you seek among the *popolo.*"

The hard smirk appeared on his face once more, but Lorenzo did not speak. The next words belonged to Leonardo.

"We know how life truly works; we men only believe we are in control. What goes on behind the closed doors of homes and bedrooms, the force of the women behind those doors, they are the true rulers." Leonardo spoke with his quiet wisdom, which was often so very loud. "It will go well with the women, with many women. I feel certain of it."

Once more Lorenzo glared at the artist.

He turned from them then, walking slowly back behind his desk to sit in the large wing-backed chair. Lorenzo steepled his hands together, long fingers touching at the tips as he tapped them against his lips. Viviana squirmed; each moment felt like the span of a lifetime.

"Make your bid, madonnas," Lorenzo returned his attention to the array of papers before them, dismissing them already from his mind as well as his chamber, "but I think I shall hear no more about it."

"How——" Isabetta stepped forward, a lunge, red splotches blooming on her face. Her beauty became a fearsome thing to behold. Lorenzo did not miss it.

Leonardo and Viviana caught her by the arms.

"*Grazie, Magnifico,*" Viviana said obediently. "*Grazie tante.*"

"Many thanks, dear friend," Leonardo added, receiving a scoff from Lorenzo that held a note of displeasure.

Together they turned Isabetta away, Viviana reaching back to close the door behind her before Isabetta could say anything that would cause the man to change his mind, but not before she caught the gleam of Lorenzo's gaze upon her friend, a blaze of attraction in his eyes.

Chapter Ten

*"Once you have set your brush upon the canvas
do not let fear create false strokes."*

"It's been announced!" Mattea burst into the studio, rubicund spots tinting her cheeks. "It has been posted!"

Their words burst in the quiet room like fireworks in a black sky. Gone were the days when only one or two of the artists worked in the *studiolo*, when some came only once or twice a week, sometimes less. In the days that had followed Viviana and Isabetta's visitation to *Il Magnifico*, since they had received his permission to bid—as dismissive as it was—more of them came more often, almost all and daily.

Today only Fiammetta and Mattea had not attended.

"You should have seen them crowding around," Mattea huffed.

"Please be quiet, everyone." Viviana raised her voice; she had no choice. "Slowly now, dear Mattea." Viviana led the animated girl to a stool and brought her a cup of watered wine. "Here. Sip, breathe," Viviana coaxed her like an agitated child. "Now, tell your story, every bit, and slowly."

"Well." Mattea let out another staccato breath as the other women gathered round her perch. "I was coming back from the *mercato*, but first I went to the Baldesi palazzo on the Via Caizaiuoli. I had to deliver a christening gown I had embroidered. It was really the loveliest work I had done in some time. I put in—"

"Yes, *cara*, I'm sure it was," Isabetta cooed, guiding the young woman's focus back toward the target. "You can tell us all about it, after you tell us about—"

"The commission, *sì, sì*. When I came back out of the Baldesis', I noticed a crowd of men around the *Arti del Medici e Speziali*. Well, it could only mean one thing, no?"

They all nodded. They all knew a crowd around the Guildhall of Doctors and Apothecaries, the guild to which painters belonged, always meant one thing and one thing only—a request for bids on a *concorrenzi* had been posted.

"Though I never expected to see *that* commission, our commission." Mattea spoke of the *cappella* fresco as if it already belonged to them. Viviana thought such resolve a powerful thing. "But then I heard the milling men speaking of Antonio di Salvestro, I saw his name at the top, and I knew. I knew what it was."

"You didn't try to read it, did you?"

Leonardo startled them with his harsh tone; it was a note he never sang.

"N—no, I didn't. There were too many men. I never could have gotten close enough."

Leonardo sighed, as did Viviana. They must tread this virgin path carefully. They must keep it a secret for as long as possible, until—or if, a brittle voice in Viviana's head tried to correct her— they actually received the commission. Things would go much smoother if they could.

"Good. Good," Leonardo told Mattea, easing the look of worry on her sweet face. "I will take myself to the guildhall. I will find out the details and re—"

"No need, *maestro*. I know everything we need to know."

Fiammetta flounced into the room. "I have spent the morning in the lovely company of one Antonio di Salvestro and his wife, Fabia."

"And?" Viviana prompted her.

"And"—Fiammetta sauntered farther into the room—"it was as we expected. They couldn't have been more thrilled to have a contessa in their home. They were effusive with their congeniality, serving me such wonderful *biscotti*, and something called barley wine. It was quite robust, I must say."

"And? The commission, Fiammetta," Isabetta prompted harshly.

"Ah, yes, well…it is to depict the Legend of the True Cross."

The pronouncement fell on the room with a loud thud.

"It is an ambitious piece," Leonardo said politely what they were all thinking.

"It is an enormous undertaking," Viviana said, stating the truth of it. She had seen such a fresco before, in the Basilica di San Francesco in Arezzo, done by the master Piero della Francesca and his studio. Francesca was an old man now, no longer painting, but his work, this particular work, many considered one of the great masterpieces of the era. And now they were to try to create another. A compendium of medieval legends that began in the time of Genesis, concluding to the seventh century, the Legend of the True Cross was a chronological sequence depicting the journey of the wood that would come to form the tool of Jesus Christ's crucifixion.

"There are so many scenes to it," Natasia burbled.

Viviana swallowed. To depict the Legend of the True Cross was to create a series of murals, from the death of Adam to the Battle of Heraclius and Chosroes, all of which spoke to pieces and relics of the True Cross, depicting the scatter of it across the lands. She counted in her head.

"Eight. There are eight depictions in all. Eight." The last word squeaked out of her.

"No, no." Fiammetta shook her head.

"Yes, Fiammetta, I have seen it my—"

"Yes, I mean no, they do not want all eight. They only want three, one for each wall. For the lunettes he wants nothing but blue sky and wispy clouds and for the bottom tiers merely serene landscapes."

The women huddled around her sighed. Too soon.

"But the scenes they do want are those with the most figures in them: *Death of Adam*, *The Adoration of the Wood and the Queen of Sheba Meeting with Solomon*, and *Exaltation of the Cross*."

"Oh, well, that's much better," Isabetta croaked. The Salvestros had chosen three of the most complicated of the eight scenes portraying the legend.

"It is, *cara*," Leonardo assured her, attempted to assure them all. "The omission of the battle scene is a great boon; it is by far the most complex and difficult of them all."

"That is true," Viviana agreed, yet her mind still felt heavy. "I suppose it would not be nearly as impressive if they had included *Burial of the Wood.*"

That scene had but three figures in it and was quite small in comparison to most of the others.

"It is what this is all about, is it not?" Isabetta postulated. "These rich people and their chapels. They do not decorate them to pay homage to any god, but to themselves and those they wish to impress."

No one could argue. As Florence had begun to flourish once more, and as luxury became ever more luxurious, such frescoes had become a standard by which to measure a family's wealth and position.

"I have no doubt you can do this." Leonardo's voice matched his straight back.

"Nor do I." Fiammetta shocked them. "I know what talent we have, what we are capable of with these hands of ours." She held hers out only to draw them back quickly. "But I do not know if I still want to do this."

"Why, what has changed for you?" Isabetta pestered her quickly.

"Time," came the answer, not from Fiammetta but Lapaccia. "Such an enterprise will take a great deal of time, many, many hours, many, many days, weeks, months. I do not know if I have such time."

"What?"

"Are you ill?"

"No, my dears, no. My illness is as it's always been, nothing more, nothing worse," she assured them quickly. "It is just…I am not as spry as I once was. I tire much more easily these days."

"We will ask no more of you than what you can do, Lapaccia, never fear." Mattea eased Lapaccia's agitation tenderly, just as a true and loving daughter-in-law would. The other women added their soothing voices to Mattea's.

"There is something else to consider," Viviana said thoughtfully. She related what Sansone had told her, what he had said about men and their possible reaction to loss of work, loss of money. She did not tell them whose words she repeated. "We must all be prepared, not only for disapproving reactions, but for angry ones."

"How much is the commission worth? Did he say?" Natasia asked, receiving a sidelong look of cynicism from Isabetta. It was easy to ask of money when the question of it in one's life was never in question.

Fiammetta's face puckered. "Fifty florins," she spat.

"Fifty!" Mattea exclaimed.

"Yes, fifty. A measly fifty florins." Fiammetta turned to Viviana. "If you will stop this nonsense, Viviana, I will give you the damn florins myself."

Mattea spun on her. "My share would feed my mother and me for a year. It is unkind of you to belittle it. But we do not do this for the money. *I* do not do this for the money."

Viviana scanned her sisters' faces. "We continue then?"

"Yes." Isabetta and Mattea voted with vehemence.

"We do," Natasia said softly.

Lapaccia merely nodded.

All turned to Fiammetta.

The corpulent women huffed a breath, stood up, grabbed a brush from the nearest table, and announced, "Of course we do."

Chapter Eleven

"How can one be themselves if they do not know who they are?"

The young woman hurried down the quiet street, grateful for the tranquility of the midafternoon rest. The heavy heat of the day would only find more at rest than usual. It also found her drenched in sweat—hunched over, chin low—beneath the cover of her hood and cloak, an uncomfortable necessity. She was a wraith, a shapeless, faceless form scurrying through the city just like the rats in the gutter.

It was not the first time she had traveled through the city alone, hidden beneath such garments. It would not be the last. The heat scorched from below as well as above, rising through her slim slippers, rising up from the paving stones. She prayed that this outing would be more productive than the last.

Had any started to notice her absences, her late arrivals, her early retreats? She flung the questions from her mind; refused their poisonous venom. She must not waver in her quest. Though she might question it—why her, why now—the answers, when they came, always comforted, always ignited the fire burning within her, the passion for the truth she sought. It scorched her as the falsehoods had her family for too long. She must make this appointment today; she was getting closer, she knew it.

She approached the front door of the church, as anxious for the coolness of its marble interior as she was for anything—any help—she might find there. The priest waited, opened the door a crack as he spied her through the stained glass of the massive arched door.

"Around back," he hissed at her, ticking his balding pate toward the right side of the church and the path that wound its way around it.

"Of course, Father," she panted, nodding and scurrying around as directed, slithering through the tall spire's shadow.

When she reached the back door—just a plain, small wooden door—he was already there, holding it open for her.

She hurried in.

"This way, my child," his words rushed at her as he rushed her through a narrow hallway, down an even narrower stairway, and into the stone basement. The coolness was a blessing; the moldy scent of the seeping stone was not.

He led her to one of the small scribe desks filling the room. "I think I may have something that will help you, but it is not definitive."

"Any help at all, Father. I will be most grateful."

She threw back her hood, leaned down over the papers, and began to read the age-yellowed parchment.

Chapter Twelve

"Journeys of great import are traveled on many paths."

In another part of the city, two other women made a pilgrimage of their own.

Viviana insisted she accompany Fiammetta on this visit, though the contessa assured Viviana that her presence was not necessary.

"You do not know how they will react," Viviana told her. "If there are arguments to be had, is it not better that I have them, not you? We do not want to remove the authority of your status in their eyes. We may need it later on."

"Well, I suppose that is true." Fiammetta puffed up. Viviana bit her lip. Manipulation did not come easily to her, but she did it when forced. Fiammetta made it easy—annoyingly easy.

It was a short carriage ride to the Serristori palazzo, just over the Ponte Trinta and onto the Via Maggio, one street east of the Piazza Santo Spirito. Viviana rode in Fiammetta's carriage, checking every thread in her finest gown and *gamurra*, preferring she herself find a fault, if there was one, before the contessa did, as she surely would.

As they climbed out of Fiammetta's carriage, Viviana's gaze rose upward, drawn to the finely sculpted capitals atop the cube-shaped palazzo, to the smooth polished stone of its façade. She thought it quite beautiful.

"Do not be fooled by what you see on the outside," Fiammetta told her, catching Viviana's admiring look. "Such taste did not make its way inside."

Viviana gave no response; whether Fiammetta was correct or simply envious that these "new" elite should have a palazzo as fine as hers, Viviana did not know. She would judge for herself.

The door was opened by the *maggiore duomo*; the mere fact that they had a *maggiore duomo* made Fiammetta squirm, as such servants belonged to the true nobility of the city, or so it was in her mind, as she had told Viviana on too many an occasion. It was an irritation wiped cleanly away as the man and woman of the house came rushing to her, effusively sycophantic.

"How lucky are we." Antonio di Salvestro de' Serristori flew toward them on his ostrich legs, his petite gazelle of a wife scurrying to catch up. "The contessa pays us another visit."

He struck a flourishing bow, far too extravagant, rising up only to take Fiammetta's hand and bow his horse-like face over it. Viviana now understood Fiammetta's desire to make this visit alone. It was not that she cared if someone witnessed such unctuousness, only that the experience of such a display should belong to her alone.

"We are so pleased to see you again." Fabia, glistening raven hair braided and twirled about her head, curtsied with drama to equal her husband's. "And you have brought a guest. How wonderful."

Fiammetta introduced Viviana to the couple, who fawned on her as they had Fiammetta simply because Fiammetta called her friend. The dichotomous couple—he so tall, thin, and gangling; she so short, curved, and graceful—led them through the house, past their sitting room—the room where they should have brought their guests—to the center of the palazzo and a grand salon.

"See?" Fiammetta scoffed softly. "Garish."

Viviana remained silent; she had no care to agree with Fiammetta, though she did. Every room boasted sculptures, frescoes, and far too much gilding.

Pleasantries passed between them like playing cards; those dealt by the couple always with a toadying dispensation. They waited as a servant brought a lovely platter with cheeses, sliced meats, and fruit along with two choices of wine. With a shrug, Viviana indulged in the delicious offering. But such tidbits and chitchat could only last so long.

They had filled their mouths with food and then words, until there was nothing else to be offered. It was time they made their offering.

With a fleeting shared glance, and an imperceptible nod, Fiammetta took the first step toward their truth.

"You are such lovely hosts"—*How smart of her to begin with a compliment,* Viviana thought—"but it is not just your gracious company we have come for today."

"Is it not?" Antonio said, even as he chewed on a piece of smoked mortadella.

Fiammetta chastised his poor manners with a withering look, but continued. "No, Antonio, I…we have come to tell you something, something you may well find a bit shocking, and to ask a kindness of you."

"Oh, you know we will do anything for a friend," Fabia twittered, a baby bird chirping for food.

"How pleased I am to hear it." Fiammetta used her guile and her status to its full potential. "My dear friend here and I belong to a special group of women."

"*Meraviglioso,*" Fabia's cheeping voice continued, "I do so love women's societies. They are so charitable."

"Well, yes, that is true," Fiammetta agreed graciously but continued righteously, "however, ours is not that sort of society."

Antonio's dark, almost singular brow rose up his high forehead. "And what sort would it be then?"

The fiddler stopped playing; the time for dancing was over.

"We—that is, Viviana, myself, and four others, including Signora Lapaccia Cavalcanti, you know her, do you not?" Fiammetta dropped the powerful name like a boulder in a puddle. "Of course you do," she continued, before they could find a way to admit the truth. "Well, we are"—she pulled in a deep breath, let it out in a rush of words—"a group of artists under the tutelage of Leonardo da Vinci."

Their hosts gaped at them. Two pairs of chestnut eyes bulged in concert.

"A—artists?" Antonio stuttered.

"Leonardo da Vinci?" Fabia breathed.

"Yes, both are true," Viviana replied to their mutterings, which were all they seemed capable of managing. Fiammetta had done her job; it was time for her to do hers.

She quickly told them of her cousin, the great Caterina dei Vigri, and her legacy, which the Disciples had chosen to continue.

The couple met her dissertation with stony-faced astonishment; they had become yet two more statues to populate their home.

"I…I…" Antonio shuddered, as if to break free of the marble that held him. "I do not know what to say."

"You need not say anything, yet," Viviana cajoled, slipping to the edge of her seat, approaching him as she would a frightened puppy. From the large reticule she had kept close to her side since the day's mission began, she produced a thick bundle of parchment, all very neatly gathered and tied with a thin, brown ribbon. She held them out to Antonio.

"Inside you will find our full proposal in response to your posted commission."

He looked at her, full-lipped mouth a cavernous maw. His narrowed eyes clouded beneath his hunched brow.

"For the commission, for the fresco you wish to have created in your *cappella* at Santo Spirito," she explained further, as if he didn't understand. It was not understanding he lacked, but comprehension.

Antonio made no move to accept the offering hanging in the air between them.

"You…you women—"

"We are called Da Vinci's Disciples," Fiammetta said with all the pretention she could muster, a potent power. "It is the name of our studio as well as who we are."

"And you wish to bid on the commission?" Antonio struggled with the assault upon his senses; it was there in every twitch, every clipped breath.

Viviana brought the package back to her lap. "You will find our proposal developed to every detail. We have seen to every aspect, a list of supplies and their cost, a well-mapped timeline for its completion, as well as basic sketches of the proposed scenes."

Once more, Viviana held the parcel out to Antonio. Once more, he made no motion to accept it. Yet the parchment slipped from her grasp nonetheless.

"I am a poet, did you know that?"

Viviana looked up at the woman who had spoken, to her hostess, who had stood and accepted the parcel from Viviana.

"I did not, Fabia," Viviana murmured; her breath quickened now. She dared a sidelong glance at Fiammetta. "I would love to read some of it."

Fabia returned to her seat, the parcel safe within the crux of her arms, pressed to her chest.

"I served *Il Magnifico*'s mother for a time, when I was but a young girl," Fabia told them, high-boned cheeks blooming with pride.

Viviana shot another glance at Fiammetta. It was a little treasure of information dropped in their laps.

"I was very young, just a girl of twelve, but I learned a great deal. Signora Tornabuoni de' Medici said I showed great promise."

Like the women of Da Vinci's Disciples, Lucrezia Tornabuoni de' Medici had been a woman far ahead of her time. Her depth of study had matched any man's; her talent as a poet was still renowned. A buzz of excitement trilled in Viviana's ears. If this woman could bring the lingering influence of *Il Magnifico*'s mother into the situation, it could only bode well for them.

"What a remarkable experience it must have been for you," Fiammetta said with unaffected tribute; any woman of an intellectual bent would be blessed with such tutelage. "We have, in fact, spoken to *Il Magnifico*." Fiammetta turned to Viviana, who quickly took up the thread.

"We have indeed. I myself, with another of our group and Signore da Vinci, were allowed an audience with him concerning this very subject."

"You spoke to him?" Antonio jumped in. "You spoke to *Il Magnifico* about my commission?"

"Not only about your commission, but about our group and our hope to complete it for you."

"I want to include his likeness in one of the frescoes. What did he say? Tell me. He should know he is included in my plans." Gone was the fawning sycophant. In his place there now sat on the very edge of his chair the social and political climber that Antonio was to his core.

"He readily gave us his permission to present you with our bid," Viviana declared, not allowing a hint of weakness, or an intimation of the flippant manner in which the permission came.

The man's stare released Viviana, darting a glance to his wife, to the contessa, and back.

"He did?" Of all the things that had flabbergasted this man this day, the draining color from his tawny face showed this to be the most staggering of all.

"He did," Fiammetta and Viviana said in concert, with a quickly shared grin at their collusion.

"Well, that it is magnanimous of him, isn't it, *cara*?" Fabia said to her astonished husband. "As devout Mediceans, it is our duty to take it seriously then."

Her husband whirled on her. "But—" he began.

"I fear we have kept you long enough." Fiammetta stood before he could protest, before he could natter at his wife for her declaration. Viviana stood quickly beside her, her stare never leaving Fabia's. She saw a strength there she would not have thought the woman owned when first they'd met, a strength that added to Viviana's hope.

"We have enjoyed your company," she guilelessly told her hostess. "I would like to come again, if I may, to read some of your poetry."

The woman rose, a shimmer of pink pleasure on her porcelain cheeks.

"That would make for a most wonderful visit. At your pleasure, signora."

In the small squeeze that Fabia's hand gave hers, Viviana felt the soul of a kindred spirit. Her own spirit soared.

"Thank you, contessa, and you, madonna." Antonio caught himself, brought himself back to the realization of his place beneath Fiammetta's, to the effusive manners his elders had taught him, and that his position demanded. He stood and led them to the door. "We are honored, as always, to have you in our home."

"Thank you, dear man." Fiammetta offered him a small curtsy; Viviana almost barked a laugh. Fiammetta was fully in the fight now. "Till we speak again," she said to him from the threshold, "which, I am sure, will be soon."

"S—soon, *sì*," he muttered.

There they left him, in the shadows of the empty hollow beneath the great arch of his front door, floundering in the thick sludge that was his confused mind.

"Well," Fiammetta chortled as they settled once more in her tasseled carriage, "I think that went well."

Viviana remembered the look on Fabia's face when she told them she was a poet, felt once more the squeeze of the woman's hand.

"Very well indeed," she agreed.

Chapter Thirteen

"Once the paint is on the canvas it is a great thing to remove it."

It had become a habit of theirs, a lovely habit. Two widows taking the early morning air, strolling to the *mercato*, making the day's purchases. Viviana often bought items for Isabetta—little indulgences Isabetta could not sacrifice a single lira to purchase herself. At first, Isabetta had argued, her pride a heavy weight. When Viviana returned to the market without her, she purchased the item, and had it sent to Isabetta's home. Isabetta had laughed at her friend's generous temerity; she no longer argued.

"Is the day not exceedingly fair?" Isabetta said, as they stepped once more upon the cobbled street of Viviana's prosperous neighborhood.

"The rain has washed the air clean," Viviana agreed. The night and all its wonders fluttered in her mind, in her stomach, and yes, even lower. It had been a night spent once more in Sansone's arms. Their lovemaking had been a thunderous thing, bursting with flashes of blinding light as Viviana found herself more and more at ease—more and more of her own unbridled self—in his arms.

"Well, where does that smile come from?" Isabetta asked, whisking away Viviana's recollections as the rain had the humidity.

Viviana felt the rush of heat upon her face. "Is it so very obvious?" *Is it still necessary to keep it a secret?* She asked herself.

"Very. I—" Isabetta jolted to a stop. "You have been with a man."

Viviana's lips spread wide; her skin tingled with the glow of his remembered touch as if it had branded her. With a laugh, she reached for Isabetta's arm again, linked it with her own, and continued their walk as she told Isabetta of Sansone.

As they reached the church of Santa Maria Degli, half the distance to the *mercato*, Isabetta, speechless throughout Viviana's confession, though her mouth never closed, sat abruptly upon one of the many benches in the small piazza in front of the church.

With her hand, she fanned herself.

"I was wrong," she said, "it is hotter than yesterday."

Viviana laughed at her friend's particular brand of humor, sighed with relief that there was not the tiniest tone of censure in it.

"How did you manage it? Such wanting, such desire, for all those years?"

Viviana shrugged, but it was hardly dismissive. "I would not become *him*."

Isabetta snickered with a grin. "And now Heaven rewards you."

If it does, it rewards me with you as well, Viviana thought. Isabetta's tender acceptance was a reward as great as any in her life.

"What are you going to do?"

"Do?" Viviana pulled in her chin. "What need I do, save enjoy myself?"

"Will that be—"

They didn't see the two men approach; hence, they did not see the glare of blatant anger on their faces until they hurled it at the women like a blast of fetid air.

"You are a disgrace to all women," the shorter of the two men harangued them.

The women flinched in surprise, in defense. Viviana feared they had been overheard; an unmarried woman having sexual relations could warrant such a reaction.

"Women cannot paint; they *do not* paint," the tall, thin man said.

Viviana looked at them, truly looked since they'd approached. Both wore long tunics; both tunics bore splotches of paint.

The tall man spat at their feet, a giant glob of phlegm turning the gray stone black.

"Return to your kitchens where you belong," his short fellow declared.

As quickly as they had come, they were gone.

The men turned the corner of the Via Strozzi, and disappeared from sight. The two women held each other tighter in the vacuum of odium in which they had discovered themselves.

"They know," Viviana gulped, though she shook her head against the possibility of it. "The city knows."

How they knew was a mystery, but Viviana was quite sure of it; somehow, the fact that there was a group of women artists and that they had bid on a commission had become public knowledge. Quickly she rejected the idea of Fabia possessing the loose tongue, but her husband...

As Isabetta scrutinized the street around them, causing Viviana to do the same, she simply nodded.

If eyes could truly throw daggers they would be in pieces, such were the scornful stares piercing them from every corner of the street.

"Do we go back?" Viviana asked. Back to their homes. There was no turning back from their challenge; neither would stand for that.

Isabetta answered, lips pulled into a sneer, "There is no going back. That moment has long since passed, and good riddance to it."

Viviana snuffled at the woman's wisdom. There truly was no direction to go but forward. They could not retract their bid without doing more harm than good. To hide within their homes would only be a surrender, a denial of their determination. It would be a fruitless one; now that word was out, they must brace themselves for such reactions whenever they were in public.

Viviana stood. "Well then. I guess we best get used to it."

She held out her hand to Isabetta who stood and took it. Once more arm and arm, they continued on to the *mercato*.

"So, tell me, Viviana, how big is Sansone's...that is, I mean..."

She laughed, as did Viviana. It felt good to do so beneath the deluge of disrespect.

"Now, now, my friend," Viviana giggled, "I am a lady. No matter what these cretins may think of me at the moment."

"Oh, please," Isabetta begged, with the exuberance of a child. "It has been too long...I cannot..."

Viviana understood her stuttering. Her husband, Vittorio, had passed away from his illness, one that had plagued him for years, not three months ago; it had altered the very course of Isabetta's life. Whatever her desires, like Viviana, her honor was stronger.

"Let me experience it through you. Tell me a little more," Isabetta pleaded, with a glimmer of a salacious grin.

"Perhaps," Viviana teased her. "Perhaps someday. But not this day."

As they had stepped into the large square that housed the *mercato*, the number of stares and denouncements increased within the highly populated courtyard. Men called out cruel obscenities; more spat at them. They were suddenly ostracized strangers in their own homeland.

They held their heads high.

"Let us get what we need and return home," Viviana muttered. "But do not rush."

If they must suffer the slings and arrows of venomous people, they would do so with dignity. Or so she thought. Never would she have expected how many farmers and vendors refused them service.

As if they carried the plague, the crowd parted wherever they walked, space meant to divide and denigrate. Viviana and Isabetta stayed as conjoined as possible, shopping together whether they looked for the same things or not. As they passed before the pungent stall of the spice vendor—whose product they need not purchase, thanks to Viviana's sons—the vendor's wife jumped up from the small stool where she sat behind the rows and rows of chopped and powdered herbs.

The plump but worn-looking woman gathered a handful of

cinnamon sticks and wrapped them in thick velum. The woman finally met Viviana's gaze as she passed the package to her.

"You are very brave, madonnas," she said merely with her breath, lips parted yet barely moving, as her eyes slipped sideways to where her husband waited on other shoppers.

Viviana accepted the package, and the woman's words, with the same wave of gratitude, straightening her shoulders. "*Grazie,* madonna." She saw the first hint of a smile on this haggard woman's face at being addressed so; it was all Viviana could give her in return.

"You should see what flowers they have today." The woman tilted her head toward a stall down the row, looking younger than she had a moment ago.

"We will," Isabetta replied with a resolute and grateful nod.

The woman operating the flower stall stood as they turned her way, as if she lay in wait—in hope—for them to come.

Her smile and the warmth of her greeting told them who—and what—she was: another compatriot.

"What is your specialty of the day?" Viviana asked the young, pale-haired beauty who stared at them as if they were the Madonna herself.

"The *primula* are especially beautiful," she replied, wiping her hands on her apron, tucking her chin and with it, her fey smile.

Viviana looked to where she pointed, looking to the burst of life and color that was the five-petaled flower, these a royal blue with a delicate yellow center, a flower whose name meant "the first."

"I shall take them all, every one you have," Viviana declared, raising her voice so those lurking around them, the far too many of them, heard every word.

The bunch of flowers—bunches—were almost more than Viviana could carry, and she shared the load with Isabetta, insisting she take some to her own home. As Viviana reached out to place a gathering of soldi in the girl's hand, the girl leaned toward her.

"Do not let any stop you," she whispered, serious whispers through the false front of a mouth wide with teeth. "There are so many of us that are proud of you and your courage."

The flower girl pulled back, pocketing the soldi, raising her voice. "*Grazie*, Mona del Marrone. Please come back again."

"Oh, you can be assured of it," Isabetta answered.

They did not obtain all they had hoped to purchase that day, but they received more than planned, things both brilliant and thunderous, espousal and evil.

Isabetta and Viviana, arms now full of primroses and cinnamon, turned from the market stalls and headed back toward the Via del Corso.

Just as they made to turn the corner onto the Via del Vecchitti, something hit Viviana in the back, a hard hit from something soft and squishy that thwacked against her. "Oomph!" Viviana cried out, stumbling as her body pitched ahead of her feet. Only Isabetta's quick arm stopped her from tumbling headfirst onto the stones.

Isabetta spun round, fury trembling in her fists; she could not tell who had thrown it. She turned Viviana around, finding the viscous, red, and pulpy remnants of a tomato, one that lay in smooshed pieces at their feet.

With one finger, Isabetta scooped some of it off Viviana's back and slathered it on her tongue.

With eyebrows raised, an approving if menacing curve on her lips, she looked back at the multitude glaring at them from the square.

"Hmmm, quite good," she called out, as if she were supping at the table of a nobleman. "Come along, Viviana."

Isabetta linked her arm once more with Viviana's and, with fear-tinged laughter bubbling from her, headed for home.

Chapter Fourteen

*"It is one thing to travel beyond our boundaries,
it is another altogether to expect companions."*

The message from Milan had come yesterday. It lay upon the desk in his old room in Verrocchio's studio. He ignored it, though it screamed out to him whenever he glanced its way. It was a nagging Leonardo wished to deny, yet he could only forestall giving in to it. Part of him longed to cede to it, longed for Milan.

As he dressed that morn, it once more cried out to him. Or was it his own longing that pestered him? He commanded it to shut up as he left the room, shutting the missive within.

The sounds reached him first. As Leonardo descended the wooden steps from the small rooms on the third floor of Verrocchio's building on the Via Carnsecchi, just steps away from the Duomo, the voices and clatter of men at work rose up toward him like the voices of a choir, so soothing were the sounds of art's creation.

He stopped; voices caught his ear, the sound of them as familiar as the grinding of pestle on mortar, of hammer striking chisel. The notion, when it came, came as if from the heavens.

"Buongiorno, Leo." Verrocchio's warbling greeted him before he had decended to the last step.

"Good morning, *maestro,*" Leonardo answered. It had been years since Andrea del Verrocchio had been his master, but the man would forever be that to him. He had been Leonardo's first and only teacher, the finest teacher one could hope to have.

Verrocchio was still the bulbous-faced, portly man he had been when Leonardo's father had brought him to the master's studio to be an apprentice. Verrocchio was still as volatile, one minute decrying mistakes in a painting his apprentices produced, the next crying at its beauty. Though now, in his fiftieth year, the thick cap of black curls sprouted far more gray than black, and it seemed as if he had grown an additional chin or two with the sagging of his skin.

"Now we will see," Verrocchio bellowed to the man beside him as Leonardo approached.

"Sandro." Leonardo gave greeting to the man without kissing his cheeks, or even a handshake.

"Leonardo," the reply came in kind.

The years had passed, but what lay between them had changed little.

Both were products of Verrocchio's studio, both brilliant. Leonardo had shone first; Botticelli had shone brighter. Each knew it was not a question of who possessed more talent—they both knew Leonardo held that distinction—but who put it best to use— that belonged wholly to Botticelli. For each man, the particular success of the other was a pebble in his shoe.

For Botticelli, his most recent work, yet another commission from the Medici, *The Birth of Venus*, was talked of in artistic circles not only in Florence, not only across the Italian peninsula, but across all of Europe. Not only was it the first canvas of its size— nearly ten feet in width—it astonished with its sense of motion. Though Botticelli did not practice, as so many of his colleagues did, the realism at the core of painting at the moment, its lack marked its success, its monumental glory, as all the more glorious.

For Leonardo, many viewed his move to the court of Milan as a retreat, if not a surrender, yet none knew of what he created there. Not yet. The duke's letter, entreating him to return, to continue preliminary work on the mural of the Virgin, was beginning to feel like a portent, but one he must shelve, at least for a while.

"Home again, Leonardo," Botticelli said from between curved lips. Seven years younger than da Vinci, his youth still hovered around him, fell down his back in luxurious waves of almond crème–colored hair, and shone in the brightness of his large if heavily lidded cerulean eyes.

"This is my home today," Leonardo answered, but turned to Verrocchio. A purposeful dismissal if ever there was one. "What is it we shall see, *maestro*?"

"Come, Leonardo, come," Verrocchio stomped through the maze that was a studio at full production to stand before a large canvas in the last stages of completion.

"Our friend here"—Verrocchio had always chosen to ignore the animosity between his two brightest pupils—"feels it is too austere."

Leonardo studied the painting, which depicted the Madonna with Saints John the Baptist and Donatus. His perusal was a silent one; even his footsteps made not a sound as he studied it first from one angle, then another, and yet another.

"I can see why he might think so," Leonardo finally spoke, but it was through the fingers of the hand that held his chin. "It has none of the brightness of his *Venus*."

Botticelli's finely curved brows rose.

"However," Leonardo continued, "it is a masterpiece of modern techniques. The architecture and still life elements place it firmly in our time. The modulated tile floor creates an amazing dimensionality. I particularly like your use of the carpet's fringe."

Over the step in the foreground of the painting, said fringe hung, making one feel as if they could walk through space, through the canvas, and into the painted scene. Of course, all three men knew the painting was not of Verrocchio's own making, but of his workshop; he had not picked up a brush since Leonardo, while still young and unknown, had added his famous angel to Verrochio's *The Baptism of Christ*. That angel had brought word of da Vinci and his talent to earth, a talent that broke the brush of Verrocchio.

"It may not be to your taste, Sandro," Leonardo addressed him directly, "but I am sure you can see the magnificence of the rendering."

It was an offering, a diffusion, as much as Leonardo could offer

Sandro, and he must if he dare ask what he planned, what he hoped both men would accept.

"Of course," Sandro agreed, readily enough. "We are all individuals. My apologies, *maestro*, for any disparagement I may have cast on your astonishing work."

"No matter, no matter," Verrocchio brushed away their compliments, but a wide grin smattered itself across his face, a rosy glow upon his plump cheeks. He bustled away from the painting and any disparagements that attempted to land upon it. "Let us celebrate with some wine."

The three men settled around a table in the middle of the chaos that was a studio at work, as solitary as an oasis in the desert.

Leonardo passed words, pleasantries, talk of their work, somehow the words forming on his lips while others haunted his mind. He must bide his time; he must wait for the right moment.

When Verrocchio patted his hand with an age-spotted one and said, "You will have your own studio, and soon, my son," Leonardo saw it for what it was: not only a sign but a blessed one.

"Well, in truth, I already have one." He made the declaration as he threw back the rest of the wine in his goblet, two mouthfuls at the least.

"You do?"

"Where?"

Leonardo filled his glass and began to talk. He capped off his tale with another chug of wine.

"Women? You are *maestro* to a group of women?"

Leonardo felt the pinch between his shoulder blades as they barged together. He fixed Sandro with a steadfast gaze, with all the fortitude he possessed. "They are not women when they hold the brush or the chisel. They are artists, incredibly talented artists. And they have submitted a bid on a chapel fresco."

Sandro laughed.

Leonardo had never struck someone in his life; however, his life was not yet over. He buried the urge; instead, he silenced Botticelli with hard eyes and a curled lip.

"And I will tutor them through it," he said as if nothing had been said in between. "I had hoped to be here for the whole of the process, but the duke has called for me to return, though it shall be a hasty trip. Nor will I leave until the work is well underway."

His mentor, his teacher, his surrogate father never blinked, never broke his confounded stare. A furrow formed between Verrocchio's pinched peppery brows.

"Have you not endured enough, my friend? After what you have been through, do you really wish to call such hazardous attention to you?"

"What makes you think it will be hazardous?"

"What makes you think the world will accept women as artists?" Botticelli scoffed.

"Is not the furthering of our vocation worthy of it? Should not the greatest art be made regardless of who makes it? We have been part of monumental change; we have changed the very nature of painting and sculpture. Does your vision truly stop there? Is not the work, the craft, no matter who may do it, the most important thing of all?"

"Great art, by women," Botticelli sniffed with a self-righteous chug of wine. "It's absurd."

Leonardo pounded a fist upon the table. "I assure you it is not. If you had seen what they have already done, you would become a believer too."

"Isn't it enough that we have to compete with each other? Now we have to compete against women as well?" Botticelli spat pugnaciously.

"Think of how many will be angered by this." Verrocchio allowed his gaze to rove about the studio, touching on the many men at work, at study. "You think any of these men's ilk will allow it?"

"It is not for them to decide, is it," Leonardo answered. "*Il Magnifico* gave the women his permission to bid."

"Lorenzo?" Botticelli sat up, closed cynical expression replaced with one of open astonishment. "Lorenzo knows and approves?"

"He does." Leonardo saw no reason to tell these men of

Lorenzo's skepticism; for him it was yet another hurdle, not one to overcome, but to extinguish. He had no doubt Sandro and Lorenzo would laugh together over it, perhaps laugh at him. He cared not a whit. Leonardo knew to whom the final act would belong. "The women have already submitted their proposal. It is—"

"Do you speak of the Cappella Serristori in Santo Spirito?" Verrocchio asked, refilling his own goblet. Of course the man would know of it; he knew of every commission, all work underway in his city. "It is scenes of the Legend of the True Cross, *sì*?"

Leonardo nodded. "It is."

"It is a difficult piece."

"And yet their preliminary sketches are..." Words failed him. Leonardo looked upward, sideward, as if the word he searched for hung in the air. "They are masterful; there is no other way to say it."

"How much of them are your own?" Botticelli quipped.

"Not a one," Leonardo answered, without sparing him a glance. "I am there to advise, to teach, not to do. One does not learn without doing." Gladness crossed his face, a telling turn of the lips, a silent acknowledgement of what he had learned by teaching.

He captured Verrocchio's gaze with an unflinching stare. "I understand now, *maestro*. I understand the thrill you feel every time you instruct only to see the instruction become brilliant performance."

The old man tilted his head to the side, eyes glazing perhaps as the faces—the years and years of work—of his greatest pupils passed through his mind: Perugino, di Credi, and, of course, Ghirlandaio. "It is a blessing as much as the gift itself," he acknowledged.

"Then perhaps you may care to be more blessed," Leonardo said, teasing. "And yes, perhaps for you as well, Sandro." He notched his arrow, released the string. "I need your help. They need your help."

Neither man across the table from him spoke. They simply stared, their silence demanding he continue.

"I will, at some point, have to journey back to Milan." Leonardo leaned toward them, hands splayed upon the scarred wood table between them, closing the gap. "While I am gone, they will need guidance. And I can think of no one better than the two of you."

Verrocchio flounced back in his chair.

Botticelli raised his goblet to his mouth. "How much have you had to drink, Leonardo? Either you need less, or I require more."

"I need nothing," Leonardo rejoined. *"They* need you."

"Do you realize what such involvement could do to us? To my studio?" Verrocchio muttered.

"To our reputations," Sandro chimed in.

"I do." Leonardo sat back, twining his arms together across his chest. "I know that to be a part of great change, meaningful evo-lution, could only lift the reputation of any man—any person—to loftier heights."

Both of the men before him had already accomplished such a feat, had been the leaders of the epic progression in art now taking place. He knew they were drunk on it. Like any drunk, they always wanted more.

"Before you answer, I request just one thing." Leonardo leaned toward them once more. "Come to their studio. Come and see for yourself what they can do."

Botticelli looked down at him, down his long and thin nose, but said nothing.

The silence, the magnitude of the request, hung above them like a rain cloud about to burst.

"I will go," Verrocchio said simply after a time.

Botticelli studied his *maestro*. He sat back, grabbed his goblet, and blew out a breath that rattled his lips. "And I shall accompany you."

Chapter Fifteen

"Fate may write the fortune; only we can seal the wax."

The women were the first to arrive and they arrived en masse. Dressed in their finest (or borrowed fineness), they would face this personal and professional gauntlet as one, no matter the outcome.

The six women and their *maestro* hovered before the closed door to the grand ballroom in the Serristori palazzo. The *maggiore duomo* was kind enough to bring chairs for Lapaccia as well as Fiammetta, which he placed at the feet of two of the many statues lining the long hallway.

A knock sounded on the outer door. From its cracked opening the sound of male voices blared. The fraught moment became even more so.

"*Dio mio.*" The words slithered out from between Isabetta's teeth. She was the first to see the new arrival.

Piero del Pollaiuolo entered the foyer, his older brother Antonio right beside him. Seeing them, both men skidded to a stop. Two pairs of matching narrowed eyes targeted the women before them.

"Da Vinci," Piero greeted Leonardo and Leonardo only. Almost of an age, their paths had crossed on many an occasion. Leonardo was ever a threat to the brothers' own notions about themselves.

"Piero, Antonio, *buongiorno,*" Leonardo replied, quietly polite as ever.

The two men didn't move, save to look at each other.

Antonio turned away first, pushing past the *maggiore duomo*.

Jostling the man against the wall, he tossed his words over his shoulder. "Come, brother. Tell your master we will wait outside." The last command he huffed to the doorman.

"Well," Fiammetta harrumphed, crossing her arms beneath her large bosom. "I never."

"You must get used to it, madonna," Leonardo counseled. "Here you are no contessa, only an artist. No, not even that, merely a female forgery of one in their eyes."

Voices within the ballroom silenced them, their need to overhear far greater than the need to argue. More than one of them leaned in close to where the two large doors met.

"They are not alone," Isabetta muttered at the others.

They realized that if Antonio and Fabia were not alone in the room, they would not be the only ones to judge the proposals, to make the decision.

"Who could it be?" Natasia asked of them all, pulling her ear away from the sliver of space between the doors.

"I fear I may know." Leonardo sounded worried, a rare sound. "It may be the *Opere*."

"*Dio mio*," Isabetta moaned.

The *Opere* were a group of four to eight men—each called an *operai*—elected or appointed to oversee both civic and ecclesiastical building projects, including whatever artworks such projects might entail. It was not unheard of for private patrons to seek their guidance when making decisions on their own personal ventures.

"I am not surprised," Viviana whispered, as if the statues hovering all around them might tattle. "Antonio is not a decisive man. His concern is for his status and little else."

"So not only do we bid against the Palloiuolo, but we will be judged by a group of men they have undoubtably worked with before." Isabetta paced the small foyer. The men's work, especially Piero's *Coronation of the Virgin* on the altarpiece in the cathedral at San Gimignano, finished last year, many considered as some of the finest frescoes in the city.

"These men know nothing of art," Fiammetta grumbled. "The *Opere* are engineers, builders, nothing more."

"That may well be," Lapaccia said, "but it is Serristori's right to have them present."

"Then we will just have to be that much more persuasive," Mattea said without a hint of worry, standing tall in one of Natasia's discarded gowns that she had altered to fit; its deep red color crept up to her cheeks.

The group took solace from their youngest member, from her strength in the face of adversity. It did not last long. Voices from outside the palazzo slithered toward them as malicious mutterings.

"I cannot make out what they are saying," Natasia whispered.

"Or who is saying it," Viviana chimed in.

"I will see." Leonardo left them before they could object. He returned just as swiftly.

"A Pietro," he said.

"Who?" more than one owl-eyed woman hooted.

Leonardo dropped his chin. "Perugino."

"*Dio mio.*" Isabetta again.

"Can you think of nothing else to say?" Fiammetta turned on her.

Isabetta gave a snide look. "*Che cazzo.*"

Fiammetta blanched; she was not alone.

"Does that not please?" Isabetta asked with a flutter of pale lashes.

"I—"

The door to the ballroom opened; another liveried servant stood in the threshold.

"All artists may come in now," he declared.

As Leonardo predicted, seated on either side of Antonio and Fabia were four members of the *Operai*, as signified by their red robes. To a one they were either bald or gray haired, with curled backs, or bulbous bellies, or both. Viviana saw one thing and held onto it: the bright smile Fabia sent their way as greeting. Viviana returned it with a dip of her head.

As the other artists joined them, as they all took a place around the mammoth table covered in embroidered silk and topped by four ornate brass candelabra, Antonio nodded at each of them. More than one noticed the small bow of his head directed at Leonardo da Vinci, the only bow offered. How grateful Viviana was for the *maestro*'s presence.

"We," he began, voice echoing off the frescoed coffers of the high, vaulted ceiling above, turning to the members of the *Opere* as well as his wife, "have been studying each of your bids for a few days now, every aspect of them. We have but a few questions, if you do not mind."

No objection came.

"To the Palloiuolo brothers, why is it you only have members of our family in *The Death of Adam*?"

Antonio looked askance at his brother; no doubt it was Piero who had rendered the sketches.

"Signore Serristori," Piero bowed his head in greeting before answering, "we thought it would bring greater attention to you if you were all present in one portion of the whole fresco, rather than spreading your likenesses throughout."

"But that is not what the commission conditions called for," Fabia spoke up; softly, yes, but firmly. "And another group has included members of both our families and in all three scenes."

Piero did not look at her. His frustration with the female sex extended to her as well. Viviana knew Fabia spoke of their sketches, for they had indeed done what she said.

"Signore Perugino," Antonio turned his attention, "your proposal states completion in nine to twelve months. Do you not consider that an extended period of time for the breadth of the work?"

The bulbous man's loose jowls waggled as he shook his head. "Not at all, signore. It is quite acceptable for a project of this magnitude."

Isabetta leaned to her left, closer to Viviana. "He is frightening."

"Perhaps he is frightened," Viviana muttered. "Now hush."

"How many artists will you put on the project?" Antonio sent another question Perugino's way.

"Three," della Francesco replied.

"Only three?" Once more Fabia engaged. "The Disciples number six, plus *Maestro* da Vinci himself."

"Disciples?" Piero Palloiuolo snorted, "What...who are disciples?"

"We are," Isabetta blared the answer, cords of muscle bulging in her neck, before any could stop her. "We are Da Vinci's Disciples."

"Oh good Lord, spare us," Piero denounced.

The other male artists sniggered, a few of the *Opere* as well.

"I understand your envious laughter," Fiammetta said with every ounce of haughtiness she possessed. She turned to Lapaccia beside her. "Who would not be envious if they could not call the great da Vinci their own *maestro*?"

"Quite true," Lapaccia answered, as if they sat alone at a café lost in their own discussion. The snickering evaporated like the steam from a pot of boiling water.

Antonio turned to Leonardo. "Am I to understand, *maestro*, that you will be overseeing the project but not participating in it?"

"That is correct, signore," Leonardo stepped forward. "These women are extraordinarily gifted. My tutelage is all they require."

Fabia smiled again. Two *Operai* nodded thoughtfully.

Antonio leaned toward his wife, whispered. The *Opere* leaned in, joined in the murmuring.

With a nod of Antonio's head, they separated. He addressed the artists before him as one.

"I believe we have all the information we need. You will hear from us in a few days' time."

"This," Antonio Palloiuolo suddenly hissed, a sharp, swollen jointed finger pointed at the women, "is a travesty, a mockery of my profession."

Before anyone—including the quick-to-quibble Isabetta—could respond, the elder Palloiuolo flung open the doors and stomped out. His brother swiftly followed, as did Pietro Perugino and the other two men accompanying him.

"What a—" Isabetta began.

The sharpness of Viviana's poking elbow cut her off.

"We are so very grateful to you, Signore *e* Signora Salvestro, and to you as well," she nodded to the men of the *Opere*, "for the wonderful opportunity you have given us. You do not know how much it means to us. *Grazie tante.*"

"*Prego,* signora," Antonio answered graciously.

The women and their master began to file out of the room. Fiammetta stopped at the egress.

"Make your decision wisely," she said, a weighty pronouncement, but one offered courteously. "History is watching."

• • •

"I am for a *pisolino,*" Lapaccia informed them outside the palazzo door. "I grow tired."

They had been in the Salvestro home less than an hour, yet it felt as if the entire day had passed.

"I will see you home." Natasia took her arm.

"And I," Fiammetta said. She had no choice; the three had come in the same carriage.

"I must see to some correspondence." Leonardo bowed his head. "I will see you anon."

The group split, the remaining three making for the studio on foot.

The day had grown dreary, threatening to rain upon their lifted spirits. They defied it with their lively chatter, their chirps of hope, their twitters of what may lay ahead. Unlike the rain, which held off, a cry brought a drenching.

"*You must stop now!*"

"Keep walking." Isabetta pulled them closer, Natasia on one side, Viviana the other.

They moved with tight, jerky motions.

"Look natural," she demanded of them and herself.

How does one look natural when one's natural state is fear? The thought tumbled around in Viviana's head.

• • •

The decision came but two days hence. Viviana found it slipped beneath the door to her palazzo. She did not recognize the crest upon the wax; it made no matter. With it clasped to her bosom, she ran up the stairs, through the short hall, and into her salon.

Viviana's hands shook as she took up the small blade used to pry off the seal. Whatever this message may bring, she would face it fully aware.

With a firm grip and precise movements, she released the wax and opened the parchment.

Greetings to the Members of Da Vinci's Disciples,

Viviana put the missive down on the desk; her fingers seemed no longer able to grasp it.

My wife and I are agreed and eager to thus award the Santo Spirito chapel fresco to the Disciples of da Vinci. It is well and good we have found your particulars and feel only the strongest hopes for their completion. However, 'tis not to be fully decided and adhered to in any manner until permission from Lorenzo de' Medici is obtained without objection. To that end, I have secured an audience with Il Magnifico two days hence. It would be of great preference if members, though not all are required, of your assemblage could be present at said audience. If so required, you as of yourself will move and persuade him thereunto, and of that he shall do, and shall answer and dissuade thereupon, any demurrals or contrary conditions he shall hold.

Please respond with all due haste as to your agreement of such noted above.

Thus I commit to you God's good grace,
Antonio di Salvestro de ser Ristoro of the Serristori

Viviana flung herself back in her chair. "All due haste," she said to no one but herself. She took up quill and ink, pulled a sheaf of her finest parchment to her, and leaned over it.

"Nunzio!" she cried, even as the tip of the quill met with the parchment, as the words tumbled from mind to paper.

Though formerly her deceased husband's valet, Nunzio, getting on in years, had stayed with the household after his master's demise. He served Viviana with the same dedication—and a lighter step.

He came to her just as she finished the few words required. Viviana peppered it with pounce, waved it in the air, then folded it, sealed it with wax, and used the stamp of her own family—her birth family—to seal it.

"Deliver this to the home of di Salvestro di ser Ristoro of the Serristori," she instructed, giving him the address and directions.

Nunzio held the message, nodding at her instructions.

"Now, Nunzio, go!"

Into her room, Viviana ran to stand before her easel. Picking up brush and pallet, she slathered the tip of the brush with the deepest shade of red; she slathered the words, those she had sent to Antonio di Salvestro, on the ghost of the landscape just begun: *We will be there.*

• • •

She had been standing at the door, shooing away any annoying but well-meaning servants did they linger too long, did they pester her with questions of her needs. She felt as if she had been standing there for a lifetime, time in which worrisome thoughts plagued her: Would the priest do as he promised? Would they be exactly as she had found them?

When the ecclesiastical novice put the package in her hands, the weight of it thrilled her. Surely it all must be there, as promised.

Running to the most unused room in the house, she unwrapped the package, rifled through it, scanning each page. Her sigh of relief did not come until she saw the signature of a notary upon the last page, one attesting the papers as true and exact copies of the originals.

Deliverance overwhelmed her, and she dropped into the closest chair. She stared at the pile of parchment. It held the key to her future, but would she truly be allowed to open the door?

Chapter Sixteen

"Generosity is a thing given, it cannot—should not—be taken."

Though dressed in his red robe of the Signoria, Lorenzo de' Medici wore steely armor.

He did not sit at his beautiful, if untidy desk. He stood before it, arms folded across his chest, lips a thin, tight line. The sun blazing in the leaded panes of glass behind him cast his hard-edged face in distorting shadow.

They filed in silently, save for Leonardo.

"Buongiorno, Magnifico."

He received no answer save a fixed, thunderous glare, the same he gave each of them as they entered, Viviana and Isabetta, Antonio and Fabia. They stood before the epitome of an angered god... and waited.

"That you are all standing here before me means only one thing." Lorenzo de' Medici did not uncross his arms. "A thing I felt sure would require not another of my thoughts."

"Magnifico." Antonio stepped up, offering his obnoxiously sub-servient and flourishing bow, yet his words held a strength belying his physical servility. "I know what we propose, what these women propose, is an uncommon venture, but—"

"Uncommon? It is that and more."

"True. Very true. But it is innovative, and you are a great believer of innovation, I know that to be true. If it pleases you, I ask only, at this point, that you look upon the sketches and the proposal they have made." Antonio took a step forward, but not another, waiting.

Lorenzo stared at him, sneered in truculent silence, and, finally, beckoned him forward with a jerk of his jutting chin.

Antonio rushed to the desk, quickly unfurling the best of the sketches that had accompanied the proposal. Lorenzo turned his back to da Vinci and his disciples.

"This is unbearable," Isabetta moaned in Viviana's ear.

"Shush." A poke of her elbow came with Viviana's response.

Lorenzo turned back, but not to them.

"Did you render these, da Vinci?"

With a shake of his shaggy head, Leonardo replied, "No, *Magnifico*, the youngest member of the group, one called Mattea, completed the majority of the sketches."

Lorenzo's brow finally broke its furrow. "The youngest, you say?"

Leonardo gave one simple nod of his head, almond-shaped eyes slanted and gleaming.

"Look here, *Magnifico*." Antonio pointed to the sketch of *The Exaltation of the Cross*. "This man, this man who arrests the eye, here is where your likeness will be. It is the figure of the emperor."

Viviana could only see the side of Lorenzo's face, but it was enough to catch his smirk.

Lorenzo spoke to Antonio in a hushed whisper, words mostly incomprehensible. Mostly.

Viviana heard names, names of those who held high positions in Florence's government, those who often opposed Lorenzo. A few words jumped out at her, "difficulties," "dissatisfaction," "growing." She heard Antonio counter, at times so meekly she wondered if he begged, at times with flashes of his subdued strength.

"You have been defying them for months now, and are only growing stronger for it."

Antonio refused to waver. Viviana did not know where per-serverance for his wife's sake ended and perserverance for his own began, but it had begun.

"Would this not make that strength stronger, show your true power? And think of the women it would please!"

Lorenzo spun round, piercing Leonardo with his gaze, the skin beneath his eyes twitching.

"Did you tell him to say that?" he asked.

"I've said not a word of it to Antonio. Anything I have said to him was only to assure him of my assistance in the project, of my guidance of these talented women."

As if summoned by the very notion of talented women, Fabia stepped forward.

"I believe your mother would approve," she said softly, the impact of her words a mighty strike.

"You dare speak of my mother?" Lorenzo spun round, features hard and blazing.

"Fabia," Antonio shushed her with a pained glare.

"I sat often at her feet when I was a young girl," Fabia began, her poise an elegant thing. "And yet I remember her words so well. I remember her poetry most of all. She was a talented woman. As are these."

As if cleansed, Lorenzo's face softened, any remnant of ire wiped away.

He had lost his mother a little more than two years ago and yet the loss was still keen within him; it was there on his unmasked face, the innocence of a son who would always love his mother. Lucrezia Tornabuoni, a daughter of a nobleman, had bridged the gap between the Medici—wealthiest of wealthy merchants they may have been—and the nobility that infused the city with its grandeur. She had held great influence not only over Florence, but also over its poets, especially female poets. Her own works were numerous, religious, and chivalrous, a value she treasured, and had passed on to her children.

Lorenzo was far more his mother's son than his father's, a man long dead, a man now called Piero the Gouty.

Lorenzo looked at Fabia, really looked at her for perhaps the first time since she had entered his study, head tilted, eyes narrowed with focus.

"Are you that Fabia, Fabia di Testaverdi?"

Fabia lowered her head, perhaps to hide the pleasure blooming on her face. "I am indeed. She was a progressive woman, your mother."

Lorenzo laughed, a surprisingly joyful sound.

"I remember you, you were a precocious child. My mother often spoke of you." Lorenzo stepped forward to bow over her hand as she curtsied. "It was always with great fondness."

Fabia rose, cheeks dimpling. "Thank you, *Magnifico*. I will always treasure such words."

He tacked her in place with his penetrating stare.

"Are you not afraid? Afraid of what this may to do your family's reputation."

"I fear more that true and great talent may go to waste," Fabia replied, fast and sure, her chin rising.

Lorenzo huffed, grinning. He released Fabia, took a quick step, and stood before Viviana and Isabetta, but it was the last to whom he spoke.

"You wear widow's weeds, as you did before," he said to her.

She didn't answer; what was there for her to say?

"How long since your husband left this world?" Lorenzo pried.

"A little more than three months," Isabetta said. She did not tell him that she had lost Vittorio long ago, to the illness that ate away at him with painful, nasty slowness. She did not tell him that her love for him had died long before that.

"And how do you fare?"

Isabetta shrugged one shoulder. "I do not starve, and if I do it is only for more living."

Lorenzo's thin lips spread. Viviana's breath caught.

"You have no fears either? Not for the consequences such an endeavor may bring?"

Isabetta laughed. "Of course we are afraid. But fear is but a spark to light great fires."

Now Lorenzo laughed well and truly. "That, my dear, is something my mother would have said. Are you a poet as well?"

"No, *Magnifico,* simply a woman who has lived more years than my age would tell."

Lorenzo paced his office, which was now as still and quiet as a tomb save for his movements and the swish of the fine fabrics he wore.

Too long, Viviana thought. *Only negativity comes slowly.*

Lorenzo broke the stillness, but only to speak to himself. "Well, I will not have to deal with Sixtus at any rate."

The pope who had waged war against him after the Pazzis killed his brother, after he avenged him, had died only days ago. While all of the Catholic faith mourned him, some did so with little grief, especially in Florence, especially Lorenzo de' Medici.

The new pope, Innocent VIII, might have Greek ancestry, but he had been raised and educated in the Italian states. The relations between the Vatican and Florence had already changed much in the few days of his reign. There were even whispers of a betrothal between Innocent's illegitimate son, Franceschetto, and Lorenzo's daughter, Maddalena.

"I have had enough of papal problems."

Lorenzo stopped his pacing, held before the mullioned windows, looking out across the piazza of the Basilica di San Lorenzo, which held the tombs of his family, including his slain brother and his beloved mother. "You are sure this is what you want?"

"We are," Viviana replied, at the same time as Antonio.

Lorenzo turned with a cynical if amused chuckle. His dreary gaze latched onto each one, moving from one to the next with somber slowness.

"It will not be easy, for any of you. There are many who will be outraged. And, as we know, *fiorentinos* are outspoken with their feelings."

Antonio began to stutter, "I am sure it will not be as bad as—"

"We know, Ser de' Medici, but we believe it is too important to allow such dissention to stop us," Viviana said, for once grateful for her quick tongue and its strength.

Lorenzo's head nodded in sluggish scrutiny. "You are a formidable woman, Signora del Marrone. I have been told so, and now I see it for myself."

"We are all formidable," Isabetta spoke up righteously. "We are artists."

Once more Lorenzo laughed; once more Viviana saw a spark in his eyes when he looked at the curvaceous blonde beside her. He threw up his hands.

"Then I wish you all the best of luck. You have my permission and my approval. Let it be known."

"*Grazie, grazie tante.*" Antonio's gratitude gushed from him.

"Thank you, *Magnifico*," Fabia said, with a bit more grace. "Your mother would be proud."

"I have no doubt she would have haunted me from the grave had my decision been otherwise." Lorenzo grinned with a bow to Fabia. "They are in your care, da Vinci."

"Of course, *Magnifico*." Leonardo gave a shallow bow as the women beside him, the artists, softly expressed their own gratitude. "We will leave you to your work."

They shambled out, bubbling with excitement barely contained.

"Signora Fioravanti?"

Isabetta poked her head back in, even as Viviana held the latch. "Yes, *Magnifico*?"

"It is my desire for you to sketch and paint my likeness," he announced, as if he were announcing the sun had risen, looking down at the spray of parchments across his desk, his pronouncement far more decisive than his attention. "Only you."

"*S—sì, Magnifico*," Isabetta replied, ducking back out.

As Leonardo led them out of the palace, Viviana fixed a hard glare upon her friend. She watched as Isabetta's face changed from confused to determined to amused.

Chapter Seventeen

"In the strangest places, treasures may be found."

The gaping balcony doors reached out as if begging for a breeze. The sharp, florid aromas of high summer held sway—the earthy scent of sun upon stone, the sharp sweetness of purple peonies. Inside, veal simmered in its pot; Viviana simmered in jitters.

She was far more nervous for this Sunday dinner with her sons and Carina than she had been for the last. That time it was Marcello and his lovely young woman who had felt the pressure of hoped-for acceptance. Today it was Viviana.

The food came in waves, the wine flowed, and she talked. Viviana talked too much and of the most inconsequential things. She dropped her two-tined fork twice. She fiddled with the edge of the embroidered tablecloth. She laughed too often and too loudly.

"Whatever is the matter with you, Mama?" Rudolfo smacked his goblet on the table. Was it that noise or his question that scorned the restless silence, that changed the air?

Viviana tucked her chin in, puckered her face. "Matter? There's nothing the matter."

"Something troubles you," Marcello echoed his brother, as always. "You are acting rather strangely."

In some ways, Viviana wished it were just her boys at table that day. Her boys understood her, knew her vagaries. Looking deeper within herself, she was grateful for Carina, for the presence of another woman, of another artist.

And there it was; just that thought was enough.

Slowly and completely, Viviana told her family what she and the other women were about to do.

Itchy silence once more took over the room. If she could have scratched it away, her skin would have been raw.

"You astound me, Mama." Rudolfo broke the silence, raising his glass to her, drinking long and deeply. "You travel roads others would never even dream exist."

She beamed at his glorious words, but there was another truth yet to be told.

"There will be many who do not approve. There are already those who do not." Viviana told them of the day she and Isabetta discovered their bid had become known, the heckling, the tomato; she told all. "My greatest prayer is that it will not affect your business."

"If it does, who it does, I would have no care to continue doing business with," Rudolfo declared.

"Perhaps this is not the wisest course for you to take, Mama," Marcello argued. "Perhaps it is not best for you or the group. Perhaps it would be better to take things more slowly."

"But such progress—" Viviana tried.

"There are other roads upon which to make progress. Small works by Da Vinci's Disciples would lead to greater works."

"Da Vinci's Disciples?" For the first time since this particular discussion began, Carina spoke.

Viviana smiled, just to hear the sound of it. "Yes, I am a member of Da Vinci's Disciples, a group of women artists under the tutelage of Leonardo."

"*The* Leonardo?"

"The very one." Viviana felt her face grow pleasantly florid.

"Yes, Carina, my mother is something of an iconoclast," Marcello avowed, eyes and brows making a quick, high jump. "About—"

Rudolfo stopped him. "She and the women with her are visionaries. Nothing more, and certainly nothing less."

With lips tight, head atilt, Marcello ceded to his brother's assertion.

"Indeed, they are ahead of their time," Marcello assured, launching into a much-censored version, to relay them to Carina, of the beginnings of what was now Da Vinci's Disciples. Not once did he mention his deceased father or the painting that ensured his death.

"And now"—Carina turned fully to Viviana—"now you will fresco a chapel, the whole group, and publicly?"

Viviana did not doubt for a minute the depths of the girl's astonishment, but her root emotion remained elusive.

"We are," she answered simply, expectantly.

"I still question if this is the best course," Marcello mumbled.

Viviana's fists twisted in the fine voluminous silk of her gown. Could she do this momentous thing without the approval and support of her sons, both of them?

"It is the only course."

Viviana's head snapped up. Such words she expected from Rudolfo; they came from Carina.

Carina preached righteously, "Such talent, and it must be great indeed for them to win the commission, should not be relegated to nothing more than their homes, or some obscure wall bereft of signature. It must be flouted before the world. It must be where all may see and learn and know." Carina pinned Viviana with her steadfast gaze. "You must do this. You all must."

"Do you truly feel that way, *cara*?" Marcello asked Carina.

Viviana suddenly realized that his reticence might have been for Carina's benefit, not hers. How blindly foolish she could be at times, seeing only walls that she herself must hurtle.

"I do, I truly do." Carina nodded, so exuberantly thick sable curls fell free of their pins. "But I have a request, if I may."

"Of course, child."

"I wish to be a part of it. I wish to watch, to learn and, if allowed, to help."

Marcello balked. "Carina, you cannot be serious."

"Oh, but I am, Marcello. It is a thing all artists dream of, and I am, to my core, an artist." As if suddenly realizing the vehemence of her words, she softly asked, "Would that meet with your approval?"

She asks my son for approval, Viviana thought, *as a wife would do.* She left this conversation to them.

"I…I…" Marcello gawped at his mother, but found nothing there to help him.

He was a man now; she would always be his mother—their mother—but she could not, should not, forever be a parent. His response would tell her how well she had done her job through all the years that had come before.

"But what of your family?" Marcello worried, with a crack splitting his voice. "Will your father deny his approval when he learns of it?"

Rudolfo once more let his goblet drop to the table. "His approval? Approval of what?"

Viviana reached out and gently poked Rudolfo's ribs, silencing him. Marcello would look to Carina's father for approval for one thing and one thing alone. Carina's lovely blush confirmed it.

"They love me, Marcello, as they love you," Carina vowed, tenderly as the dove does coo.

"Oh… *che bello!*" Rudolfo cried, finally understanding through the haze of the bottle of wine he had drunk all by himself, pouring himself yet another cupful from another bottle in celebration.

Viviana tittered as she pushed back her chair. Walking around the table, she stood between Marcello and Carina, taking one of their hands in each of her own; the three became links in a chain.

"Well, you have my approval, without question." She leaned over, kissing both on their foreheads. Rising up, she looked at Carina, studied her long and hard. The young woman never blinked; her soft smile showed no signs of running away from her face. Viviana saw in it all her hopes, her legacy as an artist.

"I must know your family approves," Viviana affirmed, fiercely pivotal words soft with joy, "of Marcello and of such activity for you. And I must, of course, make sure the other women approve as well." The drumbeat of legacy pounded in her heart, stole her breath. "But in my eyes, *cara*, you are already one of Da Vinci's Disciples."

Chapter Eighteen

"Once begun, the only path to take is forward."

More than one hand quivered as each woman signed her name to the contract. The words they pledged made their hearts beat faster, brought beads of sweat to their brows:

> *Da Vinci's Disciples, all its members, shall begin to paint the agreed to mentioned storied frescoes after first completing a detailed drawing of the said fresco which they must show to Antonio di Salvestro de' Serristori; and Da Vinci's Disciples may afterwards start this fresco, but painting and embellishing it with any addition and in whatever form and manner the said Antonio may have declared, as an act of piety and love of God, to the exaltation of his house and family and the enhancement of the said church and chapel.*

They worked as furiously as they talked.

Under Leonardo's quiet guidance, the women transformed the generalized sketches Mattea had rendered to convey the comprehensive composition of each portion of the fresco into the finalized *sinopia*, a stencil, with all its details as stipulated. They determined which techniques would be best to infuse dimension, an aspect lacking in the same work by Piero della Francesca. They knew that to prove themselves they must outshine that work in all aspects. They knew, as women, that it must be not only better, but brilliant; eyes would look upon their work differently than upon any other, and far more harshly than St. Peter's at the gates of Heaven; they must work harder than any man.

"I must say, I am still surprised we have *Il Magnifico's* approval." Fiammetta looked up now and again, quickly and analytically, to study the pose Natasia had struck for her. In using real-life models, a practice begun by Filippino Lippi, the grasp for more, and more natural, realism had found a great tool.

Natasia stood with her back and side facing Fiammetta, her right arm outstretched, her hand resting on the back of a chair, a long cape draping down her back, a draping Fiammetta endeavored to recreate. Such was the pose of the Queen of Sheba's lady as her mistress fell to her knees in worship.

In this composition, the scene that would live upon the left wall of the chapel, would be rendered the legend of the lady. As mythology told it, a tree had grown on Adam's grave, a tree chopped down during King Solomon's reign. Chopped down, yes, but prohibited from being put to any use. Paradoxically, it was then thrown across a stream to be used as a bridge. On her way to the king, the Queen of Sheba had made to step on the bridge when a miraculous vision came to her; she saw the Savior, saw that he would be crucified on a cross of this wood. Refusing to step upon it, the queen knelt, overcome by worshipful adoration.

"There is little in this world that surprises me anymore," Natasia mumbled.

"Living will do that to you," Isabetta, working on the other side of where Natasia stood, replied thoughtfully though she did not look up. "Accepting it as truth is the key."

Viviana came to stand behind Isabetta, drawn by her somber tone, anchored by the brilliance of the woman's work. "We will use the same bright coloring that Francesca did," Isabetta pointed out, studying her work and the notes she had made to the side of the sketches in the way of da Vinci. Isabetta finalized the *Exaltation of the Cross,* for it was here she would place Lorenzo. Filled with Oriental men wearing exotic headdresses, their garments were of lively color and contrast, bright violet beside pale blue, shimmering pearl white beside bursting bottle green, colors that testified to the health and strength of mankind at peace.

"I agree," Viviana said.

"As do I." Lapaccia had come upon the pair unnoticed. For the entirety of the morning, Lapaccia had fluttered from sketch to sketch, not contributing anything but suggestions and encouragement. She took up no silverpoint; she did not sit before any parchment or paper. She did not make art. And yet Viviana knew how deeply Lapaccia loved to. The question was, why didn't she?

"And I believe the men's faces should have more varied tonality," Lapaccia continued, head tilted down in the direction of Isabetta's work. "They are, after all, men of different ethnicities. They should look it."

Isabetta crowed, "Brilliant, Lapaccia, truly. Francesca did not paint them so."

Lapaccia grinned. "Then it will make our rendering all the more distinctive."

Isabetta returned to her work, her hand moving faster, more surely.

They worked for hours, the tips of their silverpoints scratching across the paper. They tutted over the *cartoni* they must create, transferring these detailed sketches to parchment the full size of each fresco square, the ultimate tool for such a manner of painting. They worked till their chatter became groans as they straightened sore backs, rubbed aching necks. "I believe we are in need of an outing," Leonardo announced.

"An outing? All of us together?" Fiammetta chirped.

"Oh yes," Leonardo confirmed brightly, but with a finger pointed upward. "Not a social outing, however, but one of learning."

With renewed vigor, the women packed up their tools and straightened their workspaces.

"Before we go," Viviana interrupted their preparations, "I have something to bring before the group."

Fiammetta flopped herself back down in her chair, dropped her chin in her palm. "More, Viviana, really?"

"'More' is exactly the word." Viviana lost her timidity. "There is a young woman, younger than you, Mattea, from a very prestigious family"—that was for Fiammetta alone—"who has asked permission to join our group."

"How extraordinary," Lapaccia responded first, quickly, and with more than one note of happiness.

"Even with what we face? Does she know what we are about to start, what we are about to endure?" Isabetta surprised Viviana with her wariness.

"In truth, I believe our endeavor spurred her to ask."

Natasia asked the questions that should be asked. "Has she been painting long? Does she possess talent?"

"She has and she does. She has brought many of her works to my home to show me."

"She came to your home?" Fiammetta badgered, as if the young woman in question had broken a sacred societal rule. "Who is this woman?"

Viviana walked a slow circle, speaking to all who gathered round her. "Her name is Carina di Tafani. And she has been to my home many times."

"I know the Tafani family," Lapaccia said. "There is a vein of minor nobility there, is there not?"

"Very minor," Fiammetta was quick to inform her. "They are—"

"*Una momento*," Isabetta interrupted what would surely be a withering report on how low on the ladder of nobility the Tafani family stood. "Why?" she asked. "Why has she been to your home so often?"

That stifled even Fiammetta's voice.

Viviana felt the flush of pleasure warm her face, felt the curve of it on her lips. "It would seem that Da Vinci's Disciples is not the only family she hopes to join."

It took them but fleeting moments of narrow-eyed thought to decipher Viviana's cryptic announcement. When they did, a meteor shower of stars fell upon them.

"Oh Viviana, how wonderful for you!" Lapaccia jumped up, embracing her.

"Which one? Which son?" Isabetta asked eagerly.

"Marcello."

"Of course," Isabetta laughed. "Rudolfo enjoys his freedom too much."

"What is she like, besides that she is an artist?" Natasia swooned a bit, still a lover of love.

Viviana reveled in the telling of Carina's loveliness, her grace and poise, her beauty.

"Does she love him?" Mattea had been silent until then. Any talk of marriage when she did not even know where her love was in the world would be painful.

"They love with all their hearts," Viviana replied gently. "From the first moment you see them together, you know it is how they are meant to be."

"I understand the joy you must feel," Natasia said. "Not only to see your son in love and on his way to marital bliss, but—"

"It is the greatest joy of motherhood," Fiammetta broke in thoughtfully. "Not only to have children, but to see them happy. There is no deeper contentment."

Viviana reached out to her. "Oh it truly is, Fiammetta. It is nearly the most supreme bliss I have ever experienced—save for when my boys were born, of course."

"But," Natasia continued with a pointed look at Fiammetta, demanding that her words be heard, "is she ready for what may come, what may come from this?"

She spun round, pointing to the piles of sketches that were the start of the task they were about to undertake.

Viviana nodded. "She is," she proclaimed assuredly, "as is her family. I insisted she discuss the entire commitment with them very thoroughly, and all its consequences. They support her to the fullest. They are progressive people, and Humanists."

"If that is the case, I see no reason why this dear girl cannot become one of us," Lapaccia declared.

"But are you sure, Viviana?" Again, Natasia pestered with her concerns. "Does the family truly realize how it may affect their standing in the community? How it may affect them for years to come?"

Viviana frowned at the normally vivacious and accepting woman. In Natasia's features, Viviana saw a face she did not recognize.

"I know they do. I spoke to them myself. There is no hesitation at all, I assure you," Viviana was pleased to report, once more a delightful memory—meeting the Tafani family—warmed her.

"Then, by all means, let the young lady join us," Fiammetta proclaimed, surprising them with her ready acceptance. She gave them all a petulant glare in response to their wide-eyed stares. "Why do you look at me so? I am not doing all this, taking these risks, putting my reputation at risk, to have this, as Viviana said, die off when we do. Young blood is just what we need."

"I agree, on both counts," Lapaccia said. "In fact, I encourage it."

"And I," answered both Mattea and Isabetta.

Viviana turned to Leonardo. "Would you mind another disciple, *maestro*?"

The tall man, silent thus far, shook his head, not at the notion but at Viviana's choice of words.

"I will always relish the opportunity to share my knowledge, such as it is, with a new artist. Learning acquired in youth arrests the evil of old age; and if you understand that old age has wisdom for its food, you will conduct yourself in youth in such a way that your old age will not lack for nourishment."

"Indeed, *maestro*, and your wisdom is far beyond your age," Viviana replied. "I may take that as a yes then?"

Leonardo tilted his head, raised one brow.

"Very well, the *maestro* is in agreement." Viviana winked at him as she informed the group.

"I shall have a key made for her." Natasia relented.

The decision made, they took off their smocks, put on their veils, and made for the door.

"Have two keys made, Natasia, if you would," Fiammetta said to her as they bustled out.

"Two?"

Fiammetta beamed; it lit her face brightly, brought a twinkle to her eye.

"Yes, one for Carina. And the other for my daughter, for Patrizia."

. . .

They strode down the Via del Gelsumino with all the confidence of a swaggering group of *bravi*, the gangs of young men with little to do other than pester and bully others.

Leonardo took the lead, the ladies behind and to the side of him in a V. He led them toward the Ponte Trinta, or so it seemed, for he refused to disclose their destination. They chatted and smiled, preened and giggled, at least until the shouting began.

"Cover your faces, you deplorable wenches!"

That first came from a window above. The women stumbled on the stones; their eyes darted about, but could not see from which window the denouncement came.

"You shame us all! You shame the city!"

There was no question from where this slander came; the man stood on his small stoop, his elaborate, expensive attire ruined by the fury burning upon his face.

"Signore Alemagna," Fiammetta and Natasia fretted at the same time.

"You know him?" Viviana asked.

"Oh yes." Fiammetta glared at the man, undaunted. "He is never happy. Ignore him."

"Go back to your homes, back to your husbands."

The most hurtful catcall came from behind, hurtful not for its words, but for the one who said them, a woman. It would seem not all of their sex would be encouraging; it was a sharp-edged blow.

"My husband is in heaven," Isabetta called over her shoulder to the woman.

"And mine is in hell," Viviana quipped. "We have no desire to go to either place just now, thank you."

"Shush!" Lapaccia whispered harshly. "You will only encourage them if you respond."

"*Puttane!*"

"Oh, this is too much," Fiammetta crackled, red splotches of anger bursting on her face. "We paint therefore we are whores? We are artists not actors. No. No, I will not tolerate this."

She grabbed the arms of the two women closest to her—Natasia and Mattea—and turned them onto the Via Santo Spirito before they reached the bridge.

"This way, *maestro.*"

"But madonna, the—" da Vinci began.

"You need not tell me where we are going." Fiammetta plunged ever forward, waving a hand in the air behind her. She whirled on a heel, pointed a finger. "But I *will* tell you how we will get there. To your father's house, Natasia." She turned to her companion, finger still demanding. "I know he has a carriage big enough for us all."

He did. Though one could hardly call it a carriage.

Within minutes, the group was back on the cobbles, once more headed toward a destination Leonardo shared only with the driver, only partially hidden by the frame of the large cart. Used for gathering goods and large items, it had no curtains to harbor them; creaking and rickety, it was but slats of wood, for the floor, the benches, and the sides, the latter to keep goods from spilling out. With their backs against the benches, only glimpses of their faces flickered out between the slats. It would have to suffice.

They jostled along, some enjoying the bouncy ride, the adventure of it, some not. It had been her idea, yet Viviana could see how loathsome it was for Fiammetta to travel in such a lowly manner. She sat, arms tightly crossed upon her chest, lips puckered as they crossed the Ponte Trinta onto the Via Tornabuoni.

Viviana turned, gaze caught by the familiar surroundings.

"Do you mean to take me home, *maestro*?" she asked of the mysteriously silent Leonardo, daring another peek over her shoulder. It did not serve them well.

"*Disgustoso*!"

This was her neighborhood; Viviana should have known better, should have realized how quickly and easily those on the street would recognize her. Like the stones thrown at the condemned, the insults hurtled toward them once more.

"*Va Via! Va Via!*"

More than one voice heckled them to go away.

Viviana hung her head. "*Mi dispiaci*," she apologized to them all for having been seen and recognized, for bringing vile words to their ears once more.

"*Sì, va via, mesollelot!*" one particularly loud and gruff man abused them.

But his cry—this slur—brought every head up, even that of da Vinci, or perhaps especially his.

"So, now we are each other's lovers as well?" Isabetta asked, voice quaking with laughter. She looked around the group, "Well, some of you are rather lovely, but, hmmm." She shook her head with exaggeration. "No, not for me. Not yet anyway."

Their laughter healed the wounds of the hurtful remarks as if some magic had dispelled the shame trying to infest them. She kept them laughing, telling them of some women she knew of who did enjoy carnal knowledge of other women, how they would secretly meet, how some of them were quite beautiful but disgusted by the male appendage.

"You only know *of* them?" Fiammetta snorted through a wrinkled nose. "You do not know them yourself?"

Isabetta could have been insulted. Instead, she slapped a hand to her bosom, batted her eyes, and said, "Me? Know such women myself? Bah!" She dramatically waved the notion away with her other hand. "I could n—"

Before she could finish, the carriage came to a halt, buffeting the surprised group sharply forward and then back.

"Of course," Viviana bubbled.

"Santa Trinta," Lapaccia sighed.

"*Sì*, Santa Trinta." Leonardo stretched out one long spindly arm to herd them toward the door. Like most churches in Florence, it remained unlocked during daylight hours. "But we mustn't tarry. I know Ghirlandaio and his crew are not meant to work this day, but with Ghirlandaio one can never be sure."

He hurried them into the Byzantine-style church, built in the eleventh century, and ushered them to the far wall near the transept. In truth, they needed no guide. The smell of paint led them, and the wooden scaffolds and piles of canvas cloth covering the floor marked their destination.

"*Dio mio*," Isabetta whispered worshipfully.

For once, Fiammetta did not scold her for it. Like the others, astonishment held her tongue.

Dominic Ghirlandaio had started frescoing this *cappella*, belonging to the Sassetti family—another Medicean, one who worked for their bank—almost two years ago. Its mammoth size, its enormity of subject matter, and the many other commissions Ghirlandaio and his workshop received, had delayed its completion far too frequently, or so Leonardo told them.

"You can see the work is almost complete, at last," he said. "But what we need to look at, what you need to study, is his dedication to depicting the true nature of life at the time of the scenes."

There were six scenes in all, a cycle representing the life of Saint Francis.

"Do you see how the clothing is not of our time? To do otherwise in a painting meant to depict a more ancient era is a crime." Leonardo lectured; his disciples hung on every word. "The same is true for the architecture."

Minutes passed, hours; their absorption was complete. Their education as artists expanded as they took prodigious notes. Only when the shadows came to inhabit the church did they realize time slipping away from them.

They returned to the cart, making their way once more through the city as anonymously as possible, their whispers frantic and frenzied over what they had seen.

As the simple vehicle once more brought them to the home of Natasia's father, as they began to disperse and make their way to their own homes in groups of two or three, Leonardo called one of them to him, leaving Viviana a few steps away, waiting for her.

"Tomorrow, Isabetta," he said, the enthusiasm born during the day evaporating. "*Il Magnifico* has informed me you should report to him tomorrow to begin your sketches."

Viviana heard his words, their discordant note. She saw too the look upon Isabetta's face, saw that there was far too much pleasure upon it.

• • •

She didn't return home as the others did; the woman made an excuse as to why she did not, hoping it sounded believable. She had only a few spare minutes to see to her errand and make it to her own home before night's darkness fell upon her, before the dangers it brought came to light. She did not care; she would not stop until it was finished.

Chapter Nineteen

"To create the correct light, one must often encounter the dark."

She wore her finest weeds. Though they did nothing to lessen her inner tumult, she was grateful for their gloomy obscurity. She wanted, most of all, to be taken seriously.

Isabetta made her way to the Palazzo de' Medici, a long walk from her meager home down near the Arno River to the center of the city, where the elite reigned and their palazzos reached ever skyward, the tall trees of wealth growing ever higher, looming over all. She walked in their shadows in more ways than one.

The door opened at her first knock. The *maggiore duomo* simply nodded and led her into the palace along the same path as on her last two visits, but this time he didn't stop in *Il Magnifico*'s study. The silent and stiff man led her onward, through a door veiled within a painting.

"Wait here," he said, but left before she could agree.

Isabetta clenched her sketchbook tightly to her chest, arms folded across it. She stood just inside the now-closed hidden egress as if rooted to the floor; only her head with its wide-eyed gaze roved about the room.

There was no doubt this was a private room, a wholly possessed, secluded chamber of a man who possessed many secrets.

Why would he bring me here? Why would we do our work in such a room?

Such thoughts intruded—nagged—as she perused the place in which she found herself.

Much smaller than his public visitation room, this chamber overflowed with many of the same singular artifacts, antiquities, books, and luxurious furniture, though in here there were only two finely embroidered chairs and a matching settee. But here there was more, more things, and of a more different sort.

Isabetta's mouth snapped closed as she spied a human skull atop a small marble plinth, its vacant eye sockets seemingly trained upon her. She had taken one step toward it when another hidden door opened and he walked in.

Free of his distinguishing red *berretto*, Lorenzo de' Medici stood before her in a red brocade *farsetto* trimmed with gold braids, trunk hose to match, and tight black stockings that hugged the muscles of his firm and powerful thighs. *Il Magnifico* filled the room, denuded it of its grandeur; his dominant energy barely left enough air for her to breathe.

With a blink, a hard swallow, Isabetta remembered herself and whom she stood before; she dropped quickly into a deep curtsy.

"Signora Fioravanti." Lorenzo raised her up. "No need for such formalities. We shall be spending far too much time together to abide by ceremonies, yes?"

Without time or the ability to think of another response, Isabetta simply nodded; he filled her mind as he did this room.

Lorenzo led her to the settee. The small table before it gleamed with crystal, carafes of wine, goblets from which to drink it, platters of meat, cheese, and fruit, some of which she did not recognize.

"Will you drink with me?" he asked, though with Lorenzo, there was never any question in such a question.

Isabetta had lost her tongue; it seemed to have run away from her mouth at the moment of his entrance. She'd be fallacious if she thought she didn't need a long draught of some strong wine. She sipped it, as a lady should, but often. It helped her find her errant tongue.

"Perhaps we should begin our work, *Magnifico*," she said, quickly adding, "if it pleases you."

Lorenzo's dark eyes slanted. He stood and walked to stand

before the three windows, the only windows in the small chamber. "Very well. I see it would please you, as I hope to do, so let us begin."

Though Isabetta had known only one man in the intimate sense, she finally knew why she was in that room. What she didn't know was how she felt about it. She clung to her sketchbook and her work as if they would save her from any decision.

"I need the light before you, ser de' Medici, not you before it. Could you please stand there," she pointed, "behind the chair in the corner?"

With a swagger worthy of a man half his age, Lorenzo stepped to the assigned location.

"Yes, that's it, now rest one hand upon its back, for your likeness will be rendered with a hand outstretched."

Once more, he followed her instructions without a word.

"Now turn, give me your left profile, but not fully, in three quarters."

Lorenzo laughed as he angled his body. "Well, that is good. There is no need to see this nose from the side."

Unwittingly, Isabetta laughed with him, at his easy self-deprecation. Their laughter slipped away like lark song at dusk, and she set to her task. Her penetrating gaze followed every curve, every sharp edge of the man from head to toe. More than once Isabetta sharply reminded herself that she was an artist in this moment, not a lonely woman.

"Tell me about yourself, madonna," Lorenzo asked with as little movement as possible; he had posed before. "How did you come to be in Florence? You are far too pale to be a native of our fair city. Your tresses of gold are those you were born with."

She ignored the fancy of his words, which took flight in her mind. Isabetta coaxed her concentration back to her task as she answered his questions, about her family, her childhood home in Venice, how she had met her husband and come to Florence with him. Time unmeasured ticked away.

"And when did you become a painter?" Lorenzo dug deeper. That question did stop her.

Isabetta tilted her head, stared far off into her past, and then simply shrugged her shoulders. "You know, I do not remember when I was not one."

"And your husband, did he approve of your work? How did he die?"

Lorenzo turned his head out of its pose; their eyes met and caught, but only for an instant.

Isabetta returned to the beginnings of the sketch before her, began to move her slim pointed piece of charcoal once more, the gritty chafe of it upon the parchment becoming the background noise of her tale.

As she worked, Isabetta told all, though why the words came so easily she did not know. She told him of the illness that had plagued Vittorio for years, how she had nursed him for years, how the business and its income followed him downward.

"Not long ago, he seemed to improve," she said without a glance upward, save to study more closely the bend of Lorenzo's arm, "but once he returned to his bed again, he never again rose from it."

"I am sorry, madonna." Sincerity laced his sympathy. "You have had a hard life."

She shrugged again, kept working. "There are many others who have suffered far worse than I."

"You are made of strong will."

Isabetta looked up sharply, not even attempting artifice as she looked him dead in the eye. "Do I have any choice?"

For once, the great *Magnifico* had no reply, not even in defense.

He returned to his pose and she to her work; she lost herself to it, wholly and completely, so engrossed that she did not hear him step toward her, or step behind her to look down at her work.

"You possess talent. It cannot be denied."

Isabetta jumped, craning her neck to see him. She followed his gaze downward; he looked at other things from his vantage point.

"Do not seem so surprised, *Magnifico*. It does not become you."

Isabetta kept her gaze upon her work; she had just insulted, if indirectly, the most powerful man in Florence, one of the most powerful men in all of the Italian states. She held her breath as she awaited his censure.

"You sketch as beautifully as you look," he purred instead of punishing her, a masculine rumble.

Isabetta turned fully; turned to face him, to see his face. She knew what it told her.

"I think it best—" She stood.

Lorenzo moved in front of the chair, stood beside her. His touch upon her shoulders was only a touch, no more, yet he drew her to him, brought his large nose to her neck.

"I knew you would smell so sweet."

For a lightning strike's worth of a moment, Isabetta swayed into him, but just as quickly, pulled herself back. For the first time in a very long while, she knew not what to do. If she turned away too quickly, spurned him, it could jeopardize their commission, the very existence of their work. If it had been any other man, her palm would have already met his face, and it would not be a tender introduction.

Yet the pull of him was so strong, and she had been alone— untouched—too long. This magnetic man ignited a surge of desire within her. It had been so long since she'd felt a strong man's arms about her, to be taken by lust and wanting. To be wanted.

Isabetta closed her eyes against it, against the picture she painted in her mind, of their naked bodies writhing together. Yet another image barged in: her dying husband as he had withered away in his bed. She took a small step backward.

"*Magnifico*, I—"

A knock came upon the door. Isabetta closed her eyes with a prayer-like sigh.

"What is it?" Lorenzo grumbled.

A young man, barely out of boyhood, stuck his head in the door he had opened just a crack.

"Signore Bernardo del Nero is here to see you, *Magnifico*," the page said, gaze plastered to the floor.

Lorenzo heaved his own sigh, dropped his hands from her shoulders as if they weighed more than he could bear.

"Tell him to wait, I'll be along presently," he instructed the page, who retreated with all due haste. Lorenzo turned glistening, dark eyes upon Isabetta. "I fear my work is forever nipping at my heels."

Isabetta had already turned from him, turned and snatched up her sketchbook and charcoal, making tentative steps toward the just closed door.

"I will leave you to your work, ser de' Medici," she said with a dip of a curtsy, one done while still in motion.

"You will come again, signora, *sì*?" Lorenzo called out.

Without turning, merely raising her sketchbook, Isabetta replied, "Of course, *Magnifico*. I must finish my work."

With those words she was gone from his sight, from his reach, though it was so very long. As Isabetta rushed through the palazzo, she could have pinched herself for her poor choice of words. She knew men well, knew a man such as Lorenzo de' Medici would take her words as encouragement. He would think it his work—not hers—that she would return to finish.

Isabetta stopped just outside the palazzo door, the busyness of life flashing past her on the street pulling her from the void she had fallen into, but not from the pinch of her thoughts.

Which business did she truly wish to finish?

Chapter Twenty

"That which we most fear is often that which we most desire."

The heavy clouds dispersed slowly, as if they feared losing one another. The sun defeated them, crepuscular rays reaching through them to touch the earth. One such ray touched Viviana's face, beyond the dark gray-green *pietra serena* stone façade, beyond Brunelleschi's simplistically brilliant architecture, to the small cross that sat upon the peak of Santo Spirito.

"May the strength of all the gods be with us," she muttered to herself, lifting her skirts and with them her spirit as she climbed the few steps and entered the church.

The light clacking of her heeled slippers broke the solemn silence so thick and heavy, pungent with the scent of incense forever clinging to the rarefied air.

Viviana could not count how often she had walked this path, entered this church, for each time she was captivated by it, its muscular energy, by the strength of the *pietra serena* columns capped by scrolled capitals, their vanishing perspective—culminating in the altar with its seemingly delicate *baldacchino*—drawing the penitent forward, ever closer to God. Its rigorous continuity of geometry pleased the eye of both the woman and the artist in her. Yet on every occasion before, the majesty of Brunelleschi's architecture— one he had not lived to see completed—had merely been a place she passed through to reach the studio. Today was not such a day.

Today her work—their work—would take place under the very eyes of God.

Viviana stepped to her left, to the side aisle that ran between the columns and the chapels. As she passed each one, she studied their ornamentation. Some boasted great sculptures, others freestanding gold and jeweled triptychs glorified with painted canvasses, while many more were frescoed. She read the names above each *cappella*, inscribed on placards of gold. She need not. The Serristori placard gleamed brighter with its newness, calling her to it.

She stood beneath its arched entryway, curved, matching those connecting the columns in the nave. The chapel was in poor repair, in its untended state as withered as flowers beneath an early frost; the frescoes—of an age she could not imagine—were faded and peeling, the coffer beams splintered.

"Well, we can most certainly do better than this."

Viviana jumped with a squeak; she pushed upon her chest lest her heart jump from it.

"Oh, Fiammetta, must you do that?"

Fiammetta merely chuckled. "Did I scare you, or are you as frightened as I am?"

"Both, I think," Viviana answered sheepishly.

Fiammetta walked past her and into the chapel. Even the corpulent woman appeared small within its depths, though it was not nearly as large as some chapels. Walled in on three sides, each measured fifteen meters. There was succor to be found in its diminutive size.

"It is a quarter the size of the *cappella* in Santa Trinta," Fiammetta mused on the fresco Ghirlandaio worked on, the one that Leonardo had brought them to.

"And our work is far simpler than della Francesca's," Viviana added.

The women faced each other. It was born then, a faith so strong it could conquer all, like the tip of a crocus that dares to break through the hard frozen ground, knowing that the sun awaited it.

"We can do this, Viviana, we truly can."

"Of course we can." Isabetta plunged in like a burst of rain feeding the flower. "Do you really question it, fear it?" She shook her head, face scrunched with dismissal. "Fear more those who wish us failure. They begin to gather."

"What's that you say?" Fiammetta asked, puzzled.

Isabetta jerked her head to the large main door of the basilica. "See for yourself."

Viviana and Fiammetta hurried to the door, opening it merely a crack, and peered out.

"Oh dear me," Fiammetta groaned.

At the base of the four narrow steps leading to the door, a small brood of men huddled together. Even from their hidden post, the woman could hear, if not the words, most surely their surliness. Their denigration of women as artists—with a paying commission—rumbled ever louder as the storm of them drew nearer.

Viviana closed the door. "We need not see them, or hear them. We need only ourselves."

They returned to the Cappella Serristori, finding not only Isabetta, but Mattea and Natasia as well.

At the sight of their surprised faces, Mattea explained, "We entered through the back, through the bell tower."

"Very wise of you." Fiammetta tipped a maternal nod.

"Perhaps we will need to—"

The door swooshed open; they heard it even within the chapel. Through the egress came the sounds of raised male voices, those who continued to huddle outside. Viviana peeked around the chapel corner. Through the door came Lapaccia, on the arm of Leonardo. Viviana's relief sighed through her; how greatly she feared what the heckling of the men would do to the ever more fragile woman.

"Ah, *buone donne*, we are all here now," Leonardo greeted them. "Here we begin."

He received naught but pained stares in reply.

Da Vinci strode into the chapel, stood with his back to the faded Madonna with Saint Anna hovering protectively above her.

"Do you think what you are feeling has never been felt before?"

He shook his head. "It is the war of art, a war we all battle. To begin such a work, any work, is to commit the soul to it. It is not any easy thing, is it? To relinquish our souls. Yet you have already done so, and on many occasions to great success. There are so many unable to take that first step, while many others are unable to finish." Leonardo spoke with commanding authority. He moved to the front left corner, where outer wall and ceiling met the inner wall of the *cappella*. "Stop looking at the chapel; look at this instead. Do not think of it as a whole, but as small parts, for it is far easier to give small parts of us to small parts. There is accomplishment when each part is finished. In that satisfaction, you will find the strength to move to the next. For now, think only of this part," he said, pointing, "for here we will begin."

What they had taken on was no small feat, not the work, nor what it might do to their lives and the lives of those around them. They may never be the same again.

No, Viviana thought, *that is not true. We* will *never be the same.*

"How do we begin, *maestro*?" she asked simply; it was all they needed.

Leonardo slapped his hands together, rubbed them with relish.

"We will begin with building the scaffolds. I have had all the necessary wood and tools delivered. They await—"

"*Mi scusi.*" Fiammetta stopped him, walked toward him with a flat palm held up. "Do you mean to say that *we* are to build the scaffolds, with our hands?"

The gleam on Leonardo's face slithered away. He took two steps, stood merely inches from the indomitable form that was the Contessa Maffei.

"Are you an artist about to create a commissioned *affresco*?"

Fiammetta slanted back. "Well, yes, but—"

"Then you *will* build your scaffold."

As if in a war of another sort, their locked gaze held. Fiammetta surprised them, surrendering as she looked away first.

"To the garden, madonnas, where our equipment awaits," Leonardo said, once more the serene tutor.

Fiammetta led them out of the chapel, and further up the aisle to the transept door.

"I have never held a hammer in my life." Her grumbling wafted over her slumped shoulders, but she did not turn—just as well, for then she could not see the amusement on her companions' faces.

• • •

Sweat covered their faces. Dust stuck to the sweat. Their smocks added another layer of heat. They had never looked so dirty; they had never felt so alive.

It took them far longer than it would have taken men, but the first scaffold was beginning to take form. Leonardo set Mattea and Isabetta to the task of breaking holes in the walls; luckily, those used when the first fresco was done were easy to spot, as the fill plaster never looked as sturdy as the stone walls themselves. The women swung their sledgehammers with gusto, grunting even as they laughed, each trying to outwhack the other. As they walloped the walls, da Vinci showed Lapaccia how long to cut the rope, taught the other women how to notch poles together and where they should intersect, how to tie them securely enough to hold the weight of at least two of them at a time.

"Dear contessa," Leonardo squatted down beside where Fiammetta had flopped herself on the floor, legs splayed, a jumble of pole crosses in her lap. She had already bonked herself twice upon the head, each time sending a sneer of derision in Leonardo's direction. "They must be at a perfect ninety-degree angle in order for the ties to securely hold with strength. You must—"

"*Maestro*," Viviana hissed at him, though her pop-eyed gaze struck elsewhere. "Leonardo!" she susurrated again from between clenched teeth.

Leonardo looked up at her, finally, following her gaze. Seeing what she did, he quickly straightened.

"*Mio bene uomini*," he cried, arms opened to greet the two men with a kiss for each of their cheeks. For his appearance there,

Leonardo gave the sort of greeting that had never before passed between him and one of their guests.

Each man returned the greeting in kind, but said nothing; it appeared as though they were incapable. The young and tall one, the older and rounder one, both wore the same mask, one of blatant astonishment.

"Madonnas, come, come meet my good men." Leonardo waved a hand at all the Disciples, no matter their chore. Viviana knew who these men were, had recognized them immediately, and yet da Vinci spoke as if they were lounging at café watching life pass by along a via.

Da Vinci introduced each woman to each man individually, Fiammetta last, not for her rank, but for the ignominy she had suffered whilst attempting to pick up her stout form from the floor. At least the venerable artists paid her the courtesy of bowing deeper than they had to the other women, save perhaps Lapaccia.

As Sandro Botticelli and Andrea Verrocchio greeted the other women, Viviana took herself to Leonardo's side. As if to take it, she pinched his arm, shushing his small yelp.

"Why are *they* here? You knew they were coming but said nothing?" She pinched him again.

"I did not tell you because I knew it would only bring you more agitation," Leonardo said, unwinding her arm from his so she could pinch him no more. "And they are here, madonna, to help."

"What?!" The tsk of her emphatic *t* echoed through the small chapel.

Leonardo simply patted her on the shoulder.

Sandro Botticelli and Andrea Verrocchio said little during the introductions. When the flummoxed daze broke, Botticelli broke it. "I see you are building your own scaffolds. Is it true, madonnas?"

How pleased Viviana was that they were, if only for the confounded look upon the genius's face; it was worth all the splinters and scrapes—every one—on her hands and arms.

"*Sì*, they are, and making good progress of it, too," Leonardo said, standing a bit taller, ignoring Fiammetta's groan.

"And they will be strong enough to hold you?" This from Botticelli.

"Oh, indeed they will," Fiammetta answered with all the frustrated determination she now carried.

"True, quite true," Leonardo agreed, ignoring the raised brows and pursed lips of the men's expressions.

"Well, making a scaffold is one thing," Verrocchio huffed as if insulted. "Painting a fresco is quite another."

"Also true," Leonardo agreed. "Would you have a care to see examples of their work?"

"Most assuredly," Botticelli replied.

"This way then." Leonardo stepped out of the chapel, holding up an arm to show the way to the side door.

As one, the Disciples made to follow, but were stopped by their *maestro*'s own halting gesture.

"It will fare better if you are not there," he explained, leaning toward them, whispering to them. "They will be more inclined to express their pleasant surprise without having to do so in front of you."

"In front of us women, you mean," Isabetta said snidely.

"The *maestro* is correct," Viviana conceded.

Isabetta huffed, with a shake of her head, "Men."

There was nothing more that needed to be said.

Leonardo took himself away, the women's malignant proclamations about his gender tagging along behind.

• • •

Da Vinci spoke not a word as his two companions made their way about the studio, as they pored over the array of canvasses, those set to dry against the wall and those still upon the easels, still in progress.

Verrocchio, the nickname given him meaning "true eye," stopped in the middle of the room, turning slowly; his face a portrait of an incredulous daze.

"These...all these...are by their hands and none other's?"

"To the one. Their talent and none other's," Leonardo assured him, chest puffed out, chin high.

Botticelli paused before Lapaccia's work, bent down, and retrieved a canvas from the crux of the wall, holding it at eye level before him.

"That is the work of Mona Cavalcanti," Leonardo told him. "You are her favorite. She strives to master your techniques."

Sandro looked at him, cupid-bow lips agape.

"She honors me," he whispered, turning back, still with the painting in his grip, still with wonder upon his face.

• • •

"Quick." Mattea slithered from the edge of the chapel where she had been spying, "they return."

Each woman picked up a tool, a pole, anything. As the three men returned to the portal of the chapel, the women looked at them with batting eyes and insipid smiles. Leonardo sniffed at their poor attempt at nonchalance.

If they had expected—hoped for—words of praise, they heard none. The words that did come were far better.

"So," Andrea Verrocchio strode toward them, arms akimbo as his experienced eye surveyed the site. "It is only the middle tiers that will hold the true scenes, so it is the top with its simple sky that we should start with. Clouds are an easy form to master, even within *affresco.*"

We. The word exploded in Viviana's mind. *He said we.*

More soldiers now stood among their ranks in this war.

• • •

The glooming of gray dusk awaited them as the women left Santo Spirito together, perhaps never more so united, never more unconquerable. Their words fell over each other's like the streams of a many-branched river cascading over a fall, their laughter the babbling.

Leonardo, Verrocchio, and Botticelli had left first, Leonardo assuring them with a wave from the door that no remnants of the aggravated horde remained. With their dispersal came the women's safe passage away.

"It is sad to think our *maestro* will be gone for a few days," Viviana mused.

"Yes, but look who we shall have to fill the void till he returns," Isabetta crowed.

"In all my wildest fantasies, I never imagined I would work under such masterful tutelage as Botticelli and Verrocchio," Natasia made a prayer of gratitude.

Isabetta walked beside her, twined their arms. "Our true *maestro* is the greatest of them all, no matter what others may say. But what he has done bringing—*aiee!*"

The rock, hurled from somewhere out of the darkness, thwacked against the cobbles as it bounced off her, smashing into pieces.

Isabetta grabbed her left shoulder with her right hand as she tumbled to the ground.

Natasia, the closest to her, dropped beside her.

"Are you injured? How badly are you hurt?" she asked urgently, trying to pry Isabetta's hand from her shoulder.

"Isabetta!" Viviana cried, running toward her wounded friend, then spinning, running toward the darkness.

"Viviana! No!" Fiammetta screamed at her, running after Viviana, and pulling her back.

A trembling group, the women gathered around Isabetta, elbows pressed to their sides, shoulders to their ears. They formed a shield about her, their heaving breath and Isabetta's moans creating a chorus of fear and pain.

"*Puah!*" Isabetta spat her disgust as she pulled away the partlet over her simple gown, as the torn and bruised flesh upon her shoulder revealed itself. She sat up, still within the circle of protection her sisterhood had created. Fisted hands trembled.

"Cowards!" Isabetta threw her head back like a wolf and cried out. "You harm women from the safety of the dark? Are you so afraid of us? You are not men, you are vipers!"

No one could be seen; nothing could be heard but the chirping of crickets and the slam of a shutter or two somewhere down along the street. Fiammetta rose slowly, standing in the circle of them still. "Things grow more serious."

With another moan, Isabetta picked herself up, a helping woman at each arm. "Yes," she growled, "and so do I. We have begun; we have Botticelli and Verrocchio on our side as well as our *maestro*. I will not allow *cowards*"—this word she yelled once more though her voice quivered with tears, though whether of pain or righteousness it was difficult to distinguish—"to stop us. Not now, not ever."

"Not now, not ever," Viviana repeated, a far-off echo of Isabetta's rectitude, yet as unshakable as the stone it reverberated off.

During all of their previous travails, their daring deeds, their criminal doings, never before had one of them been physically injured. What had they undertaken? What had she forced them to do?

"Leonardo is right," she spat. "We are at war."

Chapter Twenty-One

"Sacrifices are made in the name of love, no matter what it is we love."

A sculpted thigh slid snugly into the hollow of a hip, a small face lay cradled in the dip of a broad shoulder, a full, fleshy chest lay welcomed upon a firm, accommodating one. Nearly a foot different in height and yet their bodies entwined with the strangest coupling of precise melding. Viviana languished there, Sansone's body encompassing hers, in perfect harmony.

I am lost, she thought. *I cannot tell where I end and he begins.*

It was the most sensual moment of her life. It was an embrace one could live upon for a very long time—if needs be such.

Did he feel her smile fade? He lifted his head. "You need not fear me, nor anyone, ever." His lips lowered, paid bountiful homage to hers.

Their lovemaking had been different this time; without the aching insistence of lust, it had slowed; it had become a leisurely, lingering journey of explorations and sensations. Viviana knew not which version she preferred; in truth, she preferred both. Yet his words brought back the frightening events of the early evening, before she had returned home to find him waiting for her. The simple act had done much to alleviate the fear and anger that had accompanied her the rest of the way home.

Viviana raised her head from his chest. "If I have fear, it is not of you."

A scowl furrowed a crease at the top of his long nose. Sansone rolled them over on the bed. His fine hair fell forward. A soft ashen brown, the sun had swung its brush against random strands and glorified it with gold. The effect was a dewy color that brushed near the meadows that were his eyes. How she longed to delve forever into their depths, among the secrets, the scars, the sweetness.

"What is it then that you do fear?" he asked.

For an instant Viviana feared to tell him, feared his reaction, but the other fright was by far stronger. She told him of the rock.

He studied her, every aspect of her face.

"As there is nothing I can do or say that will make you stop this endeavor…" Viviana shook her head back and forth once and then again, her hair, tangled by their lovemaking, swishing against the linen.

"Then I will become, once more, your shadow, *tesoro mio*," he whispered in her ear, sweetly kissing it, tender touches that tingled her skin.

When Sansone rose up again, Viviana saw upon his face the same bitter sweetness, the same memories, as in her mind. How awful it had been through all those years to have him ever near, to be never close.

Viviana drew a line down the sharp curves of his face with a single fingertip; what a miracle it was to at last be so close, so dear.

"Then I will feel safer than ever before." She lifted her head to kiss him.

Their lips separated, he lay beside her, and propped her head upon his arm, their legs and linens entwined. Viviana breathed deep, aroused by the scents of their lovemaking still slick upon their skin, listening to his heart beat in time with hers. From the open window, a waft of air found them, adding its caress to theirs; laughing voices from somewhere below joined the chirping of crickets and the hooting of owls. Viviana closed her eyes, relishing the eternity of the moment.

"I would like to meet your sons." The words came from his mouth and the rumble in his chest. Viviana's eyes flew open. "And the other Disciples. I think it is time."

Viviana held so still she could have been sleeping, dreaming. She wasn't.

Sansone propped himself up on one elbow. "Do you not agree?"

She didn't answer, for she had no answer. She needed time to think on it.

Sansone smiled down at her. "If we are to marry—"

"Marry?" Viviana's pretense faded, disappeared as a shooting star does as it falls away from earth.

He leaned away from her. Though she tried to pull him back, he would have none of it.

"Did you think that this"—his eyes roved about the room, the bed, and its canopy above—"would be all we would share? Did you think it would be enough?"

"I...I..." Viviana bit her lip to stop her stuttering. "I have not thought of it, to be true. It seems such a miracle that I am in your arms, my mind has gone no further."

"Perhaps it should," he said. "Perhaps you should think hard upon it."

Viviana said not a word, for thoughts stormed in on her like a rampaging bull. To share his love, to the end of her days? Yes, that she could envision. But marriage? To once more become the property of a man, and a younger man at that? To give herself and of herself completely to another as she had once before, never having such wholeness returned. Could she do it? Would she do it? She said nothing.

With a heavy sigh, Sansone leaned toward her, kissed her once, then again and deeply, then unraveled himself from their nest and began to dress.

Viviana shot up, pulling the linen up to cover her bare breasts. "Where are you going? Are you leaving?" *Are you leaving me?*

He nodded. "You have much to think about, and much to do in the morning, *si?*"

"Yes, but..."

"I shall take my leave and allow you sleep."

"But you need not." It was the farthest thing from what she wanted.

"No." Sansone's head hung low as he laced his breeches, never fully rising. "But I think it best."

He finished dressing, kissed her once more, and walked away.

Viviana saw no anger in his languid movement nor in his stance. When he turned back for one last look at the door, she saw only his unhappiness.

Chapter Twenty-Two

"Each sunrise gives birth to new possibilities."

There were more of them and they were angrier.

The crowd of men that gathered every day before the steps of Santo Spirito had grown in number. As Viviana slithered past them and the front entrance, her heart became heavy at the sight of women. Only a few, yes, but their small numbers did not squelch her disappointment. Minds were difficult to change; narrow minds most of all for their entryways were far too small for new ideas to penetrate.

"Have no care for them, Carina." Viviana led her along the narrow Via de Coverelli and the even smaller path that wound around behind the basilica. She had told Carina about them, what had happened to Isabetta, for she wanted this young woman—this hopeful artist—to enter this undertaking in full knowledge of what awaited her. Telling was one thing, seeing another, most especially when the sight was nasty and offensive. "They come no closer than the piazza, not a foot upon a single stair. Father Raffaello has seen to it."

Natasia's brother had preached to the horde from the top step as he would have from his pulpit. Perhaps his words of Christian acceptance and generosity had not made an impression, but words of trespass and arrest most certainly had.

Viviana had waited to bring Carina until they finished the preparatory work: the scaffolds built and in place, all the materials purchased and at the ready. She wished for Carina's first introduction to the Disciples to be one of creation, for there the magic resided.

"We rarely work during services; hence we only arrive after Terce. We work only behind the canvas cloth during None, though some choose to join those prayers, so we must have the materials we need to see us through. And we always leave before Vespers."

These were not rules laid down by Father Raffaello, but ones all artists obeyed, not a one ever written or spoken. It gave the artists eight or nine hours of uninterrupted work to call theirs on any given day, save for Sunday. There was never work performed on Sunday.

"Actual work time is limited then," Carina said, keeping her eyes on the path before her and nowhere else.

"Indeed," Viviana sighed. "So we must be as efficient as possible with the time we have."

Carina answered with naught but a hesitant nod, lips a tight line on her face.

"Today will be so very exciting," Viviana said, rushing to dispel Carina's doubts and fears. "We are making the *arriccio* and beginning the first square."

Carina's face brightened; curved lips reached up to drop twinkles into her eyes.

Inside, the basilica was empty, save for one man.

"Patrizio, *buongiorno*," Viviana greeted the man sitting just outside the shrouded chapel, struggling to keep her surprise from her voice. Was he here to chastise her for entangling his wife in this endeavor, one that had become not only unconventional but dangerous?

The balding man didn't move, didn't respond. Viviana cringed, but would not shy away.

"Good morning to you, Patrizio," she said again, a tad louder, softly laying a hand upon his shoulder.

Patrizio flinched, jerking round.

"Ah, Viviana," he said, at last hearing her. "*Buongiorno*."

"Have you come to see our progress, to see how talented your wife is?"

Patrizio shook his head. "No, I have no care to see it. I will wait for the grand unveiling. I come only…that is, I only know Fiammetta is safe if I am here to know it for myself."

It was chivalric of the man, one known for the good care he took of his wife, though Viviana thought there was something else he would have had to say. She would say nothing of it either, then.

Viviana introduced Carina to the conte, and then turned to the chapel. "We are to our work, Patrizio."

The man nodded silently as Viviana led the young girl into the confines of their workspace and to the women within.

Lapaccia embraced her with all the repressed nurturing spirit churning within her.

Isabetta kissed both Carina's cheeks. "Aren't you the loveliest thing? And is not Marcello a lucky fellow?" Isabetta gave a wink and a nod to Viviana, who preened, already possessive of the daughter she would soon have.

Fiammetta greeted her as Isabetta had, with kisses, but hers came with a penetrating perusal. "My own daughter will be joining us tomorrow. I have the feeling you two will have much in common." It was the highest praise Fiammetta could give.

Leonardo came to her. Viviana watched as the girl's eyes widened, as small beads of perspiration broke out on her smooth brow. She remembered the first time she had come this close to the *maestro* and her own reaction; there were no words when faced by such a mystical, serene force.

"Welcome, child." Leonardo bowed before her.

Carina's head snapped to Viviana, jaw to chest. Viviana smiled, but made the smallest motion of a curtsy and gave a nod of her head.

Carina shook herself, quickly dropped into a deep, graceful obeisance. "I am honored, *maestro*." She rose, raised her chin, peering into his numinous, amber eyes. "I vow to you to be worthy of my place here. I know I have much to learn. I pledge to learn it well."

The corners of da Vinci's mouth twitched. "Then you have already earned your place. To acknowledge the need for learning is to be truly enlightened." Over Carina's head, Leonardo's gaze met Viviana's.

Mattea came and took Carina by the hand in an easy manner; no more than five years separated them in age. "Come, *cara* Carina, come look at the scaffold. See how it is imbedded in the wall? I knocked those holes out."

"Where is Natasia?" Viviana turned her attention from Carina now that the group had fully assimilated her charge within the fold.

Fiammetta simply shrugged and gave a small shake of her head.

"We cannot wait, I fear," Leonardo replied. "To complete this first square will take all our time today. We begin with the *arriccio*."

The manner of fresco painting was, by its very name, "fresh" painting. Upon a dry coat of *arriccio*—a combination of two parts fine sand and one part slacked lime—they would place the *sinopia*, a stencil made from their detailed sketches. Once the charcoaled lines were in place, they would smear the wall with a fine last coat of *arriccio*—the *intonaco*—which would remain wet. Then quickly, speed demanding skill, they would then ply the *buono*, the dry pigment form of color. As the *intonaco* hardened, a layer of crystal would form over the pigment, imbedding it into the surface. The surface must be painted before that layer dried. The technique—one of the most difficult for any painter—and its materials, assured that it would stand the test of time.

The mixture composed, they began to apply it to a square no more than three meters by five meters at the very top left of the chapel, small enough to apply the *buono* before the *intonaco* had time to dry. All fresco painting began at the top; in this way, there was far less chance of paint splattering down with the pull of gravity upon portions already completed below.

"Carina," Leonardo held out one of the wide brushes used for the application, "would you care to take up your first brush?"

She walked toward him, hand outstretched to take the brush, face blooming with the blush of roses, shooting stars in her eyes the color of the night sky. If her hand trembled, she paid it no heed. With a determination to make Viviana proud, Carina accepted the brush, slathered it with the plaster, and swept a broad stroke upon the wall.

"Brava," Leonardo said mellifluously.

"Brava!" Isabetta cheered raucously, as she and the others applauded.

Carina, near tears, accepted their true welcome into the group with a lopsided grin and a dipped curtsy.

The entire square, now completely coated, begged for more attention.

"Mattea," Leonardo called, "the *sinopia*. Isabetta, you are with her."

Viviana took Carina by her shoulders and stepped them back a pace or two. "Watch," she said, voice filled with wonder. She had performed this task many times on the studio walls, as had all the Disciples, but this time was different. This time the world would see.

The two women worked as one. Mattea lay the *sinopia* exactly in place; Isabetta held two pointed pieces of charcoal.

"Done." Mattea reached for her piece without looking up.

Isabetta slapped the charcoal into her palm and dropped to her knees upon the scaffold. They drew with furious precision, as if it were blades they held, not brushes. Within minutes, the skeletal form of wispy clouds and three birds in flight appeared.

"*Perbacco*," Carina breathed, though she did not need to; her surprise was as firm upon her face as her nose.

It took them less than an hour to complete the sketch upon the wall. The next step came, as it so often did, with difficulty.

"The *intonaco*, Fiammetta," Leonardo instructed.

"No, me." Lapaccia stepped quickly to the mixture and the large brush.

"Will you not be too tired to work the *buono*?" Fiammetta asked the question they were all thinking.

"I will allow you all that privilege," Lapaccia replied as she set to work, applying the last coat of plaster evenly and thinly upon the sketch so as not to smudge or obliterate any of its lines, as more than one pair of eyes locked and narrowed.

The concealing cloth opened, a gasping Natasia rushed in; her breathing and the dark splotches of red upon her cheeks told them she had been rushing for some time.

"I am so sorry," she panted, "I could not help my tardiness."

"Where have you been?" Fiammetta interrogated.

"You must be Carina." Natasia ignored the inquisition completely, stepping to the young girl, and kissing her cheeks. Stepping back, she rummaged in the small drawstring pouch hanging from her waistband and drew out a pendant hanging from a long silver chain. It was no pendant.

"This, Carina, is yours," Natasia proclaimed as she furled the chain over Carina's head, dropping the key upon the young woman's chest.

Carina reached down, took up the key, and held it to pursed lips.

"*Molte grazie a tutti.*" She thanked them all, though there was no need. They were as grateful for her as she was for them.

"What wonderful progress you have made already," Natasia said, nothing more, though more was still expected.

Indeed, the wall glistened with its own welcome, its need for the pigments as deep and intense as any desire.

"To your brushes, madonnas."

This time Leonardo took the place beside the mesmerized Carina, watching as five women climbed the scaffold and began to paint on the dry pigments, as the pigments soaked up the moisture of the *intonaco* and became moist themselves. It was a choreographed dance completed almost in the absence of words. The artists spoke with jerks of their heads, grunts, and the pointed tips of brushes, an abbreviated language only those who have worked together long and hard could understand.

Leonardo directed and encouraged them as he walked among them. "Make your work in keeping with your purpose."

Carina, enraptured, slid down the wall at her back, heedless to the dust that clung to her fine gown; she had no smock, yet. She tilted her head this way and that, high and low, left and right, a bird on its perch searching for both prey and predator, to see the women as they worked from each of their perspectives. If asked, she might not have been able to tell where she was at that moment, for she looked to be lost and flying in the azure sky coming to life beneath their brushes.

The ringing of bells, the murmuring of voices, the clanking of a thurible marked None as it came and went. First one, then another and another, raised themselves up, stretched out their backs and their knees with pops and grunts, until only Isabetta remained at the wall, finishing the small, fine lines of the last bird gliding upon a gentle breeze. The lunette might only be that of a sky but it would be the finest one they had ever created.

"*Ehi*. What goes on here?"

Not a one of them heard him push back the cloth and enter their haven. Not a one of them expected to see naught but a boy, an urchin with the dirt of the street upon him, standing with arms akimbo, questioning them.

His round brown eyes almost hidden beneath the tangle of tight black curls looked at them expectantly.

"This is no place for you, *ragazzo*," Fiammetta spared the boy the shortest, sharpest glance. "Be gone with you."

"But I want to see what they are all fussing about." A dirty thumb pointed toward the door and, no doubt, the churning crowd still in attendance.

"We create a fresco," Lapaccia told him kindly.

Thick brows disappeared into the nest of his hair. "You? Women?"

"You are correct," Leonardo informed him.

"*Mamma mia*!" the boy cried out, a palm smacking his forehead. "That is why they are angry."

Viviana scrutinized the boy. "How old are you, child?"

"I am nine and one half," he said, pulling himself straighter for he was small for such an age. Viviana smirked; more than one of the women softly chuckled.

"And I am going to be an artist," the boy said, his voice daring any to defy the contention.

"Are you?" Mattea asked, fighting her amusement to mirror his serious mien.

"*Sì*," he said matter-of-factly. "I wish to be a sculptor, but I will paint as well." This last he offered with a cavalier shrug, as if he would be doing the paint a kindness with his use of it.

Mattea hid her grin. "Then perhaps you should watch a bit as our friend finishes her work."

"Perhaps I should," the boy said, plunking himself down next to Carina.

He and Carina observed together as Isabetta finished the final touches of the first square and the Disciples began the next. They had set their *giornata*—a day's work—to two squares a day for the bottom tier and lunettes, one per day for the main scenes. Only under such a rigorous schedule could they complete the *cappella* in the time proposed and contracted; only doing so would truly prove their acumen. To fail would be a disaster, not only for them, but for Carina and those like her, for any who hoped to one day walk behind the Disciples, even if they did not yet know it.

As the six women stood back, stood beside Leonardo and studied their work, deciding where they had done brilliantly and where they could better their work, the child stood.

"*Grazie, madonnas,* and you, *maestro* da Vinci," he said, pulling back the cloth for his withdrawal.

Leonardo's bushy brows bunched together. "You know me, boy?"

The child baulked at him with a cynical smirk. "Who does not?" he said, as if it was a silly question.

Without another word, he went as swiftly as he had come.

"Visit us again, won't you?" Viviana called out, unable to name the magnetism of this child, only it's pull.

"I will," the boy answered with backward wave.

Just as he pushed the two-story, thick wooden door open a crack, allowing an orangey swath of sunlight to creep in, Isabetta called out to him as well, "Tell us your name, child."

He stopped, glowing in the sun's ray. "They call me Michelangelo."

And with that, he was gone.

"Well," Fiammetta harrumphed, "I never."

"What a delightful child," Lapaccia said. "We shall hear from him again."

"I have no doubt of it," Viviana agreed.

"Humph," was all da Vinci had to say.

The women ruminated on him as they cleaned their tools, as they organized their space. Carina pitched in without being asked, winning approval even if it was not her intent. As they made to leave by the back door, as they had come, Isabetta dug in her heels.

"This is insufferable!" Her raised voice echoed to the heights of the vaulted ceiling. "We have been awarded a commission, received permission from *Il Magnifico* himself, yet we must come and go from the back like vermin. It is intolerable, and I will not do it anymore."

Lapaccia reached out to her. "But after last night, after your injury, is it wise?"

"I would rather suffer the slings of a thousand rocks than feel myself a coward," Isabetta avowed, trembling with righteous tenacity.

"As would I," Mattea fumed, equally insulted.

"Well then," Fiammetta raised her chin, heading for the front door, "we shall put ourselves to the test in more ways than one."

Chapter Twenty-Three

"An artist's vision sees more clearly than most."

How grateful she was to sit.

Viviana arched her back with a low moan. The carriage jolted forward as it began the short journey home after bringing Carina safely to hers. Viviana slumped back on the tattered cushioned seat with a sigh, letting the rocking soothe her as if she were a baby lolling in a cradle. Her heavy-lidded gaze observed the city as it passed, the vista smudgy in the dusk, the view blurry as the lids of her eyes grew ever closer to closed.

Until they snapped open.

Something, no, *someone* in the small alley off the Via del Corso caught her eye.

"Stop!" Viviana cried, banging on the roof of the rickety carriage. Viviana's head jerked forward, then back, as the driver pulled sharply on the reins. The carriage shuddered to a stop.

Slipping off the seat, Viviana stuck only enough of her head above the opening ridge to see beyond it.

It is her! But it cannot be.

Viviana glared at the scene, at the two men talking with the woman; one she recognized as well as she did her own face. Who were those men? What would *she*, of all people, be doing talking to strange men without any sign of a chaperone or escort?

Such behavior is not in her. Viviana's thoughts continued to plague her. No, it was not who the woman had been raised to be, to act. It was not who she was.

Yet Viviana's eyes did not lie to her, she was sure of it.

"What are you up to?" Viviana asked of the woman, though she was too far away to hear her. The woman turned from the men, heading toward this end of the alley, and Viviana's carriage.

"Drive on," she said, banging once more. "Quickly!"

Viviana would not confront her; all lives held secrets. She only hoped that if her friend were in trouble, in need of help, she would ask for it.

• • •

They had been set to the task of cleaning up. A task that was theirs more often than the others'. It was the way of the apprentice, and neither Carina nor Patrizia felt anything but gratitude for it.

Of a similar age, they had attended the same social events, and seen each other, but had not come to know each other. "Were you surprised when your mother agreed that you could become one of the Disciples?" Carina asked, as she and Patrizia folded the huge drop cloths, stepping apart, the tips of the cloths in their hands, then rushing together to create a fold. It resembled a joyous dance.

Patrizia sniffed with a grin. "I am not sure if the word 'agreed' is appropriate. I believe I would use the word 'allowed.' Such is the way of her. But, yes, I was quite surprised."

They stepped apart, though not as far as before, and came together once more, the cloth growing smaller, yet thicker.

"Ah, sì, I understand," Carina replied.

"So," Patrizia observed, "you see my mother, see her truths?"

Carina's almond-shaped eyes grew into walnuts.

"I…that is, I did not mean, oh dear." Her words faded into the dust of shame.

Patrizia giggled. "Have no care, Carina. I know who my mother is better than most. She is an indomitable force, and not always courteous about it."

Carina's boisterous sigh of relief was like a gust of wind.

"I admire her," she said candidly.

"You do?" Patrizia's brows quirked lopsidedly upon her smooth brow.

Carina gave a decisive nod. "Indeed I do. She sees something that needs to be done, and she does it. If she disapproves or disagrees, she has no compunction about saying it. Brusquely, perhaps, but without hesitation. It is courageous to live in such a way."

Patrizia stopped. They were but inches from each other, only the cloth between them. She stared at Carina.

"*Grazie,* Carina," she whispered. "You have allowed me to see my mother as I never have."

Carina shrugged with a grin. "To see through another's eyes is often to see more truthfully."

Patrizia nodded silently. "And what of your parents, Carina? What had they to say of all this?"

With the completely folded cloth pressed against her chest, Carina stared out into the nave of Santo Spirito.

"My mother is a great musician, as is my father," she answered without answering. "My childhood was filled with music. It was also filled with memories, specific memories, of another sort."

Patrizia stopped her cleaning of the brushes as if Carina tied her hands with her words.

"We would go to performances or parties where my father was asked to play. I would always sit next to my mother. I would listen to my father, but I would watch Mama. She moved her hands upon a harp that was not there. She would play along with him from her seat of feminine anonymity. She was always proud of him, but it did not ease her sadness."

"She did not want such sadness for you," Patrizia offered.

"No," Carina said, shaking her head, "she did not. Nor did my father. If I were to say they did not worry, I would speak falsely. Yet they did not hesitate to agree, not for a moment. They believe Marcello came into my life not just for love, or to be my husband, but to bring me to this, to bring me here. They believe all such occurrences have more than one purpose."

Patrizia stood and stepped closer to Carina, reaching out a hand. "Then they are as courageous as my mama."

Chapter Twenty-Four

"Realities become harsh with realism."

No sunlight, no matter how bright, or birdsong, no matter how joyous, could relieve her of the heavy dread that weighed down each step she took.

Viviana had decided to walk to Santo Spirito that morning, knowing Carina would arrive by her own family's carriage, affording Viviana time to think. It was the last thing she needed.

Thoughts of what she had seen the evening before collided with those of what awaited her. She would stand by their decision. She would enter the basilica through the front door, through the throng she knew awaited her. What she wanted most of all was to run from both. There was nowhere to run, for she herself had laid the stones of her path.

"Viviana!"

The breeze carried her name to her as it did the redolence of late summer flowers.

Reaching the intersection of the Via Maggio, the Borgo San Jacopo, and the Via delle Trombe, Viviana searched its byways for the person to whom the voice belonged. Her eyes rolled heavenward and her pounding heart slowed at the sight of Isabetta, who hurried to catch up with Viviana.

"Are we ready for this?" Isabetta asked, linking her arm with Viviana's.

I would rather face that crowd than see what I already have, Viviana thought.

"I am, I think," was what she said.

"Are you members of the infamous Da Vinci's Disciples?" Though there was mirth in the call, both women spun without a smile, only to break into grins at the sight of Mattea, waving to them from further along the Via delle Trombe.

The pair slowed and waited for her, became three united as Mattea slipped her arm into Viviana's. Whatever lay ahead, they would face it together.

They chattered like crows on a laundry line. Having assumed all the artists were already ensconced within the confines of the church, the teeming horde faced the basilica's façade, tossing their malicious words toward the door as if the very sound of them could break it down. The trio of women saw nothing but their backs.

The crowd had grown, as it had every day since it had been born. The wide steps—as wide as the basilica itself—were barely discernable, as bodies ran the entire width of them, rows and rows of agitated, boisterous people.

One face could be seen, for its profile rose above the others, the man a head taller than any other. As if he knew she had found him, Sansone turned and found her. Viviana sent him a wink and a smile; he answered with a nod. She wanted more; she needed more. He had not come to her since that night. She needed to know he was not still troubled by what had or had not happened between them. Though if his clipped nod were any indication, Viviana thought he would not come to her anytime soon, or perhaps ever again.

"There is no way but through," Isabetta said to them, never moving her gaze from the wall of raging humanity before them.

"Then through it we go," Viviana conceded, turning from Sansone and her dire thoughts. "Remember, no matter what they say, stop for nothing."

They approached the back row of men and women, though thankfully far fewer women than men. So intent upon their defilement, the first row of the crowd let the women squirm through them, and paid them little heed; they gave the women not even a glance. It seemed too easy.

"There. It is them!" A gruff voice roiling with disgust rose above all, as did his pointing finger.

They were anonymous no more.

They clung tighter to each other, heads down and forward as if to batter their way through, pushing ever forward. From the side of her vision, Viviana watched Sansone surge through the crowd, heading toward them.

"Do not look at them," Isabetta hushed harshly as the crowd closed in.

Having heard such words, it was exactly what Mattea did.

"*Uffa*!" Viviana grunted, jerked back by the link of Mattea's arm, yanked back as Mattea stopped and turned into the crowd.

"What are you doing?" Viviana cried as the younger woman released her arm, broke away, and moved into the crowd. "Come b—"

The words caught in her throat, strangled by the sight before her. The same vision—the same face—that had sent Mattea flying into the crowd.

"Mama?" It was a cry as well as a question, one she need not ask. The elderly woman, who never left her house save for church, stood almost hidden amongst the rabble. Isabetta reached out—too late.

With bumps and bangs of her now-straight shoulders, Mattea plunged into the crowd, grabbed the woman by the arm, and pulled her out of it.

"Inside, Mama, now," Mattea seethed at her mother. The aged Concetta Zamperini did not possess the strength to fight her; she was but a dog on her daughter's leash. With Viviana and Isabetta on their heels, with renewed and invigorated ire careening toward them, the women rushed through the door, which snapped closed on their tail of hatred.

Mattea half pulled, half dragged her mother all the way to the Cappella Serristori, though they did not enter its confines.

"What in the name of God are you doing here?" Mattea whirled on her mother, hulking over her like a vulture did its prey.

"Language, Mattea, if you please." Even in this moment where she should have been contrite, Concetta was still a mother.

"Do not dare, Mama, I warn you. Why are you here?"

Heads poked out from the other side of the hanging cloth, on both sides, where cloth met wall. Leonardo, Natasia, and Lapaccia from one side, Carina, Fiammetta, and her daughter Patrizia from the other.

"I wanted to see…" Concetta began. Even from where Viviana stood she could see the tears pooling in the petite and plump woman's eyes, the creases fanning out from their corners etching deeper into her crinkled skin.

"You wanted to see what, Mama, the work I do?" Mattea did not change her stance nor ease the peevish annoyance in her voice. "I would have brought you. I would have gladly shown you all the work I have done."

Concetta shook her head. "I wanted to see what you were throwing your life away for." Concetta gave as good as she got, pained gaze intent upon her daughter's face as if they stood in a world where no one else existed. "What is so important you would toss away any hope of marriage—of family—for it?"

"Oh, *cara Mamina*, I have thrown nothing away."

"But you have." Concetta thrust herself to within inches of her daughter, a shaking, gnarled finger pointing back at the door they had entered through. "Do you think any of those men will have you now? Do you think any of those they know will? You will never find a husband, never find love."

"She already has."

Lapaccia's words, spoken with the beginnings of a warble of her own as she stepped from out of the chapel, cleaved the tension between them.

Concetta spun toward her, eyes widening at the sight of what was, by her clothes and jewels, a wealthy, perhaps noble, woman. Viviana discovered another note of respect for the woman as Concetta, even in the throes of such familial turmoil, remembered her manners, and dipped a curtsy, curt though it was.

"Madonna, I know not—"

Lapaccia walked to Concetta, returned the curtsy—much to Concetta's shock and dismay—and linked her arm with Concetta's.

"Your remarkable daughter solely possesses the love of my son."

Concetta stuttered back a step. "Your son?"

"Yes."

Mattea stood, her own arms wrapped about her, features drooping like a flower gone too long without water.

"Come, Mama." Mattea reached out to her mother. "I will show you our studio. Dear Lapaccia," she said, turning, "will you join us please?"

"Of course, *cara*," Lapaccia replied, joining them.

"Come, *artisti*, work does not wait, not even for passionate mothers," Leonardo said, pulling back the curtain to allow them entry.

They pretended to work—they moved tools here and there, they studied what they had done, they discussed what they would do next—but every ear, save Leonardo's, was trained on sounds outside the chapel, waiting for the sound of the back door closing. When the whoosh and bump finally came, they each, to the one, sprang back out.

Concetta walked—no, marched—back toward them with her head high, a wide, creasing smile on her flushed cheeks. To look at her, one might think she had been made a queen.

It is how she must feel, Viviana thought with a surge of satisfaction for this woman who had lived such a hard life.

"My daughter is betrothed to a great nobleman," she told them haughtily, as if they didn't know.

"Your daughter, madonna, is a great artist with important work to do," Leonardo replied.

"And *who* are *you*, signore?"

Mattea pulled on her mother once more. "This is our *maestro*, Mama. This is Leonardo da Vinci."

Even as the woman's jaw fell, she had the good grace to offer the man a curtsy. Rising back up, she leaned toward the tall man, neck almost bent in half to look him in the eye.

"Is my daughter truly a great artist?" she asked, voice as small as she was herself.

Leonardo bowed before her. Keeping his head close to hers, da Vinci whispered as if he shared a tremendous secret. "She is one of the best of her age I have ever seen."

"*Oh mio*," Concetta trilled, turning to Mattea. "Forgive me, *cara figlia*. I should never have doubted you. About anything."

"Come, Mama, I shall walk you home." Mattea wound Concetta's arm through hers, knocking her head lightly upon her mother's, leaving it there for an affectionate respite. They made for the back door to take their leave. "There is more we need to discuss. Such as how to truly keep a secret."

"It will be like keeping a firefly in the palm of one's hand," Isabetta chortled, inciting more giggles and laughter, even a smirk from Leonardo himself. "Well then, let us to work. I think ours will be easier this day than dear Mattea's."

Fiammetta shook her head as she watched them walk away. "As if we don't have enough of a battle to wage."

As if beckoned by her words, a crash shattered the stillness of the basilica, smashed to pieces one of the stained glass windows of the southwest transept.

From the jagged hole in the glass, a voice rose up. "You there! Halt!"

"Get back," Leonardo yelled, long arms stretching out to the side, corralling the women into the closed confines of the chapel. "Get back and stay back."

With them, he waited, not a breath heard among them.

Time ticked by on a soundless clock.

As the silence grew and lengthened, Leonardo poked his head out from the corner of the chapel, seeing no one, seeing only the broken window across from them and the blue sky where it had no business to gleam.

He stepped out; Isabetta began to follow.

"Stay," he compelled her.

She nodded, retreated from a man she barely recognized. Their Leonardo had been painted with strokes of fear, but much worse, anger. Their Leonardo rarely showed anger. Though she knew he felt it; who wouldn't when forced to defend one's honor as Leonardo had?

With a swiftness they did not know he possessed, the tall, lanky artist rushed across the nave, into the opposite transept, and back again.

He stood as rigid as the rock he held before him. But it wasn't just a rock. Wrapped round it was a tattered and grimy piece of parchment secured to the rock with a piece of twine.

"Well open it, for the love of God," Fiammetta blustered, blaspheming in fear.

"Mother!" the fair Patrizia gasped, pale hazel eyes agape.

A flick of a hand was her mother's only reply.

Leonardo did. As he folded it open and held it flat, they all saw the words written in a scraggly scrawl.

You must stop now.

Viviana sucked in her breath. "It is the same words shouted at us from the window."

"What, when?" Leonardo and Fiammetta badgered them.

The women told of their walk to the studio after leaving the Salvestro palazzo, of the cry that rained down upon them.

"We thought it was merely someone who did not approve of our activities. Someone harmless, for he hid among the crowd or the buildings," Viviana explained.

"Does the use of the same words mean it is the same man, or merely another who agrees with the first?" Lapaccia wondered aloud.

"Or could it be a warning of another sort altogether?" Fiammetta mused.

"I am sure they are united, come from out of the crowd," Natasia insisted.

Leonardo held up the rock. "This is not harmless. Nor was the one that hit Isabetta. I must speak to Lorenzo."

"No," Isabetta replied. "I will speak with him. I am to have another session sketching him tomorrow."

"Be careful," Leonardo warned her.

She nodded, unsure exactly to what he meant. "I will, of—"

The front door slammed opened. Once more, the women yelped in fear.

"Get back." Once more Leonardo commanded them.

"No, wait!" Viviana cried, seeing the silhouette of the man in the light streaming through the door, seeing his face once it closed. "He is no foe, I swear it!"

Sansone's long legs brought him to her in but a few strides. As if alone, he grabbed her by the shoulders, scoured her for injury.

Viviana laid her head upon his chest, feeling the flurry of his heartbeat, closing her eyes at the succor of his presence. When she opened them, she saw them. Every floundering-fish mouth, every bug-eyed stare, every creased forehead on the faces of the Disciples and da Vinci as well.

Viviana lifted herself off Sansone, pulled away from him, but only a little. Looking up into his face—one as dear as both of her children's—one side of her mouth lifted tentatively, as did one shoulder.

"I had to know," Sansone whispered. "I had to be sure you were unharmed."

"Life takes us where it should," she said as softly, "even if we do not know it ourselves."

She heaved a breath, and turned toward the ogling onlookers.

"Dear friends," she began, as she led Sansone closer to them, "please have a care to meet another, a very dear friend, Sansone Caivano."

For a shattered second, no one moved, no one spoke.

"It is my *very* great pleasure to make your acquaintance, signore." Isabetta stepped out first, dipped him a curtsy, offered him much more than just a smile, one filled with knowing mischief. "I know how—"

Any more words gurgled to a halt in her throat as she looked more closely upon his face.

"I know you—well, that is," Isabetta stammered, wide eyes blinking, "I have seen you before. I believe you accosted a carriage I rode in once."

Sansone chuckled from deep in his throat. "Ah, *sì*, that would be me, Signora Fioravanti."

"You know me?" Isabetta's brows jumped.

"I know you all, in my way." He grinned sheepishly at Viviana. "I fear my entry today had much the same lack of grace," he said, tossing a quick, skeptical glance at the others.

"Think nothing of it, signore. Were it not for you we could all be imprisoned still, or worse, deceased."

"That was you?" Mattea squeaked.

"What is that you say?" Fiammetta finally spoke, but it was not to greet the man.

Together, Viviana and Isabetta told them all of Sansone's part in saving Lapaccia; though small, it had been crucial; as Isabetta said, it had saved them all.

"I owe you my life as well, it would seem, signore." Lapaccia stood before him, her graceful curtsy belying her age. "I hope I can repay you in some way."

Sansone gently lifted her up and bowed his head nearer to hers. "You already have, Mona Cavalcanti."

"Signore," was all Fiammetta said as she dipped a shallow obeisance. There was a price there yet to be paid; Viviana knew it.

"It is well to have another male among us," Leonardo bowed to Sansone, who returned it.

"I am most honored to make your acquaintance, *maestro*," Sansone replied.

Leonardo inched closer to Sansone, lowering his voice, but it was not so low that Viviana could not hear his words.

"Was that you out there? You who yelled?"

"It was."

"And?"

Sansone shook his head. "I lost him in the crowd, I fear. But I know his dark coloring and the size of him. I will search for him, of that you can be assured."

"Sansone is a great *condottieri*," Viviana said with blustery pride. "He—"

"Was," Sansone said simply. "I *was* a soldier."

Viviana quirked him a look. "Was?"

Sansone nodded. "I have seen enough of battlefields and war. I have let it be known. There is more to life and I have a mind to live it. My days of a roving maker of war are over."

More giggles came from Carina and Patrizia, for his words and the look he cast upon Viviana's face said much of the life he had in mind. She felt her face flush, trying to hide her emotions as she told of Sansone's prowess and military victories.

"You are indeed accomplished, signore," Carina said. "Marcello will be well pleased to hear his mother is so well cared for and protected. I feel certain that when Viviana introduces you to him he will be profuse in his gratitude."

Viviana stifled her gasp; a fear she had yet to address—to realize—had been allayed as soon as it came. She should have thought of it herself—if Carina knew of Sansone, so too would Marcello. Perhaps Carina would have said something, thinking Marcello already knew of Sansone and his mother's relationship. But the young woman's words, her graciousness, assured Viviana of Carina's silence at the same time that it compelled Viviana to make the man known to her sons.

Viviana bestowed Carina with a grateful glance, her gratitude twofold.

"I certainly feel better protected to know of you, signore."

"Sansone, if you please," the man said, "all of you."

"Yes, Sansone," Isabetta said. "We are all well protected with you ever near. I am certain the worst is behind us."

Chapter Twenty-Five

"Devastation and ecstasy, both are weapons of great power."

The morning light fought its way through the stubborn fog.

With her head tucked in the crook of his arm, eyes just opened from a fit of sleep, Natasia found a peace that had eluded her for many a day. She had looked for it—searched for it—in the beauty of her husband and his love.

"How do you fare this day, dearest?" Pagolo asked, kissing the top of her head as they lay still wrapped within the linens in which they had slept. "Is everything as it should be?"

Natasia felt the small twitch of her lips; men could talk of war and death as if they spoke about the price of bread, but oh, how they dreaded speaking of a woman's body parts and their functions.

"All is as it should be. Within my body at least," Natasia assured him, rubbing small circles of assurance on his bare chest. "I feel once more at full strength."

"I am sure you would have recovered even sooner if you had not gone to paint." The small part of her husband that was fretful over what the Disciples did found its voice in his. He must have heard it himself, for he quickly tried to disguise it, kissing her disheveled hair once more. "You are strong; it is well."

His faith in her was far stronger than her own.

Turning her head upon the linens, she faced him. "I am so sorry, dearest."

Her lip quivered, threatened; she bit it. She could cry no more; she had shed enough tears to fill the Arno River to overflowing.

"You have naught to be sorry for. God will bless us when he feels the time is right. I have no doubt."

Pagolo kissed her deeply, sensually. Lifting his face up only enough to touch the tip of her nose with his, Pagolo's eyes slanted, brows rising mischievously. "It only means we must try more."

Natasia did laugh then, and then more as he rolled atop her, smothering her dimpled face with his angelic kisses. Both knew it was still too soon; the promise of it was enough.

"Signore?" The call came with a discreet knock upon the bed-chamber door. "The carriage is here."

Pagolo dropped his weight off her, back onto the bed, staring at the brocade canopy above them. "The carriage is here and I am not even dressed. See what you do to me?" His impish eyes flicked from her face to his protruding body part.

Natasia laughed again; there might come a day when such an appendage struggled to protrude, but it would not matter, for he would always make her laugh, always make her happy. She only hoped she could do the same for him. The burden that she might not grew heavier upon her shoulders every day.

Pagolo rose and began to dress. Natasia studied him all the while, lost in her own thoughts of him, and of more. He was the love she had dreamed of as a child; he was that, and more. If he knew, would he leave her? If he knew what she did, would he do worse?

"How long will you be gone?" she asked, pleasing herself with the curves of him, and the edges too.

"I shall be back before you are back in that bed. My mission in Poggibonsi is a quick one."

His mission, for *Il Magnifico* no doubt, reminded her of her own.

"And what will you do while I am gone? Are you to your work?" Pagolo asked, struggling into his *camicia*. Natasia rose, and, with the linen sheet wrapped about her person, helped him tie the laces at each shoulder.

It pleased her greatly for him to call it that, to give it the respect of the word.

"Indeed I am," Natasia leaned back slowly with a low moan, kneading her lower back, and began her own morning ablutions. "We begin the bottom tier today. I am quite eager for it. I love to paint serene landscapes."

Pagolo stopped, the laces of his breeches still in hand. "You will be careful on the scaffolds, will you please? Use those Viviana made, not Fiammetta."

This time they laughed together as they made their way to the kitchen, where Pagolo grabbed a slice of bread.

"I will see you soon, dearest." He made to kiss her, then pulled back. He stared at her—into her, before lowering his lips to hers. Natasia opened her eyes, studying him even as she kissed him. It was more than a kiss goodbye; it felt like a probing question, and a declaration as well. She took the last to be the truth of it, musing on the rest.

• • •

With one foot on the step, one hand on the door sash, Pagolo called out to his carriage driver.

"Turn right on Corbolino and a right on Benci," he instructed, hefting himself up.

"But, signore, that won't take us—"

"Just do it, *per favore*," Pagolo demanded. "Then stop near the corner of Porciaia."

"As you say, signore," the driver agreed, despite his crooked lips and narrowed eyes.

They sat for minutes, but not many. Pagolo kept one eye on the small slit of the nearly closed curtain. If he breathed, it did not feel like it.

His hand cramped with its tight hold upon the curtains; a wraithlike fist compressed his chest ever tighter. At last, Pagolo saw what he waited to see, and then what he had hoped not to see.

The fine carriage could be no other, with its fringed red velvet curtain and its gilding, a wedding present to Natasia from her parents. Like every day his wife went to the church to paint, she traveled there by carriage. This day, it passed by where his own carriage sat, heading north. Santo Spirito lay to the south.

"Take me away," Pagolo called, rapping his knuckles upon the door. "Take me to Poggibonsi."

As the carriage began jostling along once more, Pagolo dropped his head into his hands.

• • •

"I do not think I have seen a finer widow's gown in all my life," Lorenzo said to Isabetta by way of greeting. He wore the creamiest black leather Isabetta had ever seen; it seemed to flow over his body rather than sit upon it.

So, she thought, *his work begins where it left off.*

"*Grazie, Magnifico.*" She dipped him a fine curtsy, feeling far less anxious than she expected. "It was gifted to me by Mona del Marrone."

Lorenzo sniffed. "I wager she did not wear it very long."

Isabetta could not restrain the twitching of her lips. "I believe it made her itch."

Lorenzo tossed back his head with a fine laugh. "I do not wonder. Though I would wager you look far lovelier in it than she did."

"Viviana is a beautiful woman, *Magnifico*. I can only hope to aspire to her grace."

Lorenzo must have seen the rise of her hackles, for he bowed to her words.

"Shall we begin?" she asked, taking her seat upon the settee, opening her sketchbook.

"No work until we drink," Lorenzo said, pouring two crystal glasses of ruby wine, crossing to her with a swish of fine leather. The masculine smell of it found her.

"It is early for me for such a strong brew, but if you insist…"

"I do." He sat down beside her before handing her the wine.

Isabetta bent forward, stretching to place her sketchbook on the table before them, just out of her reach. When she sat back, Lorenzo had shimmied to within inches of her. His scent wafted closer, the aroma of valerian musk, civet, and man. The tangs did not repel her.

She drank a long draught, tipping her head back, revealing her neck. Did she do so on purpose? She would ask herself later. Did she come here knowing—wanting—something to happen? Another question for another time.

He needed no more of an opening. Once more Lorenzo leaned toward her, the tip of his long nose brushing against the tender skin beneath her ear, inhaling deeply. He laughed, a deep, throaty laugh.

"Your skin prickles, Mona Fioravanti. Do you find me prickly?"

Isabetta, though she didn't realize it, shook her head. "If you are going to smell my neck, I believe it only right that you call me Isabetta."

"Hah!" Lorenzo guffawed, even as he inched closer, his hard thighs now rubbing against hers, their warmth passing from his leather to her silk. "Then you must call me Lorenzo when we are alone."

"Are you ever alone, Lorenzo?" she asked, daring to turn her face to his.

His dark eyes lost their smile as they looked upon hers. "You see a great deal, Isabetta."

"So I have been told," she smirked with a shrug.

Isabetta took another sip of wine, licking a droplet from her lips.

Lorenzo groaned. He was undone; she could see it in the glaze in his eyes. When his lips fell on hers, when his tongue demanded entry, she gave it.

His hands came quickly to her waist, but oh so expertly; she quivered at the touch. With a leer that begged for a slap, Lorenzo took her glass—one she had nearly tipped over—and placed them both on the table.

Lorenzo stood up, hovering over her, looking at her from the very depths of him.

"I will not force you, Mona Isabetta. Nor will I expect anything from you merely because of who I am."

Isabetta's gaze never left his face. She rose slowly. Even more slowly, Isabetta removed the pins holding her hair, allowing the long buttery tresses to fall in waves around her.

"You need not force me to do anything...Lorenz—"

His mouth was on hers before her words were finished. She closed her eyes to the feel of his lips, his hands, not knowing which were which, not caring. With a groan of her own, she surrendered herself to him, to the moment.

• • •

What began on the settee, ended on the floor, but not before Isabetta cried out with the relief of need long unsated.

Their naked bodies, filmed with sweat, slid slowly against each other merely for the languid feel of it.

"You have not slaked your need in quite some time, Isabetta, have you?" Lorenzo asked her, nuzzling his face between her tender breasts.

Isabetta laughed, Lorenzo's head bouncing as she did. "Does it show that readily?"

Lorenzo propped himself up on one elbow, his hair a tangle, face florid, lips spread wide. "Either that or you are extremely passionate."

Isabetta stared at his lips, thinking of the pleasure they had brought her, licking her own. "Would it be so terrible if both were true?"

In answer, Lorenzo kissed her again, long and hard. She returned it in kind.

"Kiss me like that again, and we shall never leave this room."

Isabetta laughed again. Then…

"Oh no!" she cried, jumping up, gathering her clothes, attempting to put them on hurriedly. "My work! I must get to my work. Stand up, Lorenzo, strike your pose."

With a roguish grin across his face, he did as instructed, completely naked. "Does this meet your requirements, madonna?"

"Actually…" Already she was an artist again, albeit a well-sated one. The lines of his body, the hard edges of the muscles of arms and legs, the sensual curve of the lower back to the upper buttock, ignited her other passion just as well.

They spoke a little as she worked, talked of their lives. Isabetta tried her best not to show any reaction as *Il Magnifico* told her of his father's early death, his fears when he had to step into the role of the leader of the Medicis. It was a notion she never would have imagined.

"You have risen far higher than your father," she said softly, hand rustling on the page. "You hold great power. Power!"

"What?" Lorenzo's head spun about as if a threat had appeared.

"We need your help, Lorenzo." Isabetta put down her charcoal. "Da Vinci's Disciples need your power."

He listened almost devoid of reaction as she told him of the crowd, of the heckling wherever they went, ending with the rock that had struck her and the one that had demolished the church window. At that, he did react.

Lorenzo came to her, kneeling before her, oblivious to his nakedness, kissing the bruise he must have seen already. "I will take care of it. I will take care of you. On that, you can be assured."

The concern and care writ across his face touched her heart. She caressed his face with the touch of a feather. She knew what she had done was not unfaithful to the husband she had been so faithful and loyal to, yet she would be lying to herself if she did not admit to a twinge of guilt. She had lain with a married man. True, Lorenzo had rarely been faithful to his wife, no matter how many children they created together. He had, in fact, a mistress, Lucrezia Donati, a love from the days of his youth, though many believed it was a love unconsummated—a delusional notion.

She pushed such thoughts to the ignored corners of her mind, for his words, such noble words—"I will take care of you"—made it easy to do. When was the last time she had heard that from a man?

Isabetta stood up and once more removed her clothing.

Chapter Twenty-Six

"The brush struggles for truth, but some mysteries even it cannot solve."

Are they statues or are they real?

It was the first thought to burst into Viviana's mind as she approached Santo Spirito; her dread of pushing her way through the angry throng had made itself known from the moment she awoke. That dread took flight as she stood at the very back of the crowd, which seemingly grew larger with each new day, looking at the additions to the scene this morn.

Though they might look like statues, the four soldiers were very real.

"I must paint them one day," said she to herself, blinking against the sunshine glinting off their armor.

With their silver breastplates atop the bright red, white, and gold full-length *farsetti* with finely slashed sleeves worn above stripped balloon breeches, and their kettle hats with ostrich feathers dyed to match, these four men of the *Otto di Guardia* were resplendent with mighty pageantry. Splendid and deadly, as their scroll-hilted swords and their finely tipped lances testified. Their faces were impassive, save for the threatening sneers with which they surveyed the riotous crowd below them. What had once been a political police force during the days of the Cosimo I had evolved to a criminal one after the assassination of Giuliano de' Medici. These men were the fiercest of the fierce, garnered from all ranks of the military.

Viviana's lips twitched. Poor Father Raffaello's largesse, impressive in its own right, looked far fleshier as he stood beside these well-trained, burly, and muscular men. The priest must have seen her in that moment, for he leaned toward the nearest guard, nudging him, and pointing in her direction. With but a glance from that soldier, the others sprang into action, plunging into the crowd, parting it with the same might that Moses must have the Red Sea.

"Make way!" they shouted, hewing a path through the rabble, more than a few people requiring a shove from a horizontal lance before they moved.

Angry voices became growls. The shoving moved in both directions. People fell upon the cobbles. The human sea tossed angrily.

Viviana pulled her veil down, dipped her head, and plunged into the open trough they created for her. As she reached the steps and climbed them, the soldiers closed ranks behind her, at the ready once more.

With one hand on the door, she turned back to the soldier nearest to her. "Thank you for being here today, signore."

"We will be here every day until you finish," he said, wary glare never leaving the crowd. "It has been so ordered."

Viviana gave a nod of acknowledgement, hand upon the door. There she held it for the briefest moment, as her gaze caught and held on two faces, two men who surprised her with their presence in the horde. She turned from them with a frown and slipped through the door; the soldiers may guard their bodies, but invectives still wounded hearts and minds. She hurried from them, slammed the door on them.

The first woman she saw was Isabetta, struggling through the back door, arms filled with more bristly brushes and pots of pigments. Viviana corralled her before they ducked behind the cloth.

"I see we are to be protected," she said with a tilt of her head, "and by the *Otto*, no less."

Isabetta's face burst joyously. "Is it not wonderful? I feel my creativity leaping knowing they are there."

"And have you felt other things that *Il Magnifico* has to offer?"

Isabetta's joy disappeared like a candle snuffed. It was a brazen question, even if asked by her closest friend.

Viviana softened. "Did you think I would not be able to tell, as you had with me, even were they not at the door? It is painted gloriously upon your face."

Isabetta said naught. Her gaze rose to the coffers above their heads, or perhaps beyond. "There are many things I have done that I regret, as have you, that they tell us will send us into the fires of Hell," Isabetta said without artifice or shame. "If I find scattered moments of satisfaction in his arms, it is the least of my offenses."

Viviana's chest swelled and collapsed with her sigh. "I feel only joy for you. You have been too long without such moments. My care—my concern—is for your heart. *Magnifico* is a powerful, persuasive man, but he is a thief of hearts. Protect yours, please, *cara*."

"Who is to say who uses who?" Isabetta said within the shelter of Viviana's solicitude. "I have known the pain of loving one I cannot have. I promise you it has hardened me against doing so ever again."

Viviana nodded though unconvinced. She knew the magnetism of Lorenzo de' Medici, had felt it herself. She knew too Isabetta's needs. The combination was not a favorable one, not in Viviana's mind.

The raised voice of Leonardo da Vinci, distinctive though muffled through the door, broke her worried reverie.

"He speaks to the crowd? What does he say?" Isabetta dropped her bundles, hurried to the front of the church, Viviana hard on her heels. They put their ears to the crack.

"Do you not realize what this can do for our work, all our work? How it can bring it to the masses, not just to those with deep pockets? Is not that what we truly want? What is best for the craft?"

"They are women!" A cry answered him, as if being female were a contagion to ward oneself against. In this instance, perhaps it was.

"True, but they are talented, dedicated women."

"He dares to reason with them." Isabetta pulled back, fell back, knocking her head upon the door. "He may as well try to sell rosary beads to the devil."

"There are many among them from the guilds," Viviana mused. "I believe it is to them he speaks, not those who merely demand we know our place."

"Your place is within that chapel continuing the profound and beautiful work you were meant to do."

The women jumped at the presence of da Vinci before them; neither had heard his silent entry through one of the two smaller doors bookending the large, main one.

"Yes, *maestro*," the women said in concert, rising up.

"We may work safely now the *Otto* is here as well as Signore Caivano." Leonardo led them up the side aisle and to the walls that awaited the strokes of their brushes.

The guards' presence, like Sansone's, was a relief; any peripheral burden withdrawn allowed expanded creativity within. The women worked with passionate determination and efficiency, completing two sections of the lunettes before the time for None came. Though today, and the many days that would follow until their work was finished, there would be no None service offered at Santo Spirito. Father Raffaello had deemed it best for both his parishioners and the artists. Father Tutalle from the neighboring Santo Felice, on the Via Agostino just two blocks away, had agreed to shared precedency over that particular mass.

The Disciples still worked behind the cloth, if only for their own peace of mind. As they sat on the floor and the scaffolds and took a midday repast, a memory from the morning returned to Viviana.

"Natasia, dear, why were your uncle and cousin in the crowd?" she asked.

Natasia's head bobbed as she swallowed her mouthful of bread and cheese. "They were? They were here?"

Viviana nodded. "Indeed. I saw them myself. Did you not?"

"I did not." Natasia shook her head, food forgotten. "Their

relationship with *Il Magnifico* falters. Perhaps they fear this, and my action in it, will make it worse."

"It makes no sense," Fiammetta said dubiously. "He has approved of it. If they endeavor to endear themselves to him, they would agree, not oppose."

Natasia fluttered both hands as if plagued by pesky insects. "Oh who knows the vagaries of my uncle's mind? I would pay it no heed." Her eyes met not a one of theirs.

A piece of meat, half chewed, caught in Viviana's throat. There was little she could do to discharge it.

Chapter Twenty-Seven

"Loving your work does not make it anything less than work."

Their raw fingers ached, splotched with color, color that would not wash away no matter how hard they washed, no matter how roughly they scrubbed.

Bowed backs, strained necks, throbbing eyes—it was the truth of them all.

The consequences of their undertaking grew and grew. Viviana had expected derision from the community; they received condemnation. She knew they would need to work hard; she never expected it to take such a toll upon their bodies.

As the women around her stretched and moaned, unfurling hunched backs, stretching cramped fingers, Viviana felt their pain as well as hers, for in her eyes she had brought it upon them.

Or had she?

It was Isabetta who insisted they work longer. It was Fiammetta who demanded they work finer, pay greater attention to detail. It was Mattea who mixed and remixed the pigments, sometimes starting over and over again, until she created the perfect color.

To a one, they had never worked so hard or for such long hours before.

Viviana stopped her work to watch theirs, and added another pain to her list: that of her heart.

"Perhaps we should stop a bit early today, take some much-needed rest," she suggested.

Not a single agreement came in reply.

Leonardo sidled up to stand beside her; he watched her watching them.

"Tell me, madonna, do you think you are all weak women, too weak for this work?"

"How dare you, *maestro*," Viviana spun toward him, roared at him. "There is nothing weak about us. There is nothing weak about being a woman. It is only the men who govern us all who believe such nonsense, who try to tell us it is so. We can do anything a man can do, and do it better. We…"

Viviana stopped her own ranting, narrowed her eyes at da Vinci, and smiled, almost.

Leonardo tilted his head to the side as his brows rose and made ripples upon his skin.

Viviana leaned closer to him.

"If you were any one but Leonardo da Vinci, I would gladly wipe that grin from your face and show you just how weak I am."

Each day blurred into the next. Weeks passed. They began to take turns rubbing each other's backs, soaking their hands in heated water to ease their aches. The one thing they did not do—would not do—was stop.

• • •

The chapel was an agitated, buzzing hive, each woman a bee, angered at the dishonor and the taint, the same they had all encountered that morning. Like angered bees, they were a threat to sting anyone they could blame for it.

Each woman began her day in her own way. Fiammetta broke her fast with her husband and daughter, Natasia with Pagolo, and Mattea with her mother. Isabetta wandered her small home as if she looked for something, but if asked she could not say what. Lapaccia began her day in prayer, as did Carina with her family. Viviana wrote in her journal, for most nights she was far too tired to do so.

But this day had begun the same for them all, for when they

stepped outside their door, turned to close it behind them, they all saw it. Though the words all differed slightly, the message was the same.

To the one, their doors and the front of their homes—the large and the small—had been vandalized. In paint as red as a hot summer sunset, the words defiled them. Words of their indecency, their lack of legal paternity, even their physical beings had been splashed on their homes for all to see.

To the one, they gaped in shock, grew red in anger, and made their way to the chapel and their work, work that no words—no man—could stop.

• • •

The day had been plagued with interruptions, disruptions of little consequence, nonsensical thoughts in minds intent on focus. Father Raffaello asking what time they would finish that day, Mattea's mother appearing merely to speak once more of the noble who loved her daughter, the back door to the basilica opened and slammed to a shut, yet again.

"*Dio mio*, what now?" Isabetta snapped. She stood at the chapel egress, her back to the church, beseeching her fellow artists. "Have we not suffered enough? Can we not simply carry on with our work without interruption?"

"Oh dear," the soft, lilting voice answered her. "I fear I have come at an inopportune moment."

Isabetta spun, words of banishment ready upon her lips until she saw that face.

It was a face talked about by men and women throughout Florence, a face immortalized by both Leonardo and Botticelli. Her delicate beauty—the petite face upon the long, thin neck, the cupid's-bow lips, the wide, pale eyes, the long, flowing hair of the natural auburn so coveted by Florentine women—had been extolled in the sonnets and poetry of men throughout Florence, men including Lorenzo de' Medici.

Isabetta lost thought, words, in the face of her lover's true love.

The relationship between Lorenzo and Lucrezia Donati was a topic forever under discussion. Some said he fell in love with her long before his marriage to Clarice, though Lucrezia was already married. Some said Lorenzo's love for Lucrezia was naught more than platonic worship. Few believed it. Knowing the man as she did now, Isabetta knew with certainty there was nothing platonic about what went on between them, knew his lust to be too powerful, his power too strong to be denied, his insatiable desire to possess all that was truly beautiful too insistent.

Yet he protected her, feeding the fantastical notion. For a man to commit adultery, though a sin in the eyes of God, was nothing exceptional in the eyes of society. For a woman to do so was a punishable offense, one punishable by law and its biting jaw.

"Of course not, signora." Viviana rushed to Isabetta's assistance. "We are merely taken aback by the presence of a visitor. We have been forced to deny such attendants, I fear. I am sure you understand."

"Indeed," Lucrezia gave a simple bow of her head, perhaps an attempt at an apology. "I have seen those who would make for poor guests."

"And yet you found your way in," Fiammetta challenged; no matter how revered this woman was, she would not intimidate the contessa, nor would she be countenanced.

Lucrezia smiled, a gesture lovely and enchanting and, to another woman's eye, well rehearsed.

"For me, allowances are made, *sì*," she professed with a coquettish lift of one shoulder. "I confess I felt a powerful need to see the courageous women everyone speaks about."

Fiammetta replied with her own polished, "contessa" smile. They all knew her words were specious; they all knew whom Lucrezia had truly come to see.

"You are most welcome, Signora Ardinghelli." Isabetta, the master of herself once more, faced this woman with her true self, one that had become a powerful force all her own.

"You know me?" Lucrezia's perfectly plucked brows rose.

"A beauty such as yours is well known, madonna," Isabetta simpered sweetly.

Lucrezia tipped her head, accepting such sweetness, unable—or unwilling—to hear its mockery.

Isabetta took the woman's arm. "Come; let me introduce you to my fellow artists."

Names were exchanged, as were the curtsies, as if they all were performing in a play.

"May I?" Lucrezia requested, once the fallacious pleasantries finished, tipping her perfectly coifed head toward the chapel.

"As you wish," Isabetta allowed.

Lucrezia strolled about the chapel, Isabetta on her heels, following the rich aromas of rosewater and lavender that hovered about the expensively groomed woman. As Lucrezia studied and examined their work upon the walls, her hard, haughty expression softened, marveled.

"You have all done this yourselves?" Gone was Lucrezia's well-practiced speech, her postured superiority.

"We have," Isabetta stated.

The woman who surely looked upon Isabetta as a rival, looked upon her—them all—in wonder.

"Where did you find the courage?"

Isabetta tossed her head, one shoulder rising. "There are many times in life where one has no choice but to be courageous, to do what must be done to give ourselves better lives. Surely you can understand."

Lucrezia sniffed, though it sounded more like what it was, a snicker.

"Indeed I do. Do you know," she continued, "there are many who say you are to be feared?" She looked at them all. "That you are all to be feared. That the devil sent you, that you are witches. They say you will change our very way of life."

Viviana dismissed the words, fearing more the leer upon Isabetta's face. Lucrezia's gaze scuttled about the chapel and all in it. "I say that there are times when old ways not only should be changed, but must be changed."

She turned once more to Isabetta; her small, curved lips lifting at the corners, as did Isabetta's.

"I have taken too much of your valuable time, *donne artiste*. Please, continue your important work."

"We thank you for your visit today…and your encouragement," Isabetta intoned.

Lucrezia Donati dropped into a deep, respectful curtsy, her pale green eyes flitting to every face.

"Do not stop. No matter the consequences, hold to your convictions."

With such words, she minced away; only the scent of her remained, and the astonishment she left behind.

Chapter Twenty-Eight

"Any artist may paint the truth, or the truth as they see it."

The carriage tethered to the post before her home looked familiar, but Viviana was unable to place it. She stepped around it to her door, assuming it was but one of her sons' regular customers.

But one should never assume.

Her sons, like the ground floor full of employees, swirled in an eddy of frantic busyness. Viviana had no desire to get in their way, yet she needed to.

"Dinner this Sunday, *sì?*" she asked them quickly.

"Of course, Mama," Rudolfo rushed past her.

Marcello simply nodded; he had not a glance to spare her from the mounds of parchment on a desk made invisible by them. Viviana leaned over the escritoire toward him. "I think it best if Carina not attend, just this time, my son, if it does not offend."

That brought his attention to her. "Are you…is there a problem with Carina? Does she not—"

Viviana stopped him with a raised hand and a shaking head. "She is wonderful, Marcello, have no fear. It is as if she has been one of us from the beginning."

Marcello slumped with relief. "Then—"

"There is merely a private matter I need to discuss with my sons, naught more."

His brow furrowed, but he nodded. "Of course, Mama."

Viviana leaned further, bussed a kiss upon his forehead, said, "*Grazie, cara,*" and took herself away, toward the stairs.

"A visitor awaits you, Mama," he called to her back. "Signore Capponi."

Viviana stumbled, but raised a hand in acknowledgment. What would Natasia's husband want of her? What would she say to it? Jemma waited for her at the top of the stairs. "Signore Capponi is—"

"I know," Viviana stopped her curtly, removing her veil. "Where is he?"

"Your salon, madonna."

"*Grazie,*" Viviana replied over her shoulder. She reached her study, but stopped short of entering. From the side of the opened door, she peered at the man awaiting her within.

Pagolo sat slumped in his chair, arms resting on legs that jittered. This was not a social call he paid her.

With a deep, fortifying breath, Viviana put on her best smile and walked in.

"Pagolo, what a wonderful surprise." She opened her arms to him as he stood to greet her.

"Mona Viviana." Pagolo did not know the entire truth about the man Viviana had once called husband, but he did know how she preferred to be addressed. "Please forgive my unannounced presence."

"There is nothing to forgive, dear Pagolo. It is always a pleasure to see you." Her attempt at banality failed with a betraying squeak of uncertainty. "Natasia did not mention you would visit."

"That is because she does not know of it."

"Let me get us some biscuits, shall I?" Viviana rushed from the room before he could reply. As she hurried up the steps to the kitchen, and gathered a platter of biscotti and some wine, she tried to weigh her possibilities. Her loyalty lay with her sisterhood, which would never—could never—be questioned. But what if loyalty became a barrier to salvation?

"Here we are," she twittered, returning to her salon with the victuals. She poured a glass of wine for both of them, which they readily consumed. Neither touched a single biscotti.

If Viviana had hoped for small talk, it was in vain.

"I worry for my wife, madonna."

"Dear Pagolo." Viviana leaned toward him. "You need not fear. We are now well protected. The *Otto*—"

"It is not her work, your work, which troubles me."

Viviana took another, larger gulp of wine.

"I fear for her mind."

Viviana sputtered and coughed. "Why?" She croaked, cleared her throat, and tried again. "Why do you fear such a thing? What has happened?"

"Many things, too many things I fear," he said. "We have lost not one but two babies."

"*Oh buon Dio,*" she said under her breath. Not a word of such devastating losses had Natasia shared with them.

"Do not feel slighted that she did not inform you or the others," Pagolo assured intuitively. "Both were lost very early, one before we even knew of it."

She knew the pain she saw in his slacked expression belonged to them both. A piece of her heart broke for them.

"Do you think it is the stress of what we do?" The thought came to her, the images of Natasia carrying buckets of stone and sand; climbing up the scaffolds—she did not know if the losses came from such activities. The physicians were forever warning against any physical activity during such a time. If it were up to them, women would be in their beds for the entire nine months. Viviana had never set great store by such words. She had found movement and activity only made her feel stronger, made the actual birthing easier.

Pagolo shook his heavy head, dropping chin to chest. "I wish it were. I fear there is something else."

Viviana waited, for far too long it felt.

He raised his head. "I think there is someone else."

"Someone else?" Viviana jolted upright in her chair.

"Another man." Pagolo made it clear.

"What?" Viviana almost laughed the word, the thought so ludicrous. "I do not believe it. *You* should not even think it. Natasia has loved you, loves you still, for years, deeply and devotedly. She waited for you to return from war. She would have waited for you forever."

"But she has been behaving so strangely." Pagolo slapped his hands on his legs, threw them in the air. "She is forever coming and going and not only during the hours she works with you. Sometimes much earlier."

Viviana rubbed her temples and the pain that suddenly found its way there. She did not believe—not for an instant—that Natasia had been unfaithful to her husband, whom she adored. But his words and—

"I am ashamed to tell you, Mona Viviana, that I watched her when she did not know it." Pagolo's ears turned red. "On a day when she told me she was making straight for Santo Spirito while I was leaving for a day to Poggibonsi. When I left, I did not truly leave. I sat, hidden shamefully in my carriage, around the corner of my home and watched. I saw her…" Pagolo grabbed the bottle, refilled his glass, and drank all of it in one gulp. "I saw her leave, heading away from Santo Spirito, not to it."

"There could be any number of reasons—"

"None that she would not tell me about," Pagolo insisted. "We share everything. Or so I believed."

Viviana's head now throbbed; what was she to say? What *could* she say?

"What are you going to do, Pagolo? Why have you come to me?"

His dark stare held upon her, unblinking. "It is why I have come to you, madonna. I seek your help."

"My help?" Viviana squeaked.

"*Sì*. Will you endeavor to learn what she is doing, where she is going? Anything that might explain her actions?"

Viviana longed to moan, to shudder away the burden he was placing on her. But the pain painted so darkly upon his face would not allow it.

"All of us, all of Da Vinci's Disciples, are always concerned for each other's well-being. We are always on the watch for each other's care, I assure you."

It was an answer that comforted, though it was not agreement. Pagolo did not seem to notice.

• • •

The daggers felt so good in her hands, as if they were a part of them. They were second only to the brush. She did not know if it was because of the power holding them allowed her to feel, or that it made her feel as if he were with her, as if Andreano had returned and they practiced once more beneath the canopy of trees. It mattered not.

So many nights like this one, Mattea waited for her mother to take to her bed, held her breath until she heard the purring sort of snoring that always came with her mother's sleep, then rushed to her wardrobe and its secret compartment at the bottom. The special hideaway in which she had once hidden her sketches now concealed her daggers.

She quietly pushed at the furniture in their small sitting room, pushed the settee, the chair, and the two small tables to the corners of the room, leaving the center wide open. Though small, it was a place to practice nonetheless.

Mattea closed her eyes, saw him before her, saw him take his stance. She took hers. The game was afoot.

For hours she slashed, she plunged, she whirled. For those hours, he was hers again.

• • •

Pagolo's visit had left her exhausted, in both body and spirit. They needed her help—Natasia needed her—but what could she do without breaking the confidence of one or the other?

Viviana ate little of her dinner. Alone at the table, she pushed the food to one side and then the other with her fork, rarely lifting it to her mouth. When Beatrice came to clean up, she pecked at Viviana like a mother hen.

"You need to eat, madonna. You need your strength for the very important work you do," the buxom woman said as she gathered the dishes.

"Do you think it important, Beatrice, truly?"

"Mona Viviana, I have loved working for you all these years, especially the last few." They smiled together at that. "But do you think I wish the same for my granddaughters, for their daughters? To be servants in their own home as well as those of others?"

Beatrice dropped her fists and shook her head. "In my lifetime I have seen women become poets, like *Il Magnifico*'s dear mother. I have heard the music written by Lucia Quinciani." Beatrice picked up her bundle once more. "Oh yes, madonna, the work you do is very important, for us all."

With that, she was away, Viviana's gratitude trailing behind her.

Beatrice's words had lifted her spirits, but it was all Viviana could do to lift herself from the chair, to carry herself back to her salon. She sat upon her settee, promising herself it would only be for a few minutes—she needed to sketch a particularly small, incredibly detailed portion of the fresco. She did not know it when her eyes betrayed her, when they closed and sleep carried her away.

"Viviana?"

She slept; surely she dreamed.

"Viviana?"

It was no dream, but a man's voice. It couldn't be.

Viviana jumped up, rushed from the room, skidding to a stop in the short hallway.

There he stood. She had not seen him since that day at Santo Spirito; he had not come to her since the night he had asked to meet her sons, and for so much more. She thought he might never come again.

Sansone found her from his place in the balcony door. One glimpse of her, and he moved. He rushed to her and into her arms.

"I could not stay away. If this is the only way I may have you, then I must accept it."

The words were barely out of his mouth when his mouth found hers, when his lips and tongue devoured hers. Viviana tried to talk, tried to tell him, but she could not. She was lost to his mouth and to the arms that wrapped about her waist, that lifted her off the ground and held her captive against the wall at her back. She succumbed to the desire and pleasure he rained over her.

Sansone kissed her face, her neck, the tops of her breasts, never once losing his hold upon her. He pulled at her partlet, ripping it, to burrow his face into the bounty he found there.

Viviana groaned at the sensual enchantment he cast upon her; any words she may have said were lost as if cast out to sea, plunging beneath its depths. She ran her fingers through his soft hair, closing her eyes to the pleasure. Her hands moved downward, to the hard, broad width of his back, digging her fingers into to the firm muscles. Her legs came up, wrapping themselves around his waist.

Sansone moaned. One hand continued to hold her, the other to explore her. His long fingers gathered the many layers of her skirt, bunching them up, pulling them up. He swept them along the flesh of her thighs; she tingled with the delight of his touch.

Her hands moved lower as well, to the ties of his breeches. She could not see; her tremulous fingers fumbled about, brushing more of his firmness.

When he entered her, they both cried out. As their bodies crashed against the wall, swaying together in a dance she had never conceived of, they were lost together.

• • •

Sansone lowered her to the floor slowly upon legs that shook. Viviana left her back against the wall; it and his arms were all that kept her on her feet.

"I am so sorry. I was too rough. I was—"

She raised a single finger and dropped it upon his full, well-used lips.

"Dear Sansone, I have been meaning to ask you…" She looked up, lowered and skimmed her fingers along the hard line of his jaw. "Will you have dinner with me and my sons this Sunday?"

His oh-so-sweet smile was the only answer he gave; it was the only one she needed.

Chapter Twenty-Nine

"The more we desire something, the more we are willing to risk for it."

The line snaked out the mammoth door of the Palazzo della Signoria and whipped its tail out into the piazza.

Once a week the Signoria and its main councils allowed the common people to speak before them, to make requests, to make accusations. Once a week the voice of the people rang loudly.

The woman stood in that long line. Though she had arrived almost with the breaking of the day, she found her place in its middle. As the sun rose and blazed down upon them, she left her cloak's hood upon her head. As the line moved, as she made her way into the palace, the hood remained. As she reached the bottom of the stairs and the line of people upon it, she slipped away.

How she remembered what she had heard of the palace and its rooms and secret passages, she did not know. She believed she was meant to remember.

Through those passages and secret rooms she slipped, until she arrived at a door, *the* door.

The rumble of male voices chatting within was the only thing that held her. She slipped into a dark corner. She stood there waiting for the chatting to stop, for the men to leave the room for their midday repast. She waited still as they casually took themselves away, around the corner and down the stairs, out of her sight.

She moved then, quick and sure, into the room, leaving the door open just a crack behind her, having no desire to be locked within.

"*Oh Dio mio.*" She groused at herself, at the dense forest of desks and drawers, mounds of books and piles of parchment that filled the room. Where would she find what she needed? How could she, in the short time allotted to her, before the men returned?

Up and down the aisles she rushed, rifling through parchment, reading the spines of books. She grew closer; the sweat ran in a rivulet down between her breasts. They were in this section, they had to be, for there were others of the sort she sought. She rifled more, read more. When she saw the name, saw the book, she grabbed it and pulled so hard that three others fell with it, the noise like thunder. She left them upon the floor where they landed, concerned only for the one in her hands, that she read its contents before the storm could reach her.

To a desk she hurried and there she dropped it, there she scoured it.

"At last!" she cried, forgetting the need for silence. "At last, oh dear God, thank you."

She closed the book with a slap, snatched it up, and clasped it to her chest.

The jubilation in her heart, spreading her lips and filling her eyes, slowly ebbed away, a waning moon headed for darkness.

"What do I do now?"

Chapter Thirty

"Truth may be feared as a demon, so often it is an angel."

Sansone stood in the hallway watching her.

Viviana fluttered from room to room. Her movements were sporadic, staggering, chaotic. Jemma and Beatrice followed her.

"No, Jemma, not there," Viviana snapped at the girl when she placed the mammoth antipasto tray upon the table. "I told you to put it on the sideboard. Must I tell you again and again?"

Jemma cringed beneath her mistress's ire, for Viviana never hurled it her way.

"*Basta,*" Sansone said. He could no longer stand and watch Viviana suffer.

He walked to her, took her in his arms, and held her. She stilled there, stilled perhaps for the first time that day.

"Enough, Viviana," he whispered to her as Jemma slipped past them, offering him a nod as she did. They did not hide themselves— who and what they were to each other—from these women; the time for that had long since passed. It was an old house; the walls were thin.

Releasing her only as far as the length of his arms, Sansone tipped his face down to Viviana's.

"You must release this agitation. Let go of it. If your boys see you so, so too will they become."

Viviana tilted forward, sagging against him. "You speak true, *dolcezza mia,*" she muttered into his chest. When she had started calling him her sweetheart, he could not remember, only that it was so. "It is just that they…that I…we—"

"I know, *tesoro mio*, I do know."

And he did. He knew the importance of her sons in her life, knew how much their opinions mattered to her, how much their love meant to her. More importantly, he knew how afraid she was to risk losing them, their respect.

"They are devoted to you." Sansone stroked her back. "They may be surprised, perhaps a bit shocked, but they will not betray you, I am certain of it."

Viviana pulled away, pupils large as she gazed upon his face, as she cupped the sharp jag of his cheek. "I hope you are—"

"*Ciao*, Mama, we are here." A young man's voice came to them from the door at the top of the stairs. Viviana jumped from Sansone's embrace.

"*Miei cara figli.*" Viviana ran to greet her sons. Sansone retreated to the dining room, allowing her time alone with them.

He heard their kisses, heard their laughter, heard too the high pitch of Viviana's voice.

"We have a guest today," she said with an expelled breath. "I wish you to make him welcome."

"Him?" a different voice asked, a voice thick and dripping with caution.

Sansone pulled on the hem of his best velvet *farsetto*, smoothing it of any wrinkles. He stood tall as he strangled the chair before him. He had stood against many an enemy, many a finely swung sword, with little apprehension. Today was not such a day.

Viviana smiled stiffly at him as she led her sons into the room, bright and cheery with afternoon sunlight, the parrots on the frescoed wall glowing with it.

"Marcello, Rudolfo, please make the acquaintance of Signore Sansone Caivano. Sansone, my sons." With that chirp of pride in her voice, his Viviana returned.

He strode toward them, stopping to bow, as they did in kind.

"Do I know you, signore?" Rudolfo squinted at him, studying him. "I feel sure I have seen you before."

"Sansone served in many the same battles as you did, my sons. He is a renowned *condottieri*," Viviana boasted for her lover.

"That is it." Rudolfo slapped his hands together. *"Guerra del Sale.* Ferrara."

"Ah, *sì*, I was there." Sansone nodded as he took the measure of the young men before him. Though the youngest resembled Viviana more, there was something of hers—her intellect—in the eyes of the eldest.

"You were not simply there, signore." Rudolfo brushed past him and into the room, helping himself to some wine. "You led my contingent. You were masterful." He raised his full glass to the man.

Sansone bowed; his heart trilled. *"Grazie*, Rudolfo. May I call you that?"

"But of course. Though I may find it hard to call my commander by his given name."

"It is my wish."

Rudolfo raised his glass again, grinning. "Then it is my honor, Sansone."

"Were you there as well?" Sansone turned to Marcello, finding him silent and sullen, still standing at his mother's side, as stiff as the soldier he had once been.

"I was, signore, but with a different detachment."

"Why do we not sit? Everyone, help yourselves to the antipasto." Viviana sat down so hard, the legs of her chair squealed against the stone floor.

Rudolfo quickly availed himself of the bounty of meats, cheese, tomatoes, and peppers; Sansone followed with a quick glance—and a slight curve of his lips—at Viviana. Marcello took a chair beside his mother, pouring her a glass of wine from the green glass bottle sitting upon the maroon damask tablecloth.

"If I may ask, Mama, how do you know this man?"

So I am to be "this man." Sansone did not turn at the words, did not allow the slight to show upon his face. *I must change that.*

"Well, I met him quite a long time ago, at the home of the Contessa Maffei." Viviana launched into her story, a condensed version bereft of her emotions, the years of her longing, save for when she told them of Sansone's assistance in keeping her safe as they searched for—and saved—Lapaccia.

"Well done, Sansone," Rudolfo said between his many bites of food.

Marcello's eyes had never left Sansone's face as his mother spoke.

"And now? What brings him to our table?" He spoke impolitic words with soft belligerence.

"Now?" Viviana's voice had reached the tone of a strangling bird. "Well now we are…that is to say…well, he and I—"

"I would like to court your mother, Marcello." Sansone put down his fork, clasped his hands before him, and looked Marcello straight in the eye. "I have come to you today to ask your permission to do so."

Did they not sit at opposite ends of the table, Sansone felt sure Viviana would have reached out to him; he felt her touch nonetheless. He was equally as sure that Marcello would have stabbed him with his fork.

"Really?" Rudolfo blurted, though not unkindly. He stared at Sansone, who stared at his mother. He shrugged his shoulders with a big grin. "Good for you, Mama. You have my permission, Sansone, with gratitude."

"*Grazie tante,* Rudolfo," Sansone replied, unable not to smile at the young man's natural ebullience, and his kindness.

Marcello stood abruptly. "You ask my permission, signore. Yet you are already lovers." It was not a question but an accusation.

"Sit down, Marcello." The command came not from his mother, but from his brother.

Marcello did not sit.

"Our mother," Rudolfo said, pointing to her, "has not known love, the true love of a man, for the whole of her life. Do you really wish it to remain that way? Does she not deserve better?"

Sansone felt a flash of pride, for Rudolfo, for his defense and care for his mother's happiness, and even for Marcello. Any honorable man, one who loved and respected his mother as he should—as Sansone had when his own mother was alive—was a good man. How strange he should already feel proprietary towards these sons of hers.

"I would feel the same were it my mother, Marcello," he said to the young man who still had not sat down. "But I assure you my intentions are honorable. I have asked her to marry me but she hesitates."

The hard etchings of anger on Marcello's face softened, but did not disappear altogether.

"But you are..." Marcello began, then turned to his mother, "forgive me, *mia cara Mama*"—his gaze fell again on Sansone—"but you are a younger man, are you not?"

He strikes hard, to the heart, Sansone thought as Marcello would. Younger men were often with older women—especially widows—to use them, to spend their money, to enjoy their connections and their property, only to take their satisfaction elsewhere. It was a cruel truth.

"In the number of our years? Yes, I am younger." Sansone knew that only unvarnished honesty would suffice. "But we—all people—are not defined by a number. We are defined by ourselves, our truth. In that, there is no difference between us."

He gazed upon Viviana, every feeling he had for her, those so strong and encompassing, lay in that gaze.

"Your mother's beauty, her intelligence, her charms, her caring and loving nature are ageless in my eyes."

It was a declaration Sansone knew she might never have heard in her life but one she well deserved.

Viviana dropped her chin, but not her eyes, which locked securely on him. She bloomed beneath his words.

Marcello sat, but slowly, not in the rush of defeat.

"Has he asked you to marry him, Mama?"

Viviana nodded sparingly.

"But you have not answered him yet?"

"No, I…" Viviana faltered, but only a little. "I wanted you to know him, know of him." She took a deep breath. "To know myself and my truth with him a little bit better."

Marcello nodded at her sensible words. "Then I will await your answer as well."

Sansone caught Viviana's gaze once more, and saw the small shrug of one shoulder she offered. It was not the answer he had hoped for, but then neither was hers. He was content to wait for both.

At that moment, Beatrice appeared in the doorway. "The veal, madonna, yes?"

"Yes, please," Viviana replied, her relief to change the conversation palpable.

Rudolfo kept them all laughing, all charmed, with his easy banter as they ate the scrumptious meal. Marcello ate.

The afternoon turned to evening and Viviana's sons made for their home.

"It was an honor to meet you, Sansone." Rudolfo took his hand. "I hope I will see a great deal more of you."

Sansone gripped the hand in his, man to man. "Nothing would please me more, Rudolfo."

Marcello simply bowed before him. "Signore," he said, and nothing more.

Both boys kissed their mother and took themselves down the stairs.

Arm in arm, Sansone and Viviana watched them go.

"He is not happy with me," Viviana said, not needing to delineate which son she meant.

"He will come round," Sansone assured her, holding her closer. *As will you, I pray.*

Chapter Thirty-One

"Many things may be hidden, but rarely truth."

The clamorous caterwauling of the ever-growing crowd came to Viviana as if from far over the hills. She walked through the path cleaved for her by the guards, gratefully entering the contrasting silence within.

"I hoped you would arrive before the others." Fiammetta's voice reached through and into Viviana's foggy realm. "I need to speak to you." She patted the scaffold upon which she sat.

To Viviana it looked like a hangman's scaffold. The days of summer had evaporated, as had their heat, but it was not the chill of autumn, stretching its arms to settle around them, that made her shiver. Still, she sat as instructed.

"This man, Sansone, your lover…"

Viviana gurgled a laugh as her head dropped back on her neck. For all her faults, one could not fault Fiammetta for being mealy mouthed.

"*Sì*, Fiammetta, he is my lover. He is that, and more. And what have you to say to me of it?"

The contessa flinched, and Viviana straightened in triumph; if Fiammetta intended to hurl arrows at the heart, then so would Viviana.

Fiammetta sat up straighter, cleared her throat. "Very well then." She turned to face Viviana directly. "It is wrong and you will suffer for it."

"More than I suffered beneath the fists of my husband?"

"There are many forms of misery, Viviana, and you are well aware of that fact. You not only disgrace yourself, you disgrace every one of Da Vinci's Disciples."

"Ah," Viviana muttered. There was the truth of it. "You mean I will disgrace you by your association with me?"

Fiammetta's lips formed a hard line upon her face until she cracked it. "I will not deny it. Yes, I will be disgraced. Along with the others. We will all be disgraced by it, as individuals, as a group, a group of women artists who dare to do things no woman has done before. Your promiscuity will only cast more disparagements upon us. Are you prepared to pick up that burden? Is he worth it?"

"Promiscuity?" Viviana jumped from their perch, stood before Fiammetta trembling. "We live in a world where it is common place for men to have mistresses, many mistresses, where the *puttana* walk the streets openly. And *I* am promiscuous?" Viviana waved the ridiculousness away. "Is he worth it? Truly, Fiammetta? Should the question not be is my happiness worth it?"

"We must often sacrifice our own happiness for the good of others. As a mother you should know that."

Viviana's pitch swelled to reach Fiammetta's. "What? Now you are to question my duty as a mother? You go too far, Fiammetta."

"No, it is you who has gone too far! Your selfishness will only ruin me further."

Viviana opened her mouth, bitter tongue longing to snap hurtful words like a whip. Fiammetta's face stopped it. Viviana had never seen the woman looking so forlorn...so beaten.

"What has happened, Fiammetta?"

With a gaze that looked everywhere but at Viviana, Fiammetta shrugged her broad, fleshy shoulders. "You know quite well what has happened."

"But that was years ago now," Viviana replied, assuming Fiammetta referred to the downfall she'd suffered because of her friendship with the Pazzi family, those responsible for Giuliano de' Medici's murder. "Surely it is forgotten by now."

"They never forget," Fiammetta spat. "Not the Medicis nor those devoted to them." Her chin dropped, neck creasing with rolls of flesh. She stared at the floor. "Every day we receive fewer and fewer callers, less and less invitations. And of those I send, most are not accepted. I had hoped, perhaps foolishly so, that participating in a commission approved of by *Il Magnifico* would once more endear us to the faction, but it has not happened. Do you think my husband sits in this church, day after day, merely for his concern for my safety and that of Patrizia? It is because he has nowhere else to go, nowhere where he is accepted." Fiammetta raised her eyes but not her face. "The quicksand of our past draws us ever downward."

Viviana struggled for words of encouragement, words to wash away the anguish she was witnessing. She struggled in vain.

"Do you not see, Viviana? To be so closely associated with a woman who is being intimate with a man she is not married to may be the fatal blow."

Viviana knuckled her forehead as a battle of thoughts warred within. How much of her life had she squandered on doing what was best for others? How much had she sacrificed already? It was not her doing, the relationship between the Maffei and the Pazzi— that Fiammetta and Patrizio had done themselves. Now Fiammetta asked her to sacrifice for them, sacrifice her happiness for their misguided loyalty? She shook her head. No, now it was *her* time, her time to think about herself. There was but one answer, one thing to be said.

"Sansone loves me. He has asked to marry me."

"Marry? A younger man! What will they say?"

"I will say something," the coarse male voice jammed a wedge between them.

Seeing Andrea Verrocchio both women took a step away from the other. Neither could have said when he entered beneath the draping, or how much he had heard.

"I may not know of what you argue, but I do know this." The elderly man stepped further into the chapel. "A workshop divided is a workshop that cannot work."

Verrocchio stomped his way to the corner, where they piled their supplies at the end of each working day. Grabbing a brush, he stomped back to them. "If there is to be cohesion upon the brush, there must be cohesion in hearts and minds. I have seen discord destroy more than one studio in my life."

"Wise words, *maestro*," Fiammetta said, in her best contessa voice. "But this is more than a discussion between fellow artists. It is one between longtime acquaintances, and I have but one more thing to say. No, to ask."

Verrocchio shook his head, threw the brush back toward the pile of supplies, where it smacked against the wall, landing with a dull thud.

Fiammetta leaned toward Viviana, all civility gone from her voice. "You have said Sansone loves you. He has told you so?"

Viviana nodded with clenched teeth, leaning forward as well.

"But do you love him?"

"Yes I do!" The cry burst from her, unbidden, unforced.

Verrocchio grunted, stepping between them.

"I believe that is all you need to know, contessa," he said, walking away.

Viviana could not know what lay upon her face. She saw only Fiammetta's and how it had softened.

"Viviana, I—"

"Here we are, please forgive our tardiness," Isabetta chirped as they stepped through the concealing shroud cloth. "We were…what goes on here?"

"Nothing to concern yourselves with," Fiammetta answered, stepping away from Viviana. Trudging to the pile of supplies, she began to set them out.

Isabetta looked at Viviana, raising her brows. Viviana shook her head.

"Let us to work, yes," she said only. "We are so close now."

"Indeed you are," Verrocchio blustered, with a nod to the other women as they too began to file in.

Once all were there, all greetings made, he spoke to them as one.

"First I tell you that Leo had to leave for Milan, but," he said, staving off the peeps of disappointment and worry with a raised hand, "but that only means you will have Botticelli and I for the next few days. We will take turns, but one of us will always be here if you need us. Though I am not sure we will not merely be superfluous."

His gaze flew up and around, to the walls and the women's paint upon them.

"There was a first," Isabetta said. "Is there a second?"

"Hmm, *sì*, there is, but they are words that taste bitter to me." Verrocchio brought his gaze back down to them, but lifted his chin. "I owe you an apology, all of you."

To the one their mouths closed, their ears opened wider.

"I knew you possessed a degree of talent, but—"

"A degree?" Mattea muttered.

"But," Verrocchio continued, as if he hadn't heard her, "I did not believe you could fresco or, if you attempted to, I believed it would be a disaster."

"And now, *maestro*?" Viviana prodded gently.

"And now I realize that though I may think I know everything, I actually know very little. "This…" He waved his arms to encompass the whole of the chapel. "This is nothing less than a masterpiece, and I am honored to be here."

Patrizia and Carina squealed softly. Mattea and Natasia preened. The four older women simply shared satisfied looks. They knew what such words truly meant, coming from the master that was Verrocchio. They also knew the struggle he must have had to say them.

"To your work, madonnas," he said, rising up only to take himself to the finished wall on the left and plunk himself down on the scaffold. "I will be here if you need me. Wake me should I snore."

• • •

They worked until dusk; they accomplished far more than most days.

In dribs and drabs, they took themselves home. Fiammetta, her husband, and Patrizia in their carriage, Lapaccia and Carina in theirs. Verrocchio on slow feet, though he had in fact slept through most of the day. Viviana left as she had for many a day, on Sansone's arm, Isabetta on his other, for they often walked her and Mattea home.

"Are you not for home?" Isabetta asked Mattea.

"I will stay and help Natasia with the cleaning up."

It was Natasia's turn, but Mattea longed to stay within these walls as long as she could. She hadn't felt such hope as that given to her by Verrocchio in a long time; she would savor it.

"'Tis you and I then," Natasia said merrily. "We will walk to my parents' home after, if you would like, perhaps nip some of their dinner while we are there."

Mattea blinked. "I would be honored, dear Natasia. What of your husband?"

"He is off on another trip for *Il Magnifico*. He will not return till tomorrow, so we need not rush."

In companionable silence they worked, cleaning brushes, folding drop cloths, until all was righted.

"Well done," Natasia said, surveying the chapel, fists upon her hips and a grin upon her face. "Now for some wine."

"And I believe you mentioned food?" Mattea said eagerly, having rarely supped at the table of such wealthy people; she could only imagine the treats in store.

Natasia laughed and linked her arm in Mattea's. "Yes, *cara*, and some food."

In this manner they quit the church, going out the back way to put some unnecessary implements back in their studio.

The path behind the basilica was hard to find in the darkness. They laughed as they struggled to maneuver their way, tilting when they inadvertently stepped off the path's stones, linking arms once more as they landed on the smaller alley along the side of the church.

"Are you still astounded by Maestro Verrocchio's words?" Mattea asked, pulling her shoulders up to her ears in her own wonder. How she remembered feeling the same when Leonardo had spoken similar words. To hear it from *two* masters made it far more real.

"I am overjoyed," Natasia replied rapturously. "He did nothing today, and yet we accomplished more than we had on any other. It shows one just how powerful words can be, does it not?"

"We are so close to the finish," Mattea mused. "Is it wrong to feel such pride for what we have done, what we have achieved?"

"And how truly well we have achieved it?" Natasia joined Mattea's self-praise. "No, I do not believe it is wrong, though pride is a sin. But I believe there is nothing sinful about feeling one's true worth. Do you feel—"

The two men came out of the dark as if they had risen from the dead. The two women shuddered to a stop.

"Let us pass, if you please," Mattea's voice dropped, rigidity surged, stiffened her limbs.

"Not possible, dearie," said one man.

He jumped toward her, grabbed her by the waist, and tore her from Natasia's hold.

"Help—" Mattea tried to scream.

He clamped a hand upon her mouth. It smelled as foul as he.

Mattea felt bile rise in her throat, but still she took in the way of him. Short, stout, and bald; he was not a young man. The same could not be said for the man who had grabbed Natasia.

He was tall, with a full head of black hair; his long arms captured her friend swiftly, pinning Natasia against the high outer wall of the palazzo beside Santo Spirito.

Mattea heard Natasia's whimpers. Her own fear was one thing, that of her innocent friend quite another. She bit the rancid flesh muzzling her mouth.

The foul man yipped and pulled his hand away.

Mattea kicked him.

He yelped again, jumping away, out of range, as far as he could without losing his hold.

Natasia slid to the ground; the tall man still clenched her.

Mattea twisted her arms up and out, releasing the older man's final hold upon her.

"Natasia!" she cried as she ran to her, dropped to the ground beside her. Her once-abductor following but not attempting to regain his hold.

"You have to stop. You know not what you do, what it will do if you continue." The man holding Natasia squatted down beside her, his venomous words spittling their faces with phlegm.

Mattea brought a fist down upon one of his arms, again and again, hoping to dislodge it from Natasia. She hammered a nail that would not plunge.

"It is only a painting, a fresco, it hurts no one!" she shouted as she struck.

"Shut your mouth," he snapped, without taking his glare off Natasia. "This has nothing to do with you or the stupid fresco."

"These men are too powerful." These words were for Natasia; he leaned ever closer to her. "You cannot fight them on this. You will not win."

"What is he talking about, Natasia?" Mattea cried, still pounding on the man's arm. "What—"

From the darkness to her right, deeper into the alleyway, came another sound, a shuffling. She turned, she saw it, she saw the shape of a person, though man or woman she could not tell.

"I care not for their power," Natasia screamed at the man, a vanquisher aflame. Her words, her vehemence, shocked Mattea as well as her captive.

Mattea's mind tumbled. *What is she saying? What is she doing? Who is this man?*

Her head swiveled.

The shuffling, it came again, closer.

"Stay back," Mattea yelled, too late. The form was but a few feet away now. Scoundrels surrounded them; or so it seemed.

We are lost, came the thought, on the heels of others, on the exasperation she felt. *Why me? Why is it always me? First with Isabetta, now with…*

The dagger hit her hand as the scrapping of metal upon stone pummeled her ear. It was her answer.

"Take it, Mattea."

She heard a voice, but not just any voice. It was the voice from her dreams.

"Mattea!" the voice nagged her into action.

Mattea reached down. Her fingers grasped the hilt of the dagger. Just the feel of it brought her out of her paralytic shock, stopped her from crying out his name. For an instant, she closed her eyes, found the other her, the one who, after her mother slept, practiced, dagger in hand. She was again the one who craved the power of the steel.

"Now, Mattea! Now!" the harsh whisper commanded. She obeyed.

Mattea jumped up, pulled the short man who hovered about them not away, but toward her, pounding his chest against hers. The move set him off kilter. Just as she wanted. She controlled his body now; his balance was in her command. The hand without the dagger shoved him backward.

Beside her, somewhere in the dark, came the grunts and thwacks of fighting. From below her rose Natasia's whimpers.

Mattea sucked in her breath, shut out the sounds. All she heard, all she saw, was the man before her. A man she had to stop.

With another push, Mattea dropped into a crouch, swinging her right leg beneath him, hitting his ankles.

He fell to the ground, his body thudding upon the stone.

Mattea kicked out her skirts, straddling him, dropping on his chest. Leaning forward, she pressed the edge of the dagger against his throat; put her face an inch from his.

"Run. Run now or die. Return, ever, and you will die."

She kept the dagger to his throat as she rose, pulling him up with her by his ragged doublet, letting him see the bloodlust in her eyes.

A scream rent the air beside them, the pain of it even louder. It was not the voice she knew and loved. It was the other; that was all that mattered. In that moment, she had to stay on this man.

"Do you wish to die?" she menaced the man frozen by the

blade at his throat. Mattea pressed harder, breaking the skin, drawing blood; her threat was real, no matter that it came from a woman.

"No," he whined, not daring to shake his head.

"Then run," Mattea commanded, "run and tell any others the same fate awaits them."

She lifted the blade, barely an inch, and he was gone. Her glare stayed on him, until he turned the corner out of her sight. She listened until she could no longer hear his frantic footfalls.

Mattea swiveled round, finding Natasia still huddled at the base of the wall, sobbing but safe.

"You are all right? You are unhurt?"

Natasia nodded, wiping the tears from her grimy face, looking at Mattea with fire in her eyes. "I will not stop."

Mattea felt her lips spread, felt admiration for Natasia's strength, understanding it.

"I know not what you do, Natasia, nor will I try to dissuade you of it. But you will tell us all."

Natasia only nodded again.

Her friend secure, Mattea jumped back up, spinning round.

The images bombarded her hard and fast: the dead man on the ground, the fatal wound to his gut spilling his lifeblood. The man standing above him, gasping for breath. The man she loved.

Mattea threw herself into Andreano's arms. "You are here. You are here."

"I am always with you," he whispered as his lips lowered to hers, softly at first, a touch of love, then growing harder, the agony of need.

"What goes on there?" A man's voice came out of the darkness at the end of the alley at the Piazza Santo Spirito. Someone must have heard the ruckus in the quiet, wealthy neighborhood. Someone drew near hesitantly.

Andreano tore Mattea away from him, tearing both their hearts apart. "I must go."

She shook her head, refusing his words. "Stay. Oh please stay."

"Soon, my love, my life. Soon." He kissed her once more, tasted

her, a taste to last. He pulled away from her even as he promised
to return.

Mattea's arms, still outstretched, were now empty, as her heart
was once more. She watched him turn, watched him run, his raven
hair unfurling behind him.

He was gone.

Once more she stood in the void without him.

"Mattea," Natasia's tender whisper came from her side. "We
must go, Mattea. We cannot be seen near him…near that." She
nodded toward the body on the ground.

Without a word, Mattea took the hand ready for hers. Together,
they ran.

Chapter Thirty-Two

"To hear the tune, one must pay the piper."

It mattered little that he had approached the castle upon this very same road many times. Each time he shivered as he drew ever near.

Leonardo had waited as long as he could to make an appearance in Milan. The last letter from Ludovico Sforza had made it plain he would wait no longer. Leonardo's horse crested the hill, and before him, the great peak of the Torre del Filarete poked at the sky, rising seventy meters tall.

"There is nothing for it," Leonardo mumbled, as much to himself as to his horse. He spurred it forward toward a challenge of his own making, one he must now manipulate to his advantage. The unpaved road brought him to the very door of the tower. Before he could dismount, liveried servants appeared, to relieve him of his horse, to bring him to Ludovico. It was nothing if not a well-run castle.

They walked him through the tower, through the Courtyard of Arms, without a word. Leonardo took nothing from their silence; they were always silent, as silent as the stone sarcophagi from the Roman era forever standing guard along the courtyard's perimeter. The courtyard spoke far louder, echoing the past. Its shape and mighty appearance begged the castle's military genesis to be remembered.

The first duke of Milan, Galeazzo II Visconti, ordered the construction of what was then to be a simple fortress. By the time of its completion in 1368, it consisted of four walls, each 180 meters long, with a square tower guarding each corner. Galeazzo's successors, Gian Galeazzo and Filippo Maria, redesigned the structure, converting the military stronghold into a palatial home. Neither man was beloved by his people. Both died without heirs. The people had their say, razing the palace to the ground. Their mistake was turning to Francesco Sforza for help.

Within three years, Francesco ruled Milan, declaring himself duke.

One of his first acts was to rebuild the castle. While much in keeping with the original design, Francesco had added the tall central tower and two, smaller round ones to flank it.

"Leonardo, you live!"

The cry resounded and repeated, tossed against the curved coffers of the surrounding, columned walkway.

Ludovico Sforza marched toward him. Leonardo dropped into a bow.

"*Buongiorno, duca,*" Leonardo greeted him. "And to you, *giovane duca.*"

Ludovico looked at his nephew as the thorny crown Ludovico wore, no matter his attempts at disguising it. A duke in his own right, Ludovico was but regent of Milan, in the service of his nephew, Gian Galeazzo Sforza. A boy of seven when his father passed, the cherubic child with the long curly locks of strawberry gold was quickly ascending to the height of both his deceased father and his uncle.

"It is a good day, Leonardo," Ludovico countered, "for it at last finds you here." The ruggedly built, handsome man showed little of his welcome upon his swarthy face.

"I came as requested, signore," was Leonardo's only reply. If the man wanted more, he must ask for it.

Round, almost black eyes studied the artist. Thick brows rose, hid beneath a copious cap of straight black hair, rounded under at their ends.

"Come, Leonardo, let us show you our progress."

Thus began a tour of all the rooms under renovation, nearly all in the vast castle. With the full power of Milan in his hands, if only temporarily, Sforza was determined to bring the castle into its true magnificence, with the full power of the rebirth of the arts and architecture that were at his disposal. Unlike the more military-minded of his family, Ludovico cherished the arts and those who made it, architects included. Ludovico saw Leonardo as one who would assist him in transforming the castle into a palace.

From room to room they strolled. Ludovico lectured and Gian followed quietly. It was a large castle; it was a long walk. It was his penance, and Leonardo knew it. He paid it.

In truth, Leonardo would be false with himself if he only feigned interest. Sforza's plans were magnificent, modern yet classical. The man laid a gauntlet before Leonardo, one he likely knew da Vinci would be hard pressed not to pick up.

"Ah, here. I most especially wanted to show you this room," Ludovico declared, as they entered a large, rectangular room, fully enclosed within itself.

It was an empty space full of promise.

"Why is that, signore?" Leonardo asked, gaze drawn upward to the pointed, vaulted ceiling, the point of each vault buttressed to the wall two stories above his head. It was the most astounding feature of the room. It was the only feature of the room. To Leonardo's eyes, the rest looked like a blank canvas.

The dark man with eyes of midnight stopped and pinned Leonardo with his stare.

"This will be your room, to do with as you wish," Ludovico asserted, with both a superior nod of his head and a convincing grin upon his lips.

"I... *grazie, signore*," Leonardo's tongue twisted, as did his mind. What he could do with such a room. What he could do *in* such a room. The images burst and flashed in his mind. "I am sure you will find the work pleasing."

Ludovico strolled away from him, his footstep echoing sharply in the empty cavern.

"I am sure I will." Ludovico spun back. "But you must be here to do it. You must be in Milan to do all we hope you will do, all we know you are capable of doing."

There it was. A veiled threat, perhaps. A dangling treasure on the long stick of Milan, most certainly.

Leonardo knew nothing but the truth would suffice. He told it, the truth of what he was doing and for whom he was doing it.

Ludovico studied him for the length of a fortnight, or so it felt.

"It is a new world, Leonardo," he at last murmured, and set to pacing the large room once more. "How much longer?"

"A month's time, perhaps a bit more," Leonardo responded. It would have to be, as that was all the time remaining for the women to finish the fresco in keeping with the contract's specifications.

Ludovico returned to the artist's side, a breath away.

"I am a believer in change, in *evolere*. But not to my own detriment." He patted da Vinci's shoulder. "A month, *no* more, *sì?*"

Leonardo once more let his gaze wander the room, and then fly out of it to include the castle, all of Milan. Possibilities flew with it. There was so much he could do in Milan; there was so much to do. He could not let it, and them, slip from his grasp.

Leonardo dipped his head.

"*Sì, duca*. A month."

Chapter Thirty-Three

"Burdens, once shared, are no longer as heavy."

Verrocchio slept propped against the wall on the scaffold as he had the day before, and the day before that. He stirred only when they stirred him, muttering answers to their questions, instructing with half-opened eyes but extraordinary mastery.

The days Botticelli had been there had been very different. He stood behind each of them throughout the day, tutoring, criticizing, complimenting. They learned a great deal from each, no matter their differing approaches.

"Tell us, Natasia," Mattea whispered. How glad she was for Verrocchio's snuffling slumber. She did not know what Natasia would tell them; after the events of the other night, she knew only that it must be told to the Disciples alone. How strangely she looked back at that night. They had been accosted, threatened, and yet *he* had been there. A curse and a blessing.

Natasia hung her head, picking quills from a feather brush as if it held all her concern.

"Tell us what?" Fiammetta asked from her perch upon the scaffold, nose inches from the wall as she worked a fine facial detail.

Mattea glared at Natasia, urging her to speak, but the young woman remained mute.

"Very well," Mattea huffed. "As Natasia and I were leaving Tuesday evening, we were set upon by two men."

Urgent questions rained upon them.

Natasia looked up at Mattea as a younger sister would an older sister who had tattled, at the women crowding around them, all work forgotten.

"Mattea does not tell the truth," Natasia finally spoke.

"What? You cannot—"

"She was not detained nor warned—only I was. Her misfortune was merely in being with me."

"Tell us, Natasia," Viviana repeated Mattea's words with quiet concern. "We can only help if we know what goes on."

Natasia did not lift her head; she spoke in low tones. "When I was but a girl, no more than eight or nine, I overheard my father talking to my brother. Half of what he said I did not understand; the more terrible things I did."

She paused. No one spoke; no one moved.

"My father's grandfather was proclaimed a bastard, the illegitimate son of a prominent Soderini and a woman of France."

Natasia plucked at the quill in her hands still. "That man, Emiliano by name, knew it was not the truth. Though his parents both died young, he knew them to be married, for they had told him so and he believed them. His belief carried him far, to France itself. There he found the papers attesting to their marriage, to his legitimacy. But when he brought them back to Florence, those in league with the great Cosimo—those sycophants beneath him—denied the authenticity of the documents, of Emiliano's words. He demanded they listen, that someone listened. He showed them to as many people as would see them." Natasia looked up at her sisterhood, pain writ sharply upon her cherubic features. "They charged him with aggravated fraud. They absconded with all the documents that he, in their words, 'flaunted about the entire city.' They executed him when my father was but a boy of two.

"When my father was on the cusp of manhood, he and his brother Niccolò found Emiliano's journal. It had remained hidden for nearly two decades. In it, they read of his searching, his travels to France. It told of the documents which proved his contention."

Natasia laughed; the bitterness clung to it spitefully. "My uncle's reaction was fierce. And of this some of you may know."

"He stopped a plan to assassinate Rodrigo Santoro." Fiammetta told what she knew; she knew the truth.

Natasia nodded. "He did, for Rodrigo's father was one of the few who believed Emiliano, who tried to help him." She shrugged. "In the end, it helped my uncle, and my father too to an extent. The Medici once more welcomed them. My uncle has risen higher, being far more ambitious."

"But your father has not forgotten," Viviana thought aloud.

"Nor forgiven," Natasia sniffed. "For he was—we all are—looked upon as descendants of a bastard. One who lost his life to repair the family name. My father has always craved the justice that his *nonno* died for."

Mattea sat down on the floor beside Natasia. "Is that what you are doing? Is that what this is all about? Are you continuing the work of your great-grandfather?"

Natasia sat taller, straighter. "It is. I had to. It is the only way the Lord will allow a baby to grow in my womb."

"Oh Natasia," Patrizia groaned. "Why would you—"

"I have lost two already." The scathing words negated all others. The women sagged with her burden of sadness. "I have to prove we are not bastards, or the progeny of a bastard. I cannot—God will not allow me—to bring another into this world as such."

"*Uffa!*" Isabetta bellowed. Caught hold of her impatience, and said more kindly, "Do you truly believe God is so cruel?"

"How can you not believe him to be so, after what your own husband went through, and you with him?" Natasia turned the question round on Isabetta. "After the pain Viviana and her children suffered?"

"God works in ways we cannot begin to understand. We must trust there is a reason for it, dear one," Lapaccia proclaimed.

Viviana sat on the other side of Natasia and took her hand. "You must tell your husband. He knows you have been doing something clandestine. He believes you have taken a lover."

It was Natasia's turn to blanch. "He what…how—"

Viviana told her of Pagolo's visit, of his words, and of his fears.

Natasia dropped her head into her hands. "I never meant to hurt him. I never meant to hurt any of you."

"Us?" Fiammetta blurted. "How have you hurt us?"

"Those men, those men who blocked our way, who yelled at us? Many of them yell only at me. 'You must stop now.' These words are not to stop what we do here, but what I have done."

"But they are not the only men out there," Viviana tried to comfort her. "They are not the men who spat at Isabetta and me when first they learned of our intent to bid. They are not those who vandalized our homes. There are far more men, and women, who decry our actions than those who try to stop you from repairing the good name of your family."

"But who are such men? Who would be harmed by your actions?" Mattea asked.

Natasia shrugged, hung her head. "I care not to think of it, or speak of it."

"Men who have no desire for your father and his line to gain any more power with the Medici." Fiammetta spoke where Natasia would not. "Men who fear losing their own positions with him. Men such as your uncle."

Natasia closed her eyes against Fiammetta's words. Her silence gave them validity.

Instead, she knelt beside Isabetta. "That rock. It was meant to strike me. Can you ever forgive me?"

"There is nothing to forgive, *cara*," Isabetta soothed her with a whisper.

"I should have stopped then, but I could not. I kept on. I searched as Emiliano once searched. I knew, somehow I knew, that the documents he found and gathered were still somewhere." Natasia smiled; it lit her face as surely as the sun did the earth. "I have not failed. I found the papers, where he tried to prove it, where he *did* prove it. The papers he was killed for."

"*O Dio mio*," Fiammetta intoned.

"Language, please, Fiammetta," Isabetta teased. Natasia laughed first; Fiammetta laughed hardest. It was laughter they all needed.

"You must take this to *Il Magnifico*," Mattea said.

Natasia's shoulders slumped once more. "I have tried to get an audience, but was turned away."

"I will get you that audience. I will get him to right this wrong." Isabetta plunged her hands upon her hips.

Fiammetta glared at her. "Please, Isabetta, getting the Medici to provide us with guards is one thing, a thing he benefitted from as well. But this…this is something far greater altogether. How would you do this? What power do you have?"

Isabetta raised her chin high, eyes aglow as she smirked. "I have the power all women have, but rarely use. I am his lover."

Chapter Thirty-Four

"Justice is but another path to peace."

Isabetta tossed throughout the night. All manner of consequences for what she planned played over and over in her mind as if she were watching plays. Each play differed, but the ending never did.

She had sent the request the day before; she had received permission within a few hours. Already her deceit had begun.

When she arrived at the Palazzo de' Medici with Natasia beside her, she saw the *maggiore duomo* show a speck of emotion for the first time. It was a heavy harbinger.

He led them to *Il Magnifico*'s public chamber. He did not lead them through the hidden door. Isabetta did not expect him to.

"Cara Isabetta," Lorenzo entered from that concealed entrance, his words coming faster than his glance, "why are we not—"

He saw her, saw them.

His dark glare narrowed; his head tilted almost imperceptible.

"I see you bring a friend, Signora Fioravanti." Of all the things Lorenzo de' Medici was—the good and the bad—he was no fool. He knew the moments demanding caution.

"I have, *Magnifico*," Isabetta said, not a quiver in her voice. "I realize it was wrong of me to do so under the pretense of our work, but this is far too important. This is Natasia di Soderini Capponi. She has an urgent request of you, *Magnifico*."

"Soderini, you say?" Lorenzo finally spoke. "Which Soderini is your father?"

"Crispino, *Magnifico*," Natasia answered with a wobbly curtsy.

"Ah." Lorenzo's eyes narrowed once more, upon Isabetta. She saw in that glare that he knew why they had come.

"All I ask, Lor...*Magnifico*, is that you allow her a few moments to speak, to show you what she has uncovered."

He stared at them far too long. *Il Magnifico* stepped to his desk and dropped himself into his chair. He did not speak. He merely opened his arms wide, palms upward. Isabetta prodded Natasia forward.

Isabetta stood back, silently cheering Natasia, for once the woman began to plead her case, to display the irrefutable evidence, all visage of fear and hesitancy vanished. Righteousness dispelled it with fisted hand.

Lorenzo listened. Lorenzo picked up each piece of parchment, intelligent gaze reading each one. The last he dropped upon his desk and sat back in his chair. A suffocating silence, the sort that followed a scream, engulfed the chamber.

At last he spoke.

"If I acknowledge this, acknowledge the true paternity of your line, I will make many enemies."

Natasia's head waggled, jostled by the potent wind of her passion. "But it is the right thing to do, *Magnifico*. It is true justice. Is that not what you fought for after your brother's death?" If she went too far, she showed no concern for it. "This is no different. I will not let my children be the progeny of a bastard when he was not." Natasia punctuated her resolution with a pound of her fist upon his desk.

Isabetta saw her pull back—rein in her fortitude—though she had no need. Isabetta had never respected Natasia more; her righteous conviction was a beautiful thing to witness.

"I understand, signora, truly I do," Lorenzo said, the fire of his ire cooling. "But this is a difficult time. It is not the time for me to make such a bold statement."

He disappointed Isabetta; it was the first time he had. It was far too bitter a pill to swallow.

"And what will your wife say when she learns you have taken

another mistress? What will Lucrezia Donati say if she hears she is being usurped? She has already visited me—us—at Santo Spirito."

"She did?" Lorenzo flashed the question. For the first time Isabetta saw the truth of his feelings for the woman. It lay slathered on his face as if applied with a brush.

"She did. But I gave her no reason to fear me. Perhaps now is the time to do so."

"Isabetta, no," Natasia cautioned in a breath.

Lorenzo forgot Natasia, spoke to Isabetta, his jutting chin crumpling. "You would do this?"

Isabetta took two steps to stand beside Natasia. "*Sì*, for my sister, I would."

He stared at her; in his eyes, she saw all that had passed between them, all that could have.

Dropping his gaze from her, Lorenzo stared once more at the papers and their undeniable truth.

"It is done."

Isabetta heard the heartbreak in his voice, for she heard it in her mind, felt it as well.

Natasia breathed a gasp, hands fluttering to her cheeks, body swaying. Isabetta took her hands and squeezed, shaking it. Natasia must remain the strong, determined Natasia.

"We have your word?" Isabetta asked.

Lorenzo stared at the two women as if he stared at them all, all of Da Vinci's Disciples. "We men are fools."

Isabetta laughed though with little joy. "Yes, most of the time you are."

She stepped around his desk to stand behind him. Without shame, she turned him and kissed him, knowing Natasia was watching, not caring. It was a kiss of goodbye; they both knew it.

"But now and again you do the virtuous thing."

Isabetta released him, walked away from him.

Nudging Natasia as she passed her, she made for the door. At its open egress, she turned back, turned to look at him for one last time as her lover rather than her ruler. She would miss him, his nimble hands, and the joy they brought her. Upon his face, she saw her own sadness.

"I will paint you gloriously," she whispered, though he heard.

She turned then, turned away from him for the last time, with a small, bittersweet smile.

It was worth it, for Natasia, for her sistren it was.

She held out her hand for Natasia, who took it. It was a touch of profound gratitude. It was enough.

• • •

"Papa? Papa, where are you!" Natasia cried, as she and Pagolo burst into her parents' home.

Within seconds, both father and mother came rushing to them, the two couples colliding in the public sitting room.

"What is it? What is wrong?"

"Nothing is wrong, *mia cara famiglia*. Everything is right, as it always should have been," Natasia exclaimed, thrusting the papers into her father's hands, not only those that proved their paternity, but those from *Il Magnifico*, those that decreed them as true.

Her father's dark eyes, small in sockets of heavy, wrinkled flesh, flashed between her and the papers. They began to quiver in his hands. His legs wobbled; jagged footsteps barely brought him to a chair before they failed him. His shoulders began to tremble. When he finally looked up, Natasia saw tears upon his cheek; she could not recall ever seeing him cry before. She rushed to him, dropping to her knees at his feet, delving into the embrace that awaited her.

"You and Tomaso are the greatest gifts the Lord has deemed worthy to bestow upon me, but this is the greatest gift *you* could ever give me."

Crispino Soderini looked up to his wife, eyes moist with wonder. "I am a bastard no longer."

Chapter Thirty-Five

"Gifts given often come without ribbons or bows."

It was a finely rendered portrait, a perfectly captured moment of serenity. Seemingly a happily married couple whiling away the evening together.

Viviana and Sansone had supped together, talked, laughed, and simply reveled in the company of the other. As if creating the scene, giving it its final touches, he sat in her chair in her salon while she stood beside him before her canvas, brush in hand. They did not speak, and yet they were more intimately together than they had ever been.

Sansone put down his book, rose, and quit the room. Viviana listened as his footsteps moved him about the house and back again; he returned with a small goblet in each hand.

"*Grappa*," he told her as he handed her a goblet, kissed her forehead, and returned to his chair and book.

Viviana sipped the strong brew, a digestive drink, one to relax the body and the mind for a good night's slumber. She stared at Sansone over the rim, feeling a jolt but from more than the wine. Comfort and happiness nudged her. No, they slapped her in the face, a hard slap for her foolishness.

Floating out beyond the boundaries of her body, Viviana saw them studying the painting. She saw the ease of them together and the comfort it brought her upon her face; she glimpsed the years ahead and the happiness she could claim as her own. Why then, did she not claim it?

Viviana put down her brush but not her drink, took herself to Sansone in his chair, and knelt beside it.

"Sansone, I—"

The knock upon the door took them both by surprise. With all that had transpired over the last few months, it was a guarded surprise.

Viviana quickened, began to rise.

"Stay, Viviana," Sansone commanded, a hand upon her shoulder as he stood and made for the door.

The softly spoken "*buona notte*" that came with its opening was so very familiar to Viviana and yet no less of a jolt.

She did stand then, just as Sansone returned, brows high upon his forehead, her son, Marcello, walking in his wake.

"*Buona notte, Mama*," Marcello greeted her. "I hope I do not disturb you."

"Of course not, Marcello. You are always welcome, no matter the time." She leaned toward him to kiss his cheeks. He grabbed at her, enveloped her in his arms. Over Marcello's shoulder, Viviana cast a concerned look at Sansone.

"Would you like some *grappa*, Marcello?" Sansone asked, already heading for the door.

Marcello at last released his mother from his grasp. "I would, Sansone, *grazie*."

Sansone took himself away. Getting him the drink was nothing; hearing him call Sansone by name was something.

"Sit, Marcello." Viviana led him to her settee and pulled him down beside her. "Are you well? Has something happened?"

"Something has happened, *cara Mama*," Marcello said, hanging his curly-haired head. "But I am well for it, at least I hope so."

Despite his words, Viviana could not shed her concern. For all his words to the contrary, he did not look well.

Marcello lifted his head; Viviana's work caught his eye. For the first time, Viviana saw a lightness return to his features.

"*Nonni*," he said, lips curling upward ever so slightly. "It is as lovely as she herself was."

"*Grazie.*" Viviana thanked her son hesitantly; he did not come to discuss her work.

"Tell us what you have come to say, Marcello," Sansone urged him softly, handing the younger man his drink, grinning as Marcello downed the potent liquor in one gulp. "Or perhaps you would rather speak to your mother privately. I could—"

"No!" Marcello answered, quick and sure. "I am glad that you are here, that I may say these words in your presence."

Marcello sat so very still, chin once more to chest, both hands wrapped about his now-empty goblet.

"I have been a fool, Mama. You have given up so much for us, protected us, stayed when you should have left, for your own safety if nothing else. You suffered so much for us, Rudolfo and me; you suffered terribly."

Viviana grabbed his hands. "I did no more than any mother would do. It is what mothers are meant to do."

Marcello laughed without mirth. "It may be what mothers are meant to do, but not all do it. You did. And how have I thanked you? What did I do the first time my loyalty to you was put to the test? I failed you." Like the child he had once been, Marcello's lips quivered with the tears threatening to drop from his eyes.

"Oh my son." Viviana held his head to her chest. "You can never, could never, fail me. Think not of it, for it is a lie."

Marcello pulled himself up, slapped at the tears that her embrace had released.

"I realize now that your happiness is all that matters, not how it finds you or with whom it finds you."

Without releasing Viviana's hands from hers, Marcello spoke to Sansone.

"Signore, I thank you for the happiness you have given to my mother and only wish that you continue to do so."

With a sharply drawn breath, Sansone stood and reached out a hand. Marcello stood and took it.

Viviana rose, stood between these two precious men. "Now we are a loving family, as we have been, as we always should have been."

Chapter Thirty-Six

"Achievement, in and of itself, is a gift we give to ourselves."

They finished on a Monday in January.

Every day save Sunday, they had come in on the murkiness of dawn, left on the gloaming. Yesterday they had applied the final touches, the most intricate of them all. All the brushes had been put away in their proper cubbies in the studio, along with the drop cloths and pigments. The scaffolds were gone, far more easily demolished than constructed.

They were all there, every member of Da Vinci's Disciples, the old and the new, as well as their *maestro* and the two who had taken his place in his absence.

They stood in one long line, shoulder to shoulder, from one side of the *cappella* to the other. They spoke not a word; their elation was no less brilliant for its silence. Their eyes roved about the walls, every inch, from the simple landscape to the many-figured, finely detailed scenes, then up, up into the deep azure sky with its wispy clouds and fluttering birds.

"I do not know what they will say of this, Viviana, but I thank you for bringing me to it, for bringing this joy to me," Mattea spoke, but any one of them could have said the words. It mattered not to Viviana who said them; they were a gift given.

They had at last made their mark, one that would endure for many lifetimes. At last they had said to the world, "We are artists." Great hope realized was a many-splendored thing.

"I have learned a great lesson," Fiammetta said, both to them and to herself. "I have learned that doubt, of any sort, is a useless thing. I will never doubt again." To Carina and Patrizia she prophesied, "This is your beginning, a far grander beginning than we had. Do not let it end. Promise me you will not let it end."

"I promise, Mama," Patrizia breathed.

"I swear it, Contessa," Carina declared.

"It is well then," Fiammetta sighed.

"Wait!" Isabetta suddenly cried, and ran off, out the back door, letting it slam behind her.

"What is she about now?" Fiammetta mumbled.

Before any could speculate, the door flew open once more, and this time the bang came with the tinkling of glass upon glass. Isabetta rushed toward them with three flat-sided bottles, the amber-colored liquid within sloshing as she cradled them in her arms, a basket of wooden cups hanging from her shoulder, and a smile that filled her face and dimpled her cheeks.

As she passed out the cups, as she filled them with the expensive peach brandy, their numbness waned; elation now throbbed to life. Their own disbelief at what they had done left as quickly as it had come. Joy and laughter took its place.

"To us!" Isabetta raised her cup once everyone's was full.

"To us!" they chorused, and drank.

"Will they drink to us next Monday?" Natasia asked the question, though, once more, any one of them could have.

The mention of that day, the day their work was to be revealed in an ostentatious ceremony Antonio di Salvestro had insisted upon, sprinkled the sourness of a lemon in their sweet brandy.

"Or throw drinks at us?" Fiammetta mused with a smirk.

"Does it matter?" Isabetta asked.

To the one, all looked back up at what they created.

"No," Viviana said. She said it for them all.

They left together then, out the front door, heads in the clouds where their spirits soared.

Chapter Thirty-Seven

"Hate is a burden that walks a path of destruction."

She walked from room to room, looking in each, not knowing what she looked for.

As a specter tethered to the world, Viviana had haunted her home for the two days since they had finished the fresco. She tried to sit, to read, to write in her journal, but such pursuits were far too frivolous; they could not keep her. Neither food nor drink held appeal.

Instead she walked, never leaving her home. If she had walked as many steps from her door as she had taken within it, she would have been halfway to Rome by now. Her mind traveled only as far as her feet. She paced her house, searching every room as if in one of them she would find the answer to the question of what nagged at her, insisting she be somewhere else.

"*Uffa!*" Jemma cried out as, yet again, Viviana barged into her as the young woman went about her duties.

"You are bringing me to madness, madonna, do you not know that?" Jemma huffed as she pushed herself off the wall she had fallen against, picking up the linens she had carried. "I will have to wash these again."

"I am sorry, dear Jemma, I..." Viviana stammered as she helped Jemma gather up the sheets.

Jemma snatched them back. "Go, madonna. Go do something. Go paint."

For a moment Viviana hovered, utterly still.

"That is it, Jemma! That is what I should do! The studio is where I need to be!"

With a *grazie mille* tossed over her shoulder, Viviana donned her heavy cloak and flew from the house. She hurried down the Via Porto Rossi, her cloak billowing out behind her like the wings of a bird as she muttered to herself.

For an artist, one of any creative sort, to finish a creation meant losing possession of it; it lived no longer in the artist's heart and mind, but in the world. Finishing then became both exhilarating and mournful, for it could never belong to the artist alone ever again. The artist could never again live in the world of that piece of art. Such a separation could be disconcerting indeed.

When she reached the Piazza de Spirito Santo, Viviana found it more crowded than ever. The crowd of those who wished to see them fail continued to grow; their oblivion that they fought to stop a thing already done brought her a snide satisfaction, though she would not let them see it.

She could enter by the back; there was no more reason to face the crowd any longer. She had faced them; she and the others had already triumphed merely in the completion of the work, though these people did not know it. Yet Viviana wanted to walk past the chapel, to look upon it once more before the rest of the city did.

The guards cleaved her a path through the rabble; she walked it with head held high, and lips spread. With her hand upon the latch, Viviana hesitated at the door; a sound in the crowd stopped her, a sound she had not heard before from this horde.

She heard laughter.

A shiver crawled up her spine. She straightened her shoulders to shove it away and entered the basilica.

Viviana stood at the apex of the nave; the utter quiet and ever-present aroma of incense greeted her. Normally they calmed her. Yet her stomach reeled, the knot a warning, but of what she could not say.

As soon as Viviana turned into the side aisle, she knew something was wrong. The cover cloth they had left in its place, to conceal their work until the unveiling, now lay pooled in a puddle on the floor. She froze at the sight of it; then she ran.

"*Oh Dio mio, Dio no!*" Viviana cried out at the sight before her. Her knees quivered, collapsed. She dropped to the floor, dropped her head in her hands. Her sobs, her anger, racked her body. She dared to look up once more.

Their brilliant work, the delicate flora beneath the tender sky, the commanding figures, and the detailed story they told, was in ruin. Someone had decimated it with splashes of paint, onerous paint of puce and moldy green. Splatters of it dotted each wall.

Viviana glimpsed a waking nightmare.

Once more, her sobs felled her. She clutched her chest as it too fell against the floor.

"*Accidenti a te, maledetto tutto!*" From the floor, she screamed; from the floor, she damned them all as she pounded a fist upon the marble. She felt no pain save that of her shattered heart.

"Mona Viviana! Madonna!" Father Raffaello came to her, calling her name, brought out of his refectory by her shrieks. When she did not answer, he took her by the shoulders, shaking gently.

"Mona Viviana?" Once more he tried; once more she did not respond. He pulled her shoulders off the floor, lifting her until she sat. The fingers that held her twitched, his face drained of color.

"*Caro Dio,* what has happened to you?"

Viviana could not speak; sobs still shuddered through her. She could only point.

The priest turned his head; his gaze hesitatingly followed her trembling finger. He dropped to his knees.

"*I bastardi.*" Father Raffaello quivered with rage; his face burned with it. Viviana did not know if he knew the vile words he spoke.

His head fell back on his thick neck, quickly snapping back up. He threw his heavy, strong arms about her, pulled Viviana to him, held her as she continued to shudder and sob.

"I will get the others," he whispered in her ear. "Vanni! Vanni, where are you?"

These words he yelled; their vehemence came back to them as it echoed off the walls and ceiling of the empty church.

Viviana heard slapping footsteps from far off. Were they far from her mind, one stricken, unable to think, incapable of thinking of anything but the desecration of their work, their masterpiece?

"Vanni will bring them. They are coming," he whispered to her once more. "Come with me, madonna. Come wait in the refectory."

As he spoke, he tried to pull her up; he might well have tried to pull a giant oak from the earth.

Viviana shook her head. "I cannot leave. I will not leave it. I cannot."

Father Raffaello nodded, dropping from his knees to sit beside her, never loosening his hold upon her. "Very well. We will wait together."

The concept of time became elusive, for in Viviana's mind six months had been stolen from her, six months of her life had been lost, as their creation had been lost. She laid her head upon the priest's shoulder and stared at the devastation. She knew she cried still; she could not stop.

And then they came; they all came, not just the Disciples.

No one spoke a word; they screamed. To the one, every Disciple wept and moaned, blasphemed and cursed; their keening filled the basilica. Together they all huddled, a churning whirlpool of gloom and heat.

Lapaccia was the only one of them to walk into the *cappella*, two steps, then more, further and further in. Viviana feared the shock was too great upon the older woman. Lapaccia stood within inches of the back wall and its rendering of the *Exaltation of the Cross*, now with its brownish-purple splotch and small smatters. She gasped, wobbling backward. Isabetta hurried to her; gentle hands tenderly turned Lapaccia, brought her away, brought her back into their fold.

Viviana felt Father Raffaello's arms slip away from her. She thought she would tumble off the earth, until another set of strong arms replaced those of the priest. These arms she knew. With

Sansone's presence, her sobs, barely abated, grew harsh and terrible once more. Once more, time became irrelevant.

"Such evil man can do does not surprise me, but it breaks me." Verrocchio's warbling voice, never more tremulous, rived the brutal silence.

"This is not the work of those who tried to stop me." Natasia gulped the words through her tears, muffled by Pagolo's hold upon her.

"No, this is the work of men who think lowly of women, who believe we are not worthy to be artists, who have screamed at us in the streets and from their windows, who vandalized our homes," Isabetta said, teeth snapping. Viviana saw she did not cry; her body shook, eyes slinting. "Men who think women are not even human."

Botticelli stepped away from the ring of people, stepped into the chapel.

"Verrocchio, Leo, come, look." He compelled them with his words and a beckoning hand.

They went. They looked. They whispered together.

Leonardo stepped from them, returning to his Disciples. "The paint is still wet, madonnas," he whispered, as if his message demanded it. "This can be fixed. You can fix this."

"In three days? Three days!" Fiammetta roared.

"No, four," Father Raffaello corrected. "I have no doubt God would forgive you to work on Sunday, to do *this* work on this Sunday."

"But still, even with four days, we must fix what took six months!" Fiammetta threw her arms up to the heavens, her swollen, red eyes rolled up in her head still quaking with her anger. "We must make the date of reveal or we will be seen as failures. It cannot be done in time."

Botticelli came to her, pulled down her arms, and pressed them to her sides. His gaze captured them all.

"Yes, it can." The artist was not merely calm; he was deadly calm. "It can be done and we will tell you—show you—how."

Chapter Thirty-Eight

"One's true character does not show itself when all is well, but when all is not."

Each woman wore the same face.

It mattered not if some were more creased than others were, some darker, some rounder. Dark crescent moons shadowed swollen eyes; lips drooped at the corners, and shoulders slumped and curled inward.

Yet they came. Their *maestro* and the two others had assured them it could be fixed; if their doubt hung heavy upon them, it would not stop them from trying.

With them came their families, their husbands, their sons, Viviana's lover, and even Mattea's mother. Only Lapaccia was not among them.

"She took a fall," Mattea told Viviana when asked. "She claims she stumbled upon a step."

Viviana's brows jumped. "Claims?"

Mattea merely shrugged, falling into silence as the others joined them.

The beginning did not begin with brush strokes, but with words.

Leonardo stood before them wearing the strangest thing: a smile.

"Have you gone mad, *maestro*?" Isabetta asked when she saw it, one foot tapping an annoyed rhythm. "Or have you been in your cups all night?"

Da Vinci laughed softly.

"And now you laugh," Fiammetta cried. "This is no time for laughter."

"I do not smile or laugh at our task, but at what I see before me." He walked toward them, walked among them. "I love those who can smile in trouble, who can gather strength from distress, and grow brave by reflection. 'Tis the business of little minds to shrink, but they whose heart is firm, and whose conscience approves their conduct, will pursue their principles unto death. You are just such brave souls and I am so proud to find you all here."

"Did you think we would not come?" Mattea questioned softly.

"Not for a moment," Leonardo heartily replied. "And that is why I smile."

"*Sì*, we are here, *maestro*," Viviana ceded, "but what do we do now? How can this be fixed?"

Leonardo held up one finger, moved it in an arch before all their expectant faces.

"You must first possess one thought, one piece of knowledge you already have learned but have forgotten." Leonardo crossed his arms upon his chest. "What makes the fresco different from other forms of painting?"

The original Disciples looked at each other askance, as if he had insulted them; it was a question for a novice.

"It utilizes dry pigments on wet plaster, rather than wet paint upon a canvas," Carina asserted, eager to display all she had learned in so short a time, eager to earn their respect.

"You are correct, *piccolina*," Leonardo lectured. Viviana almost smiled herself at the sight of Marcello's chest puffing with pride. "And what is the end result of such a difference?"

"*Affé!*" Isabetta gasped her astonishment, stepping out of the group, walking slowly into the chapel.

Leonardo nodded with yet another smirk. "What do you see, Isabetta? What can you tell us?"

"Applying dry pigments to the plaster causes them to dry quickly." She spoke as if in a dream, softly, liltingly.

"And how long ago did you finish?"

"Three days."

"And how long does the fresco take to dry?"

Isabetta spun round, to Leonardo, to them all. Her eyes crinkled at the corners as she raised both shoulders and opened her arms. "Hours. No more than hours."

Patrizia jumped out of the crowd, and ran to one of the larger, lower splotches. With the tip of a finger, she laid a delicate touch upon it. She turned, beaming. "It is oil. Oil."

The remaining Disciples gasped, realization captured their breath.

Leonardo clasped his hands together as if in prayer. "Oh *miei cari artisti*, you make me so proud."

"What?" Patrizio interjected, round face a crumple of confusion. "What does it mean?"

Fiammetta tucked her arm into her husband's. "It means, dear one, that the slow-drying oil paint was thrown upon dry, plastered pigment already sealed. It should not have penetrated."

"It did not penetrate," Botticelli insisted. "The trick is to remove the oil paint without penetrating the fresco paint, without dampening the plaster and removing the seal. And we"— he pointed his chin toward da Vinci and Verrocchio—"we know all the tricks."

"*Di preciso!*" Leonardo proclaimed. "Isabetta, Mattea, take yourselves to the studio and bring all the clean cloths you can find."

Without a question, the two women ran off.

"Sansone," the artist addressed the able-bodied man, "if you would be so kind as to retrieve a large case of wine from Father Raffaello's refectory, I would be most grateful."

"I hardly think this is a time for drink," Fiammetta accused him.

"My dear contessa, we will not be drinking it. We will be cleaning with it."

Sansone returned moments later, shoulders straining under the weight in his hands, the glass bottles tinkling in their box.

Leonardo retrieved one of the twelve bottles in the wooden crate and held it up for all to see.

"This is Greek wine. And Greek wine is made from Greek grapes. This one comes from the *Athiri*. Its skin is much thinner, as is its pulp. The Greeks also use greater quantities of citrus in their wine, especially orange citrus." He turned from them. "Who was it, Verrocchio, that discovered the powers of this wine on paint?"

The older man shrugged and tucked his chin down against his crepey neck. "I am too old to remember. I do remember it was first used to remove grime. But with the many mistakes I make, I can only tell you I have used it often, too often."

"It removes paint?" Viviana gulped.

"It does indeed," Leonardo confirmed, as Isabetta and Mattea hurried back to them, arms full and overflowing with pristine cloths of all sizes, not the tiniest dot of paint on a single one of them.

"Ah, now you have all you need. I will show you." Botticelli took one cloth from Isabetta and the bottle of wine from Leonardo. Uncorking the wine with a small knife, he turned it upside down as he held the cloth to its opened neck. Quickly he strode to the closest splatter on their creation and gently touched it to the oil paint, only to lift it off and quickly touch it again.

"The trick, madonnas, is to dab," Leonardo instructed, "never rub."

"Never, ever rub," Verrocchio repeated.

The assembly scurried closer, spellbound as Botticelli dabbed some more, found a clean spot on the rag, wet it with wine, and dabbed again, and yet again. In no more than a few minutes, he turned to them, holding up the cloth, revealing the garish green upon it and the exposed spot of the fresco now showing through once again.

They cheered, they hugged, and they ran. They ran to the cloths, grabbing at them; they ran to the wine, pouring it. All of them, including the families, until Viviana stopped them.

"Dear ones, you show us your love by taking up these weapons," she intoned, "but if this is to truly be the work, and the war, of Da Vinci's Disciples, then it is the Disciples who must do it alone."

"But, *tesoro mio*, the work will go much faster if we assist you," Sansone argued, Patrizio and her sons grunting their agreement.

Viviana reached up to cup his cheek. "There will be many other ways you can assist us, I promise you."

* * *

For two days, the crowd outside the church watched as only men went in and out. The women they took such pleasure in jeering and insulting were nowhere to be seen, neither coming nor going.

Sansone's task this midday was that of quartermaster, stocking the church's meager pantry—meant to feed but three: the priest and his two novices—now to feed them all. And to bring fresh gowns.

With his foot upon the bottom step leading to the basilica door, rancid words smashed against his back.

"Do you see?" One heckler yelled, one who stood but a step away from Sansone. "They have to get their men to do the work."

The crowd laughed. Sansone spun on the man, towering over him.

"They are in there, you buffoon," he growled, loudly enough for all to hear. "We only bring them food. We cherish and support our women." He cocked one brow and grinned. "You should think of such things. I heard your wife say so to her lover only last night."

With a snarl of his own, the man lunged at Sansone. Bigger, faster, Sansone dodged the outstretched arms deftly. The man found nothing but himself in a chokehold in the arms of one of the *Otto di Guardia*.

"*Grazie*." Sansone dipped his head to the guard.

"*Prego, paesano*," the guard replied, pleasing Sansone as he acknowledged him as one of their own.

He forgot the man and his rancor at the sight awaiting him within.

The Disciples, all save Lapaccia, whose health had confined her to her bed, had after a day and a half finished their work with the Greek wine. The chapel and all its frescoes were not returned to their pristine glory, but there were but wraiths remaining of the splotches.

"Now we are to work with linseed and walnut oil." Viviana took the packages from Sansone and showed him their work.

"And will that remove the rest?" he asked as he strode about the chapel, forced to lean close to the walls to see the faint stains— ghosts that continued to mock.

"Not entirely, but it will make them ever more transparent. It renders paint thin and translucent," Viviana asserted. "Where the fresco colors are deep and dark, it may be enough."

"And where it is not?"

The light in her eyes dimmed. "In those places we will be forced to repaint."

He looked down at her, at the hollows beneath her eyes, at the thinness of her lovely, curved body. "All that in the two days remaining? Can you do it?"

"Two days and two nights," she avowed. "We can and we will."

Viviana gave his arm a squeeze, leaving him to return to her work, muttering to herself when he could not hear, "I pray we will."

Chapter Thirty-Nine

"Secrets and fears once whispered, become strengths."

Night had fallen upon them darkly.

Every candle, oil lamp, and lantern they could find staved it off. They were shadows within the light. Hovering apparitions that swayed and drifted, seeming to float, not walk, as the work moved them from wall to wall.

Most of the others—their families and friends—had gone home to their beds; only three remained, there but not. Sansone, Leonardo, and Patrizio were soundly asleep. They slumped on the floor, their backs to the wall just outside the chapel. Fiammetta peered down at them fondly as she passed, returning from the studio, clasping fresh brushes.

"Viviana?" she called softly. "Come see, Viviana."

Carrying her brush with its bristles of wheat pigment, Viviana answered her call.

"Ah, sweet," she whispered tenderly.

Leonardo's lips sputtered with snorting exhalations. Patrizio had shifted in his sleep, his head finding rest upon Sansone's shoulder. If Sansone knew it was there, he did nothing to move it.

"*Sì,*" Fiammetta marveled. "They are sweet men." She pulled her gaze from the three slumbering forms to face Viviana. "Sansone is a sweet man. He does love you," she said to the woman beside her. Or did she speak to herself, announcing a discovery of her own to herself?

Surprise and then fondness came over Viviana's face.

"He is, Fiammetta, the sweetest man I have ever known."

"Then you must not let anyone pull you from him," Fiammetta insisted. "Not even me."

It was as close as the contessa could get to an apology, a retraction of words that had come before. It was as close as she would come to giving Viviana her blessing.

"You are both dearly blessed." They had not heard Isabetta creep up on them, but both heard the longing in her voice.

"Love will find you again, Isabetta." Viviana pulled her into their small circle. "You must have faith."

"Faith." Isabetta blew out a breath with a small shake of her head, and slipped back into the chapel. They followed her.

"Faith is not something you can conjure, not something I can conjure," she mourned. "I know only what life has given me and what it has not. In these messages, my expectations have formed."

"Did you fall in love with *Il Magnifico*?" Mattea did not cease her work upon the wall, nor did she ignore the conversation.

"Ack, no," Isabetta rejoined, though her gaze held more than denial. "I loved his body, his hands, and what they made me feel. But I could never love a soul such as his."

"That is true love, is it not?" Natasia whispered from the tallest scaffold. "We are drawn in by their beauty, their words, but love does not come till all the layers are folded back and the true soul of the man is shown to us."

Viviana climbed up on the scaffold beside her. "You have become rich with wisdom, my friend."

Natasia shrugged. "Does one become wise, or is wisdom thrust upon us?" She shrugged again. "I did not love Pagolo when first I met him, when our betrothal was arranged. I was besotted with the folderol of the marriage ceremony, with becoming a wife. I thought little about love, true love."

Work stopped. Their hands could not move when their minds were so engaged with other matters.

"Nor can I say I loved him through the years of waiting for

him to return from war, though I made a good show of it," Natasia lamented. "It was only after we were married and living as man and wife that my love for him revealed itself."

"How?" Patrizia whispered the short, if monumental question.

Natasia turned to her, features soft and wistful. "I woke up one morning and he had already left. When I took myself to table to break my fast, I found a note from him."

"What did it say?" Carina coaxed.

"It said, 'You are always beautiful, but when you sleep you are a beautiful angel.'" Natasia shook her head even as she grinned. "It was the spark. It was enough."

"I thought Patrizio looked like a gnome," Fiammetta squawked; giggles followed. "I fought against the betrothal from the first moment my father informed me of it."

"Mother!" Patrizia protested.

"You did not," Isabetta objected.

"Oh indeed I did, but I did my duty as I was taught to do. Well, almost," Fiammetta insisted. "Our marriage was not consummated for months, though not for his lack of trying."

"You love him dearly now, I know it to be true," Viviana interposed. "What changed?"

"Nothing. Everything." Fiammetta looked beyond the confines of the chapel. "I suppose it was his refusal to be refused. He courted me though we were already married. He was charming."

"A charming gnome?" Mattea grinned.

"The most charming gnome I have ever met," Fiammetta's plump cheeks dimpled.

"I loved my husband from the first moment I saw him," Isabetta began. "I was swept away by him, by it. Swept away from my family and my home in Venice. I do not remember when I stopped loving him, but it was long before he became ill. I was a child when I met him, when I fell in love with him. And then I became a woman. I always loved him, but somewhere in our life together I was no longer *in* love with him."

"You need not punish yourself for it," Viviana intoned. "Many happy marriages exist with no more than that."

"I know, I do know," Isabetta mused. "Still. He deserved better."

"We all deserve to be loved, but our first love should always be for ourselves," Viviana decreed. "Without self-love and self-respect, we show others how they may treat us."

Words faded to grunts, and talking to painting. They brushed respect on the walls as they would on their lives.

Chapter Forty

"When one thing is revealed, many others may follow."

The crowd of people in front of Santo Spirito had never been larger. The line of those eager to enter its doors was far greater than it had ever been for any mass or service. It snaked through the piazza and down both the Via delle Caldaie and the Via del Gelsumino. Like a snake, much of it was poisonous.

Never before had the need for the *Otto* been greater; never before had they been on duty whilst inside a church. All eight of the guards stood in attendance, including the eldest, whose place Sansone would take. Four stationed themselves outside at the doors, and the other four waited inside, awaiting the arrival of *Il Magnifico*.

The Disciples fussed with each other's gowns and headpieces; they had had but a few hours after laying the last stroke of the brush, hours snatched only at dawn. They flew to their homes, quickly washed and dressed for the occasion, only to fly back, having agreed that they would await each and every arrival, that no one should be there before them. Father Raffaello had guarded the chapel hid behind its concealing cloth, lest a curious citizen or vengeful vandal impinge upon its secrecy.

"You have done it, madonnas? You have completed the work?" Such was the greeting of Antonio di Salvestro de Serristori. Upon his gangly legs, he rushed toward them and his chapel, his eyes beseeching, his voice squeaking.

"Of course they have, *cara*." Fabia de Salvestro took her husband's arm. "Would they all be standing here looking as pretty as a portrait themselves if they had not?"

Her words did not stop Antonio, but they did slow him.

"We have finished, signore," Viviana spoke for the group, a group that had agreed their sponsor need know nothing about what they had endured to complete his commission. "We believe you will be well and truly pleased."

"Ah, *sì*," Antonio exhaled sharply, scrawny chest filling and collapsing. "You do know that *he* is coming? You have been told?"

"Lorenzo informed me himself, signore," da Vinci assured him. "All is ready for him. You have seen the guards?"

"Indeed I have," Antonio stormed. "I never expected such a deplorable reaction. I knew, that is to say, I thought there would be those who struggled with the notion of women artists, but such anger?" He shook his head shamefully. Would he have been such a man, with such anger, were it someone else's chapel? "I would not have put you through such an ordeal had I seen it coming."

"Then it is well that you did not," Isabetta contested. "For if you had stopped us, not only would you not be able to boast one of the finest frescoes in all of Florence, you would have stopped progress itself. And you are nothing, signore, if not a progressive man."

Viviana clamped her teeth upon her lips, willing them not to curve upward. Leonardo coughed. They knew her sweetness for what it truly was.

"If you would be so kind, signore," Father Raffaello interjected, "could you stand at the door and tell the guards who should, and more importantly, who should *not* be let in? It would be a great assistance to us all."

"Of course, of course." Antonio rushed away as quickly as he had come, puffed up in his role as host and sponsor.

"The time, brother," Natasia pleaded with the priest, who looked about the chapel at the shadows of the sun.

"Nearly there," he answered. "A handful of minutes, no more."

The women clasped hands; the time of reckoning had come.

From the front of the church, they could see their sponsor

pointing to people in the crowd, could hear him informing the guards, "Him, her, them."

As the crowd trickled in, the Disciples stood in a resolute line before the hanging cloth, donning their widest smiles, no matter that their faces felt as if they would crack, nodding to those they recognized, and some they didn't. Footsteps beat upon the stone, each *clack* a tick of time. Low murmurs became a hum, filling the church, like the hum in the artists' ears, filling their heads. On some faces, they saw approval. Their family and friends stood before them in the front row; the women needed them there, needed to see their faces more than any others.

What Viviana saw was a sight that made her forget all the hours of aching work, all the heartache. Rudolfo stood on one side of Sansone, Marcello on the other. They were not her sons and her lover; they were her family. Any questions that may have lingered, she banished to the past along with all the pain of it, where such doubts belonged.

"This way, *Magnifico.*"

Antonio's words of greeting, louder than any he had spoken yet, erased all thoughts. All eyes turned. Viviana wondered how many attended to see the fresco and how many attended to see them.

Lorenzo de' Medici walked up the side aisle, his wife's hand resting upon his raised one.

Il Magnifico wore the red gown and *berretto* of his office in the Signoria; his wife wore all black.

Clarice Orsini de' Medici had lived a little more than thirty years. She had married Lorenzo when she was but sixteen. In the few years since, she had given birth to ten children, three of which had already passed on. Her beauty had taken on a dark-edged humanity.

She walked straight and tall beside her husband; her grand *ghirlanda* covered all her hair, its thick braid of velvet with its gold thread formed a U above her head, its ends reaching just beyond her shoulders. Her black velvet gown, belted high beneath her breasts, did much to hide her widened body. Her countenance did much to intimidate.

Viviana looked sideways at the woman beside her; Isabetta straightened her shoulders and held her head high. Viviana squeezed her hand before dropping it as they all dropped into a curtsy before the commanding couple.

"Ah, *le donne artiste*, the day has arrived and you have all survived." Lorenzo stepped before each and every one of them, greeting them all, lifting each woman from her bow. If he lingered a tad longer before Isabetta, no one noticed, save for Viviana and his wife. "Are you ready for what comes next, no matter what it may be?"

Viviana stifled any urge to harangue him for his persisting doubt.

"We are ready, *Magnifico*," Isabetta testified. "And we know what comes next. We are sure of it."

Lorenzo snickered with a slight shake of his head. He leaned in closer to the Disciples and whispered, "For all our sakes, I hope you speak true."

Encouragement came then, but not from Lorenzo.

"I am in awe of your bravery, madonnas," Clarice Orsini de' Medici said, her voice soft and high-pitched, her diction fittingly perfect. "I cannot say I understand why you felt it must be done, but I applaud you your convictions."

"*Grazie,* signora," Viviana answered for the group with another quick curtsy, believing Clarice to be done. She was not.

Instead, she leaned in close to Isabetta, and lowered her voice, though not so low that Viviana, beside them, did not hear.

"I envy you, not for what you had of my husband, but what you have for yourself."

Isabetta looked upon the woman in a way Viviana would never have imagined she would; Isabetta looked upon her former lover's wife with respect.

"Come visit our studio, madonna. You would be most welcome."

Clarice tilted her head with one brow raised. "Perhaps I shall. Perhaps I will bring some of my daughters."

The creaking of the doors closing squelched the vociferous

chatter that had been filling the church, muting it as it marked the moment.

Antonio and Fabia rushed back up the aisle to stand beside the Medicis. Antonio wore upon his face the same fear that churned in Viviana's stomach. He gathered himself, prodded by the elbow of his wife, cleared his throat, and addressed the assembly, one that filled every corner of the basilica.

"Thank you all," he began.

"Louder," Fabia whispered.

Antonio raised his head upon his scrawny neck, tossing his voice to the back row.

"Thank you all so very much for coming. I know what we have done may seem a bit outlandish."

"What *we* have done?" Viviana heard Fiammetta huff, turned and saw Natasia poke her elbow into Fiammetta's ribs.

"However we felt the tenderness of the subject matter required a tender touch." Antonio continued, "These women"—he gestured back and across to the Disciples—"these artists are extreme talents despite that they are of the fairer sex."

How does one look complimented at such an insult?

It took all of Viviana's strength not to ask the question.

"I have no doubt what they have created is a masterpiece. And I am sure you are all as anxious to see it as I am."

The rafters shook with resounding agreement, even if some of it came in hopes of disaster.

Antonio laughed, once more oblivious to all the types of truth filling the church. "Very well then. Fabia?"

His wife nodded and took her place on one side of the cloth, while Antonio took the other side.

Expectancy swallowed them whole; the entire church seemed to be holding its breath.

With a nod of Antonio's head, they pulled. With their pull the cloth fell.

The cloth fell on silence; a loud, deep, frightening silence.

"What do we—" Patrizia croaked to her mother, but she didn't finish, she need not.

The applause began then, not with hesitant, sporadic claps, but with a spark of lightning and the fury of thunder. The cheering came—rousing, vibrant, brilliant cheering.

Viviana closed teary eyes; she would capture this moment, make it hers to be brought out again and again whenever she doubted herself or the purpose of Da Vinci's Disciples.

"*Dio mio*," Antonio di Salvestro de' Serristori blasphemed. He blinked and blinked again. He looked at the women artists and back to the fresco. As the rousing adulation washed over them, he flitted his gaze between the women and the fresco again and again. He stepped to them and bowed.

"I am not the most intelligent man, nor the strongest, but I should never, ever, have doubted you. Do you forgive me, madonnas?"

Fiammetta stepped forward, placed a hand upon his head as if she were the Pope blessing him. "You know only what you have been taught. You have been taught something different today. Now you must teach it."

Antonio rose, wonder still blanching his face. "I will. I swear I will."

He stood tall once more, raised his head, his voice, once more. "Da Vinci's Disciples!"

The cheering became a roar. The women curtsied, words of "wondrous," "a masterpiece" flowing over them like the freshest, most cleansing water, the water of baptism, of rebirth, not as women, but as artists.

As she straightened, Viviana heard other words, not far behind her.

"When did they have time to fix it?"

She whirled, just had she had done that day in June, that day she had first heard of this chapel and its commission. Unlike that day, there were too many words, too many people; she could not tell who spoke them. She would not forget; she could wait.

Lorenzo de' Medici stepped into the chapel. The crowd in the church grew quiet as they watched his keen study of the frescoes. His wife walked with him, pulled upon his shoulder, and whispered in his ear. He nodded, turning to the hushed crowd.

"It is as beautiful as the women who created it. How beautiful do I look?"

The cheering began again, this time spiced with amiable laughter.

He raised a hand, calling for silence; it came swiftly.

"We have all learned something here today, perhaps myself most of all. Take heed, gentlemen; we are no longer the only purveyors of creation. Perhaps we never were, for with God we are created in a woman's womb."

In a far more orderly fashion than Viviana would have imagined possible, all those allowed into the church began to file through the chapel, to gaze upon the women's creation.

The Disciples stood just outside it, their families among them now, accepting the accolades with gratitude, not even noticing those who said nothing. The long snake of people once outside slithered slowly through the chapel.

Soon the crowd began to disperse. They left in pairs or fews or in virulent groups poisoned by their bitterness, swirling whirlpools of frustration and rage. They told Viviana more than all the other words she had heard, that had eddied around her this day.

Their work was far from over. Perhaps she would not live to see its end.

She closed her eyes and saw flashes of the years, the pain, the need—named and met. No, she might not see its end—she opened her eyes to look at the fresco—but she had seen the splendor of its beginning.

Before long, only the Disciples and their *maestro* remained. Their men and families set off to the *trattoria*, where they promised a feast would await the women.

They remained behind, to savor the last moment of possession of their work.

"The faces are all so different," Carina said. "Just as they should be, yet we do not see it often enough."

"The colors in *The Death of Adam* could have been richer, deeper," Mattea said, analyzing work she herself had done.

"We will do so next time," Viviana chortled. The others laughed; they were all far too tired to think about the next time.

They swirled around the chapel, and such words were repeated again and again: what they had done wrong, where they had triumphed. Each had an opinion save Lapaccia, who had not left the corner of the chapel where she stood leaning upon the wall.

"Dear Lapaccia, we have not heard what you think of the finished fresco."

Lapaccia moved her head toward Viviana, but did not seem to look at her.

"I have not said…because I cannot see it."

Chapter Forty-One

"See what is true; render only that."

Beneath a blanket, they huddled together upon her balcony, counting stars.

Viviana let her hair down, let the crisp breeze and Sansone's fingers ruffle it.

"There is something that happens to soldiers after they have won a battle," Sansone cooed in her ear as he stroked her. "Though victorious, they grieve. Not for those they have slain, but for the excitement that had thrummed through them for so long. That left them when the battle ended."

Viviana lifted her head.

"They were no longer quite as alive," Viviana slurred, tongue thick with fatigue.

"It is what you are feeling, I think."

Viviana chuckled weakly. "I think you know me too well."

He turned her and her chair as if they weighed no more than a butterfly upon a leaf. Sansone's mossy eyes looked through her, into her.

"I know you as the most beautiful and courageous woman I have ever known." He kissed her hands. "I know you as the woman who graces my life as it has never been graced. You have much to look forward to, much to make you once more feel so alive."

Viviana slowly leaned down, resting her head upon the knot of their limbs.

"I know you speak true. You always have. If I have done the things I have, things others have not dared to do, they tell me the past is in the past, and all its remnants should be left there."

Viviana raised her gaze to his. Blue and green swirled together as they did in the oceans surrounding the Italian peninsula.

"If you would still have me, *dolcezza mia*, I would be honored to be your wife."

Sansone did not move, did not blink. Without a word he stood. In the silence, he drew her up and, for a moment, simply stared at her.

"Sansone, I—"

He crouched, arms flashing, one gathering her behind the neck, the other behind her knees, and lifted her off her feet.

As he carried into the house, toward her bedroom, he answered her with his lips upon hers.

"What of society? What of Fiammetta?"

"Society has already damned me," Viviana chuckled. "I feel I do them a service to give them yet another reason."

Sansone plunged across the threshold, dropped Viviana upon the bed, pounced upon her.

"And what of Fiammetta?" He nuzzled her neck.

Viviana wrapped her legs about his back.

"*Puah*," Viviana giggled. "Fiammetta is only jealous, for Patrizio does not perform as he once did."

Together they laughed. Once more, their laughter became part of their lovemaking. Viviana hoped it would always be so.

Chapter Forty-Two

"For all that longing is appeased, there is always more to long for."

It could have been a day like any of so many that had come before. But it was not.

They were all there, all working, busier than they had ever been, all save Lapaccia.

Yes, busier than they had ever been, but not with projects of their own choosing. The commissions flowed in—portraits and landscapes—enough to last as far as their vision could reach. The original Disciples became the teachers; Carina and Patrizia came to the studio as much as, if not more than, they did. Viviana saw it in their eyes: the desire, the longing, the need to know, to learn, to create. She knew that look, for she had seen it upon her own face for years.

They had done what they set out to do. They had become what they had always dreamed, a true, working studio occupied and populated by women.

Leonardo had returned to Milan. Verrocchio and Botticelli visited often, always entering by the back door.

Their chatter was as lively as ever. Until Mattea stood and retrieved the overstuffed satchel from the corner. Fiammetta stood with her. Their merriment drained away as surely and completely as if the ocean called to it all the water of the Arno River.

"Are you sure, Mattea?" Isabetta asked. "Is there no other way?"

Mattea tilted her head with a lopsided grin. "There are other ways, but they are all too dangerous. I will not put Andreano's safety in peril."

"But is it necessary—" Natasia began.

"I must find him," Mattea said, stifling Natasia's pending objection with her resolve. "He must know of his mother. He must be by her side. She must see her son's face before she cannot see at all."

"What have the physicians to say?" Viviana queried gently.

"It is the clouding," Mattea said woefully. "Her sight is limited to but a few inches before her face and it dwindles still."

"But where will you look?" Carina asked.

They all gathered round her now, gathered as close as they could before she traveled so far.

"To the north. It is as much as he has told me. Venice, I believe. I have always wanted to see Venice."

She smiled at them, though sadly. Each one embraced her in turn. "Come back to us," Viviana whispered in her ear.

"I will." Mattea nodded. "*We* will." She turned to Fiammetta. "It is time."

"Patrizio and I take her as far as Ferrara. We go to hear the Friar Savonarola speak again," Fiammetta informed them.

"You go often these days," Natasia said. It was as much as a question as a statement.

"I do." Fiammetta shrugged. "I am compelled. There is a different sort of solace in his words, though I cannot tell you what it is. He speaks to the me I am now."

There was no need for her to elaborate; all knew her ever-descending status in the community plagued both her and her husband.

"And there is also something magnetic about him, something that makes one listen."

"Perhaps we will all hear him speak someday," Viviana said.

Fiammetta brightened, eyes radiating with a manic glow. "Oh, I am sure you will. I hear he is being transferred back to Florence."

La fine, quasi
(The End, almost)

What Is Historical Fact
and What Is Not

"Upon a soft pillow rests a clean conscious."

The murder of Lorenzo de' Medici's brother Giuliano, and with
it the betrayal of so many Lorenzo thought were his friends and
colleagues, did forever change the benevolent man. His revenge
upon them was fearsome, as accurately portrayed in book one of
the Da Vinci's Disciples series. His actions plunged the city-state of
Florence into war with not only the Vatican but also the King of
Naples, whose forces first attacked the outlying regions in Tuscany
under the rule of Florence. The ill effects of the war upon the people
turned many against Lorenzo. As the pain and rage of his brother's
death diminished—it would never leave him completely—Lorenzo
knew he had to salvage the situation, realizing his wrath, his pain,
had taken him out of control and had put his people in danger, a
danger he knew they resented him for.

In the most bold and daring move of his life, Lorenzo—without
the knowledge or blessing of the Florentine government—traveled by sea to Naples, placing his life and the fortune of his city in
the hands of King Ferdinand I (Don Ferrante). According to the
Encyclopædia Britannica Eleventh Edition, "Ferdinand was gifted
with great courage and real political ability, but his method of government was vicious and disastrous. His financial administration was
based on oppressive and dishonest monopolies, and he was merci-

lessly severe and utterly treacherous towards his enemies." Among the many interesting hobbies the king participated in, hunting was one of his favorites, both of the four-legged and the two-legged sort. And like those that lived in the forest, were this king to success-fully make a kill, he would have his prize stuffed. Dead, embalmed, and dressed in the costumes which they wore in life, his deceased enemies lived on in the king's "museum of mummies." This was the man to whom Lorenzo entrusted his life.

The gamble proved fruitful; Lorenzo charmed and persuaded with great acumen, convincing Ferdinand that it would do great harm to all of Italy to be divided by a war such as the one beating upon their doors. With the gift of peace in his hands, Lorenzo returned to his homeland, received with the open arms of the people and the great joy of all. At least for a time.

In 1481 Battista Frecobaldi, along with two others, members of the Baldovinetti and Balducci families, did conspire to assassi-nate Lorenzo de' Medici, once more planning to take his life on Ascension Sunday. Their enterprise was not so stealthily managed; friends of Lorenzo learned of the plan ahead of time. The three were quickly arrested, and even more quickly executed.

The Medici family did claim Averado as their ancestor. A seventeenth-century manuscript now in the Biblioteca Moreniana records a story crafted to elevate the origins of the Medici legacy and its coat of arms. This tale offers a certain Averardo de' Medici, a name that recurred in the family between the thirteenth and four-teenth centuries, as a founding father of the clan. Averado served as a captain in Charlemagne's army, the emperor and "founder" of Florence. As the legend has it, the valiant Averardo, while battling the Longobards' invasion of the Tuscan territory, defeated a giant called Mugello who terrorized the area of the same name, located in the upper valley of the Sieve. During the violent confrontation, the giant Mugello dented, with either a spiked mace or the balls of a flail, Averardo's gilded shield. The indentations made upon the knight's armor came to symbolize the heraldic emblem of the balls or *palle* of the Medici escutcheon. As traceable genealogy attests, the first Medicis, from whom Lorenzo descends, did in fact live in Mugello.

By this time, Leonardo da Vinci had indeed become dissatisfied with his life in Florence. He was not receiving as many commissions as Botticelli, Verrocchio, and Ghirlandaio, and those he did receive he struggled and faltered with, leaving many unfinished. His highly active mind had turned elsewhere, primarily to science and invention. A letter exists, written by da Vinci himself, to the Duke of Milan, wherein he offers his services as a military engineer to the duke. It is unclear if this letter was ever actually sent.

Ludovico Sforza, and Milan and its strategic location, were often part of military contentions within the states of Italy. A primitive war tank and a chariot with scythes upon its wheels were just a few of the many military designs da Vinci created during his time in Milan. Initially, the duke brought da Vinci to Milan to cast an equestrian monument in honor of the duke's father. Leonardo da Vinci's actual first completed work in Milan is the masterpiece known as *The Virgin on the Rocks*. Da Vinci returned to Florence in 1489.

Piero della Francesca did complete a fresco of the entire *Legend of the True Cross* in the main choir chapel, the *Cappella Maggiore* commissioned by the Bacci family, in the Basilica of San Francesco in Arezzo in 1447. It was not only his largest work but it is also considered by many to be his finest. The descriptions of those frescoes included in this work that form the entire pictorial of the legend are factual. Though there are a number of frescoes in the thirty-eight chapels of Santo Spirito, *The Legend of the True Cross* is not one of them.

The process of artists hearing of and receiving commissions is accurately depicted here. Though in truth, most often there were far more competitors. The contract Da Vinci's Disciples signed is written to match as closely as possible the contracts that existed at the time.

Fillippino Lippi was, in fact, one of the first to use real models, excluding portraits, when painting figures.

The story of Emiliano Soderini is a true one, though his first name is fictionalized. The man was proclaimed an illegitimate child, though exactly where the designation originated has not been unearthed. This man did claim to have found documents that refuted his illegitimacy, and presented them to the government of Florence. The government, run in part by the other branch of the Soderini, proclaimed these documents fraudulent. He was executed for his attempts to bring honor to his family name. Natasia's father, Crispino, is a fictional character, though the "illegitimate" Soderini did marry and have children.

All the street names and building names are as they were in the fifteenth century. To walk with Da Vinci's Disciples is to walk upon those very cobbles. Such authenticity of geography was made possible through the work of R. Burr Litchfield and his students at Brown University.

And, as always, the direct quotes, the bread crumbs of wisdom Leonardo da Vinci left behind, must be acknowledged:

> *"Beyond a doubt truth bears the same relation to falsehood as light to darkness."*

> *"Although nature commences with reason and ends in experience it is necessary for us to do the opposite, that is to commence with experience and from this to proceed to investigate the reason."*

> *"It seems that I was always destined to be deeply concerned with vultures; for I recall asthat in one of my earliest memories, that while I was in my cradle, a vulture came down to me, and opened my mouth with its tail, and struck me many times with its tail against my lips."*

> *"Marriage is like putting your hand into a bag of snakes in the hope of pulling out an eel."*

> *"When once you have tasted flight, you will forever walk the earth with your eyes skyward, for there you have been, and there you long to return."*

> *"It has long since come to my attention that people of accomplish-*

ment rarely sat back and let things happen to them. They went out and happened to things."

"Learning acquired in youth arrests the evil of old age; and if you understand that old age has wisdom for its food, you will so conduct yourself in youth that your old age will not lack for nourishment."

"Make your work in keeping with your purpose."

"I love those who can smile in trouble, who can gather strength from distress, and grow brave by reflection. 'Tis the business of little minds to shrink, but they whose heart is firm, and whose conscience approves their conduct, will pursue their principles unto death."

Acknowledgements

"It is far better to ask for help than to lose your way."

The writing of a book is a solitary affair. Bringing the book to the world is anything but. To those who helped me bring this book to the world I express my undying gratitude: Shannon Hassan, my ever-dedicated, ever-supportive, and encouraging agent; Randall Klein, my understanding, insightful, and expert editor; and the entire marketing, design, and sales teams at Diversion Books for their terrific support and covers that are truly works of art.

For their technical and historic advice, I must thank and acknowledge the team at the Palazzo Medici Ricardo and the *Castello Sforzesco*, for their depth of knowledge and their willingness to share it.

Yes, writing is a solitary affair. But belonging to a community of writers dispels some of the loneliness. I consider myself extraordinarily blessed, calling as my own the most talented, caring, helpful, and funny community of writers: C. W. Gortner, Stephanie Dray, Diane Haegar, Kate Quinn, Anne Easter Smith, David Blixt, Heather Webb, Christy English, Marci McGuire Jefferson, Nancy Bilyeau, Lynn Cullen, Sophie Piernot, Kris Waldherr, Leslie Carroll and more. Love you guys!

And to my family…my mother Barbara Di Mauro Russo, without whom my life would exist somewhere in a cardboard box. My sons, Devon and Dylan…I know it couldn't have been easy growing up with the emotional, turbulent, manic creature that is a writer, but we always had fun, didn't we. You've been "in" so many of my books because you are my greatest motivation. I haven't been able to give you the world; I only hope I taught you how to get it for yourself. And my dear partner, Carl; oh the places we will go. To my family, I not only give thanks, I also love and cherish you.

Bibliography

Learning never ends, it is always the beginning.

BOOKS

Alberti, Leon Battista. 1435. *On Painting.* Trans. Cecil Grayson. 1991. London, England: Penguin Books.

da Vinci, Leonardo. 15th Century. *Philosophical Diary.* Trans. Wade Baskins. 2004. New York, NY: Barnes and Noble Books.

Dersin, Denise. Editor. 1999. *What Life Was Like at the Rebirth Of Genius.* Richmond, VA: Time Life Inc.

Earls, Irene. 1987. *Renaissance Art: A Topical Dictionary.* Westport, CT: Greenwood Press.

Field, D. M. 2002. *Leonardo da Vinci.* New York, NY: Barnes and Noble Inc., By arrangement with Regency House Publishing Ltd.

Fine, Elsa Honig. 1978. *Women and Art: A History of Women Painters and Sculptors from the Renaissance to the 20th Century.* Montclair, NJ: Allanheld, Osmun & Co. Publishers Inc.

Machiavelli, Niccolò., *History of Florence and of the Affairs of Italy from the Earliest Times to the Death of Lorenzo de' Medici*; with an introduction by Hugo Albert Rennert, Ph.D., from a Universal Classics Library edition, published in 1901. No translator was given. Presented in eight books comprising 55 chapters and an introduction.

Lemaitre, Alain J; Lessing, Erich. 2003. *Florence and the Renaissance.* Paris, France: Finest SA.

Martines, Lauro. 2003. *April Blood*. London, England: Random House.

Mee, Jr., Charles L. 1975. *Daily Life in Renaissance Italy*. New York, NY: American Heritage Publishing Co.

Najemy, John M. 2006. *A History of Florence 1200-1575*. West Sussex, England: Blackwell Publishing/John Wiley & Sons.

Rogers, Mary and Tinagli, Paola. 2005. *Women in Italy, 1350-1650: Ideal and Realities*. Manchester, England: Manchester University Press.

Simonetta, Marcello. 2008. *The Montefeltro Conspiracy*. New York, NY: Doubleday.

Toman, Rolf, Editor. 2011. *The Art of the Italian Renaissance*. Postdam, Germany: h.f.ullman.

Vasari, Gregorio. 1550. *Lives of the Artists*. Trans. Julia Conway Bondenella and Peter Bondenella. 1991. New York, NY: Oxford University Press.

INTERNET

R. Burr Litchfield, Online Gazetteer of Sixteenth Century Florence. Florentine Renaissance Resources/STG: Brown University, Providence, R.I., 2006.

"Lorenzo de' Medici." *Encyclopedia of World Biography*. 2004. *Encyclopedia.com*. (September 12, 2012). http://www.encyclope-dia.com/doc/1G2-3404704367.html

The Museums of Florence: http://www.museumsinflorence.com/musei/medici_riccardi_palace.html#

Castle Sforzesco: http://www.museumsinflorence.com/musei/medici_riccardi_palace.html#

Reading Group Guide

"Many is the pearl hidden in the oysters."

1. In chapter 1, mention is made of the long years after the death of his brother Giuliano wherein Lorenzo de' Medici did not allow festivals, new construction, and public art commissions. Can grief be so all-consuming as to last so long? What other possibility—what other form of grief—might Lorenzo have been suffering from?

2. Mattea says, in chapter 3, "my mother will be livid." But she does so with a smile. Where does her amusement stem from? Is it an attitude of the era or one of every era?

3. Also in chapter 3, Leonardo da Vinci tells the Disciples (a documented quote), "Beyond a doubt truth bears the same relation to falsehood as light to darkness." What did he mean in the context of this story? What does it mean in life?

4. It is said of Viviana, in chapter 5, that she "cared little for riches; to her honor held far more value than gold, no matter how much of it there was." Is this in keeping with her character, even in consideration of her actions in *Portrait of a Conspiracy*? Why or why not?

5. In chapter 8, Marcello reveals to his mother that Carina is a painter. Why? Was it surprising that he did so? If so, why? Were his intentions appropriate, even knowing of Da Vinci's Disciples and what they had done?

6. In chapter 12, when Fabia di Salvestro talks about learning

to write poetry from Lorenzo de' Medici's mother, Lucrezia Tornabuoni, what does it also say about women of the era, of Lucrezia's era? Is it a surprising conclusion? If so, why?

7. In chapter 14, it is written that Leonardo da Vinci considered the Duke of Milan to be "another who knew of vultures." What does he mean? Why would that draw him to the duke's court?

8. What is meant by this sentence, in chapter 15, "To this man and his brother, Leonardo was ever a threat, a threat to their own notion of themselves." Did other men feel this way and, if so, why? What did it mean to Leonardo? What action in the same chapter supports the contention of the sentence?

9. In chapter 16, Isabetta responds to Lorenzo de' Medici by saying, "Of course we are afraid. But fear is but a spark to light great fires." What did she mean? Is there truth in such words, and if so, why?

10. A passage in chapter 18 speaks to the quality of the work the Disciples must produce: "They knew, as women, that it must be not only better, but brilliant; eyes would look upon their work differently than upon any other, and far more harshly than St. Peter's at the gates of Heaven; they must work harder than any man." Is this surprising? Why or why not? Does it apply to today's woman?

11. At the beginning of chapter 20, Leonardo and his Disciples discuss "the war of art." Define what this means. What does it mean to these women? Is their war a greater one and, if so, why? In this chapter, Leonardo brings Verrocchio and Botticelli to see the women's work, but does not allow any of the women to accompany them. Why?

12. In chapter 21, Sansone assumes he and Viviana will marry. Her reaction is not what he hoped for. What is her hesitance? Is it understandable in the context of her life? If so, why?

13. Throughout the book, more truths of the life of Leonardo da Vinci are revealed. Discuss what some of them are. What, if anything, came as a surprise?

14. Discuss this passage in chapter 26: "Who is to say who uses

who?" Isabetta said within the shelter of Viviana's solicitude. "I have known the pain of loving one I cannot have. I promise you it has hardened me against doing so ever again." What does Isabetta truly mean by her first statement? Who has she loved before in vain?

15. Natasia and Mattea are accosted in chapter 31. During the assault, Mattea's exasperation leads her to question, "Why is it always me?" How is the dagger hitting her hand the answer? What is the larger force at work in these events? How does it relate to a conversation between Viviana and Leonardo earlier in the book?

16. In chapter 33, Patrizia and Carina find out more about each other, and discuss the courage they will need. Why do they need this courage? How may things differ for them in contrast to the original Da Vinci's Disciples?

17. Discuss the meaning of this passage from chapter 37: "For an artist, one of any creative sort, to finish a creation meant losing possession of it; it lived no longer in the artist's heart and mind, but in the world. Finishing then became both exhilarating and mournful, for it could never belong to the artist alone ever again. The artist could never again live in the world of that piece of art. Such a separation could be disconcerting indeed."

18. The "unnamed" woman who sneaks to churches and other places alone, as glimpsed by Viviana, turns out to be Natasia. Were there clues that it was her? What were they? Why did she feel so strongly about her mission? Was the mission worthwhile?

19. When the truth of Lapaccia is revealed at the end of the book, did it come as a surprise? Why or why not?

20. The book ends with Fiammetta telling the Disciples that Friar Savonarola is coming to Florence. What are the possible reasons for ending the book in this manner? What could it mean?

CPSIA information can be obtained
at www.ICGtesting.com
Printed in the USA
BVOW08s0055220317
479137BV00001B/2/P